Half
a Heart

OTHER TITLES BY KAREN McQUESTION

FOR ADULTS

A Scattered Life
Easily Amused
The Long Way Home
Hello Love

FOR YOUNG ADULTS

Favorite
Life on Hold
From a Distant Star

THE EDGEWOOD SERIES

Edgewood (Book One)
Wanderlust (Book Two)
Absolution (Book Three)
Revelation (Book Four)

FOR CHILDREN

Celia and the Fairies
Secrets of the Magic Ring
Grimm House
Prince and Popper

FOR WRITERS

Write That Novel!: You Know You Want To . . .

Half a Heart

KAREN McQUESTION

Text copyright © 2018 by Karen McQuestion
All rights reserved.

No part of this book may be reproduced, or stored in a retrieval system, or transmitted in any form or by any means, electronic, mechanical, photocopying, recording, or otherwise, without express written permission of the publisher.

Published by Lake Union Publishing, Seattle

www.apub.com

Amazon, the Amazon logo, and Lake Union Publishing are trademarks of Amazon.com, Inc., or its affiliates.

ISBN-13: 9781503954663
ISBN-10: 1503954668

Cover design by Shasti O'Leary Soudant

Printed in the United States of America

For Greg, patron of the arts and keeper of my sanity

CHAPTER ONE

He'd never seen his father so angry, and that was saying a lot, because he'd seen him plenty mad the last few years. Tia really was to blame, not that it mattered. He should have known not to listen to her.

After their parents left the house that Saturday, she lured Logan out of his bedroom with the promise of marshmallows.

It started with a polite knock on the door. "Open up," Tia said. "It's me."

He opened the door partway, and there she stood, holding a marshmallow at nose height, her face innocent and friendly. "Come on out, Logan," she said. Glancing down, he noticed she had the whole bag in her other hand. "They're gone, and they're not gonna be back for at least an hour. They'll never know. I promise I won't tell."

Logan knew they were gone, so that much was true. After he'd heard them leave the apartment, he had gone to the window and peeked down at the parking lot, watching them get into the car and drive away.

"Come on, Logan. Stop being such a scaredy-cat and come out and have a snack with me."

He knew better than to trust her. In the four months they'd lived together, he'd figured her out. Tia was a fooler, all sweetness and light to the parents, but vile to him: pinching and poking, taking his things, mocking him when they weren't looking. She knew she could get away with it because he wouldn't say a word.

Not a word.

Every part of him said that Tia couldn't be trusted, but that bag of marshmallows dangled from her hand, inviting and near. So tempting. Even thinking about it made him salivate. Logan could imagine how gooey and sweet a marshmallow would taste after not having eaten for so long.

"Please?" Tia took two steps down the hall, holding the bag in her outstretched hand to draw him out. Logan knew he'd catch it if his father found out he'd left his room, but if he was back before they returned, how would he know?

Maybe just one marshmallow and a drink of water to wash it down. He sucked in a breath before stepping out of the room and following her. The rubber sole of his left shoe had come loose earlier in the week, and he'd wrapped it with duct tape, so now his footsteps on the bare floor sounded uneven. *Step. Thud. Step. Thud.* Logan imagined he was a pirate with a peg leg, making his way across the deck of a ship, heading toward the marshmallow treasure. The idea would have made him laugh out loud, except he didn't do anything out loud anymore.

They ended up in the kitchen. Tia acted nice then, pouring each of them a glass of milk, getting out two plates, and divvying up marshmallows between them. She popped a CD in, and the voice of Keith Urban filled the room. He'd wondered at her boldness. How was she going to explain the half-empty bag when the parents got home? Warning bells went off in his head, but once he started eating, there was no stopping. The milk was creamy and delicious, and the marshmallows were heaven for his taste buds.

"Good, huh?" Tia asked, popping one into her mouth. Everything about Tia was round: eyes, face, body, and her crazy curly hair. They were the same age, nine this year, but she was a head taller and the opposite of Logan in every way. Tan skin to his pasty white. Glossy black locks as opposed to his head of thin brown hair that swirled at the top. A cowlick, his grandma Nan had called it, tracing it with her fingers like it was something special. He was a string bean, and Tia was pudgy, almost fat, but her protruding tummy did not bother her one bit. Tia was all confidence. She was loud and brash and went through the apartment dancing and singing, while Logan knew the world was ready to beat him down if he got too full of himself. He stayed quiet and tried not to attract attention. It was better that way.

Logan ate one marshmallow after another, each time thinking it would be his last, but he couldn't seem to stop. His stomach had been an empty, painful knot, and with each bite, he felt it relax. Oh, it was good.

"I knew you'd want some," Tia said, watching him intently. "I know that marshmallows are your favorite and that you must be super hungry by now." Marshmallows *were* his favorite. At Grandma Nan's, the two of them would make s'mores in her outdoor fire pit. Their fingers would get sticky, and he'd make a mess with the crumbs, but she never got mad.

Tia picked up her plate and glass and went to the sink. After turning on the faucet, she quickly rinsed them and stuck them in the dish rack. The sink was full of dirty dishes. Tia and her mother were lackadaisical about cleanliness, and his father didn't seem to care. Logan tried not to care either, but it was hard. The messy apartment bothered him. Piles of mail and magazines. Sticky spots on the floor. Hair in the bathroom sink. *Yuck.* His mother had always kept things so neat.

He continued eating the marshmallows, slowing down now, nearly satisfied. Tia hopped over to the CD player and turned it up, then danced to the tune that was his grandmother's favorite, trying to make him smile.

The music was so loud that he never heard them return. All the warning signs—the footsteps in the hall, the doorknob turning, the squeak of the door swinging open—were lost in the noise. It took him by surprise because it had been only fifteen minutes since they'd left, and Tia had said they'd be gone an hour. When his father's voice boomed out, "What in the hell is going on here?" Logan's breath caught in his chest. He froze the way he always did, but Tia had no trouble speaking up.

"I told Logan not to do it," she said, shaking her head so that her curls bounced. "I said he should stay in his room 'cause he was being punished, but he just didn't care. He came right out and drank up all the milk and tore open the brand-new package of marshmallows. And then he played that horrible CD. He must've fished it out of the garbage after you threw it out."

Logan frantically shook his head, but it was too late. His father's face reddened as he lunged right at him. Then the hitting began, rapid slaps raining down on his head. Logan held up his arms to shield himself from the blows, infuriating his father even more. "What did I tell you?" his father screamed. "Didn't I tell you to stay in your room?"

This, Logan knew, was a trap. If he nodded yes, it would provoke his father even more because he'd be admitting he disobeyed. If he shook his head no, he'd get in trouble for being a liar. There was no getting out of this. Logan felt the knot return to his stomach, and his gut began to churn in a sickening way. He swallowed and ducked down in his chair, hoping each blow would be the last.

"I'm asking you a question. Didn't I tell you to stay in your room?" Each word was punctuated by a slap. "Answer me, dammit!"

Logan nodded and slid out of the chair down to a kneeling position. Sometimes this helped, and his father would relent and send him to his room. It was worth a try. Anything to keep his father from hitting him with his belt.

But his attempt to change the dynamics of the situation backfired. "What do you think you're doing?" his father asked, grabbing him by the back of his T-shirt and yanking him to his feet.

The fabric cut into Logan's neck, making him gag. Panic rose up in his throat followed by the contents of his stomach. He tried to hold it back but couldn't. Projectile vomit the color of bird droppings spewed from his mouth, hitting both the floor and his father's shoes in a wet splat.

"Why, you little—" his father started, letting go of his grip on Logan's shirt.

Logan rushed over to the sink, turned on the faucet, scooped water into his mouth, and then spit it out. He turned to see his father frozen in place, throw-up splashed on his shoes and pants.

Tia had slipped out of the room, but her mother stood in the doorway. She shook her head at Logan—a slow, sad gesture that spoke volumes. Tia's mom didn't talk much, and although he sensed her sympathies were often on his side, they both knew she couldn't show it. Logan understood, but it made him miss his mother even more.

His father pointed at Logan and then down at the mess. "You did that on purpose." There was murder in his voice.

Behind him, Tia's mother raised her eyebrows, turned sideways, and tilted her head toward the hallway, a subtle gesture that Logan understood. A way out. In an instant, he made a decision and darted for the door, jumping over the stream of liquid on the floor and past his father. He felt his father's fingertips graze his back, but Logan was too quick. He brushed by Tia's mom and was all the way to the stairwell when he heard his father's roar of fury.

Fueled by fear and adrenaline, Logan took the stairs two at a time and burst out the front door of the apartment, startling Mrs. Smith, who was on the other side, her arms filled with grocery bags. "My goodness, Logan," she said, but he didn't stop to help the way he usually did.

For an afternoon in August, it was fairly cool, more comfortable than inside their apartment anyway, and Logan felt a rush of air as he took off down the street. Apartments lined both sides of the street in this part of Chicago, and the streets were crowded, cars parked on both sides, kids playing on the sidewalk. He rushed by two teenagers, older boys with skateboards tucked under their arms. "What's the hurry, little brother?" one asked as Logan ran past.

He was a block away when he heard his father bellowing his name. The knot in his stomach returned, and this time it wasn't hunger but terror. A boa constrictor of fright that tightened around his chest, making it hard to breathe.

"Logan!"

He didn't turn back. He could never return now. Not after leaving his room, vomiting on his father's shoes, and running out of the apartment without permission. It was all too much. A thought filled his head: *he will kill me.* Logan could imagine how it would happen. His father's beefy hands would wrap around his neck; one quick twist and it would be over. He'd be a goner. Small for his age, Logan could easily be folded into the lawn and leaf bags they used at the landscaping company where his father presently worked. One toss into the dumpster and that would be it. Game over. Life over. They moved so often no one would even know there'd ever been a boy named Logan. Who would even care that he was dead?

"Logan, get your ass back here. Now!"

He could tell his father was gaining on him, and fear fueled his pumping legs. His chest burned as he gasped for air. He scanned the street, looking for a place to hide. He ran alongside one building and then paused to try a doorknob, but he found it locked. Maybe he could crouch between parked cars? No, too exposed. He kept going.

"Logan! I mean it!"

Logan had rounded the corner, nearly banging his leg on a fire hydrant, when he saw it: a moving van, the back open, the inside nearly full. Almost an invitation. He made a snap decision, scrambling up the lowered ramp of the van and diving underneath a kitchen table. A cluster of plastic garbage bags stuffed underneath the table became his refuge. He nestled in the middle, completely obscured by the bags, which were so soft and cushy he knew they had to be filled with clothing or blankets.

He held his breath when he heard his father nearby, screaming out his name, then exhaled when he ran past. He was safe for now.

CHAPTER TWO

When Logan woke up, it was dark and quiet. His entire body thrummed from the vibrations of the moving truck. Plastic bags stuck to his sweaty body. The air was thick with humidity. It took a moment for him to realize where he was, to remember being too afraid of his father to come out from his hiding spot.

There was a moment when it had almost happened. He'd been just about to scoot forward and ease his way out of the truck when he heard his father's voice again, calling out to some unknown person. He must have backtracked, realizing Logan had to be nearby. "Have you seen my kid?" he'd asked. "About this tall. Little pissant is in big trouble."

Logan had hugged his legs close as a woman's voice answered with a no. He was still in that position when the ramp was lifted and shoved back into the slot under the truck, and the door lowered and banged shut. The click of the latch made his throat close in alarm. It hit him then that there was no escape now that the door was locked from the outside.

For the millionth time, he wished he had a voice. One yell or scream could make this right. When the engine started up and the van pulled away from the curb, he scrambled to his feet, ready to bang his fist against the metal door. Boxes skidded forward, one of them sliding from the tabletop and slamming against his back. Loud music suddenly pounded from the cab of the truck, the melody overridden by the thump of the base. Even knowing he probably wouldn't be heard, he pounded on the side of the van.

When the van started down a hill and everything slid forward, he took the opportunity to dive back under the table to safety. It was overly warm there, and dark, too dark. He curled up on his side, surrounded by the bags. He decided that when there was a break in the music, he'd try again.

That was the last thing he remembered. He must have fallen asleep.

Sitting up, he rubbed his eyes, then pushed the bags away from his body. How long had the van been moving? Most of the time people in apartment complexes stayed in the city, sometimes moving only a few blocks away, but he didn't think that was the case. He had a sick feeling that a good chunk of time had passed. Maybe hours.

He was in so much trouble.

In the darkness, Logan felt past the plastic bags, his hand brushing against the metal floor and the table leg before finding what felt like a good-size, textured plastic box. Running one finger along the top, he found an indentation, a place for his fingers. After lifting the lid, he cautiously lowered his hand until he touched something cold and wet. Ice. He'd found a cooler full of ice and beverage cans. Logan pulled out a can and touched it to his forehead, then grabbed some ice cubes and rubbed them on his neck and face. Ah, so much better. After snapping open the can, he lifted it to his lips and took a sip. Cola had never tasted so good.

Drinking the cola helped with the heat, but he needed to get out of this van before it traveled any farther. When he finished the drink, he tossed the empty can back into the cooler and pulled out another, pressing it to his forehead. When he was done, he scooted out from under the table and pulled himself up to a standing position. Boxes were stacked on top of the table, and furniture was crammed on each side. There was just enough space for a boy his size to stand between the table and the back of the van. Logan pounded on the back door with the side of his fist. Even with the absence of music, it didn't make much noise, the sound lost in the vibration of the tires against the pavement. He put the can between his legs and slammed both fists now, frantic to make himself heard, but the van kept going, no sign the driver had heard him.

Finally, after what seemed like several minutes, he felt the vehicle veer to the right. He gripped the table as the van slowed. Once more he pounded, involuntarily opening his mouth, but of course, nothing came out. The van lurched as it turned, going over a bump before coming to a stop. He knocked again until he heard the opening and closing of the truck's cab doors. The sounds of men's voices coming around the side of the truck made his stomach tighten. Would they open the back? What would happen when they found him there? He'd wanted the van to halt to keep from piling on the miles between him and home, but now he wasn't so sure what would happen next.

Suddenly he was afraid. Afraid they'd call the police and charge him with trespassing, afraid of the trouble this would cause his father, who would probably take it out on him. Not probably. He'd *definitely* take it out on him.

The metal door flew up, just brushing past his nose. He blinked from the brightness of the sun before taking in the two men standing in front of him. They were young, with dark close-cropped hair and bulky shoulders. They both wore T-shirts and jeans. The taller of the two had pockmarked skin and a tattooed neck. "It's a kid," he said, his voice incredulous.

The other one said, "What the hell?"

"What's your name?"

Logan shook his head, once again frustrated at his inability to communicate.

"Kid! How'd you get in there?" Now he sounded mad.

The other one spoke up. "He's not gonna tell us anything."

Logan froze with fear, his eyes darting back and forth, taking it all in. His legs locked in place, and his feet tingled from being asleep. He could see now that they were parked next to a gas pump in front of a mini-mart. He heard a truck rattle past on the expressway nearby. The men seemed more puzzled than menacing, but that didn't stop Logan's heart from hammering. As he stood there, the two men discussed whether they should call the cops and report the stowaway.

"What if they want to search the truck?" The guy jerked his thumb in Logan's direction.

"Why would they do that?" the shorter one asked, running his fingers through his hair. His friend shrugged. "I don't know, but I can tell you I'm not going to jail because some kid decided it would be fun to hop a ride."

They turned to each other, their voices lowered, debating how to handle the situation. Logan caught something about kidnapping charges and stolen property and violating parole. When they were done talking, the taller one looked Logan square in the eye and said, "Tell you what, kid. We aren't going to call the police on you. But you're on your own to get home." He bobbed his head in the direction of the mini-mart. "Go inside and ask to use the phone." He paused to pull his wallet out of his back pocket and fumbled for a bit before pulling out a wrinkled five-dollar bill, which he pressed into Logan's hand. "If anyone asks, we're gonna say we never saw you. Now get outta here."

CHAPTER THREE

Joanne stood in the shade of her garage, her hand shielding her eyes from the sun. Her eyesight had gotten less sharp over the decades, but it was good enough to spy on the people at the new house, the one next door, close to the road. They were technically neighbors, her closest neighbors, really, since her house sat on a country road where the houses were generally a mile or so apart. She'd still have that spacing if her son, Glenn, hadn't talked her into selling off half her land to the couple she was spying on now.

Glenn, who was a financial adviser, had made a convincing case for selling the land. She hadn't been using it for anything, after all. A few years earlier, a cell phone company had offered her half a million dollars for the same scrap of land, and she'd turned it down, not wanting a cell phone tower hovering overhead, infecting her and her dog, Samson, with God only knows what kind of rays. When Glenn had seen the offer and heard what happened, he'd nearly burst a blood vessel. "You turned this *down?*" he'd asked, waving the paper in the air. She hadn't seen him so exasperated since his teenage years.

"Are you thinking I'm shortchanging your inheritance?" she'd asked, only half joking.

"No, I'm thinking of your future security," he'd said, a bit hurt at her insinuation. "I don't think you realize how many expenses can crop up late in life." Left unsaid was the conversation about long-term nursing-home care. Joanne knew both of them were thinking about it, but she'd brushed the idea away.

Going to a nursing home was out of the question. She planned to die in the middle of a good dream, safe in her bed, having fallen asleep after a long day of working in her garden.

Once Glenn got stuck on the idea of selling the land, his stubbornness reminded her of Samson gripping his rawhide. Eventually but reluctantly, Joanne had admitted he was right.

As a widow who lived alone, her expenses were low, but there were still updates needed to the house, and property taxes to be paid, as well as utilities and car repairs. She had some money and Social Security too and was managing fine for now, but an added nest egg would be reassuring.

So Joanne had let her son take charge. He'd had the land legally divided and worked with a Realtor to find a buyer. A buildable lot, they'd called it, showing photos of the wildflowers, the fruit trees, and the small creek that snaked around the back. The description had made it sound like a bit of Eden. The creek itself was too shallow for anything but wading in, but Glenn had enjoyed playing in it as a kid, and now Samson did too.

When the Realtor got a good offer, she'd left it all to Glenn. He'd handled the transaction so that all she had to do was sign the papers. "They're such a nice couple," he'd told her. "He's the new principal at the high school, and she works from home. They're super friendly. You're going to get along great."

Joanne was sure they were lovely people, but she didn't expect them to take on the old lady next door as a project, and they never did. She'd been relieved when they built their house downhill, closer to the road and away from the creek.

She could see their patio and the backside of their house from her living room window. It was a clear shot since her front yard was all lawn, but that didn't bother her. Her best view had always been the woods in back. The new neighbors had stopped in only once to introduce themselves, and after that, they had kept their distance. Both parties seemed content to give a friendly wave when they happened to drive past each other on the road.

After the money had been safely deposited into a special account at Joanne's bank, Glenn went back to Seattle to join his wife and two daughters. "Now you can come and visit us more often," he'd said, giving her a peck on the cheek. "We worry about you, Mom."

"Nothing to worry about," she'd said. "I'm fine. Busy and happy." She'd told him to give her love to Belinda and the girls. She waved as he got into the rental car to head to the airport.

During that particular visit, he had invited her to move in with them. Their new house had a bump-out with a bedroom and private bath, he'd told her. "And space for a small sitting area. We would love to have you come live with us," Glenn had said enthusiastically. "It has a separate door out to the backyard. Perfect for this guy." He'd pointed at Samson, who slept at her feet, one paw draped over his nose. Such a goofball.

"I do believe that some people call that a mother-in-law suite," she'd said, following his lead. "Thankfully for Belinda, she never has to worry about me moving in. I'm not going anywhere."

"It was Belinda's idea," he'd said.

Joanne believed it. Belinda was a total sweetheart. Glenn had lucked out in that department.

"I've always felt kind of bad for moving away after college and leaving you behind," Glenn had continued. "Especially after Dad died."

"I know," Joanne had said.

She'd always known. It might have been easier if she and John had more than one child, but one was what they got, and back then that was all there was to it.

"But you couldn't be who you wanted to be here. It would have held you back. That's fine. I understand." Glenn had nodded appreciatively then, his guilt melting away.

She knew her son's family had been bored visiting her in central Wisconsin, and she understood. It had been different when the girls were younger. All it took then was helping her bake muffins, playing fetch with Samson, and having tea parties in the tree house out back, a sturdy leftover from their father's childhood.

Once they were teenagers, everything changed, and it took more to entertain them. They became crazed at having to leave their friends, even for a week. Their lives and everything that was important to them was in the Pacific Northwest. Besides, cell phone coverage in her area was spotty, which prompted her granddaughters to have a kind of meltdown she found amusing. Her lack of cable television caused a different sort of withdrawal. After they'd reached a certain age, they all came to the conclusion that Wisconsin didn't have much to offer.

She'd visited her son's family in Seattle several times and loved the area. The landscape was picturesque. Mountains! The ocean! Hiking trails! Nirvana for the senses, and the people there were so lively, all of them coming and going with their backpacks. Tattoos and dreadlocks and body piercings so much the norm that after the first day, she barely noticed them. When she got back home to the Midwest, she noticed that the other shoppers at the grocery store were noticeably drabber and less physically fit than those she'd seen on her trip out west.

Over the years, Glenn and his family had visited less frequently, but she'd traveled to see them, and they called fairly often. Belinda too was good about mailing family photos. Every now and then, she considered Glenn's offer. Usually after a funeral. At her age, the number of funerals for people in her generation happened at the same rate as the weddings she'd attended in her twenties. Bit by bit, there were fewer of them on the planet. Her husband, John, had set the whole thing off when he'd died twenty years ago at the age of sixty-three (so young!), and after that, all her siblings had passed away, one by one, along with most of her friends. It seemed like every time she turned around, there was more bad news. Sometimes she thought to herself, *And then there was one.* Illogically, it felt like being left behind. Not that she wanted to die, of course.

It occurred to her that the best strategy might be to make younger friends. Easier said than done.

She didn't have much to complain about. Each and every day was full. In the warm weather, she spent as much time as possible outdoors, gardening and hanging wash out on the line. Nothing smelled fresher than sun-dried clothing. On Sundays, she went to church and then to bingo afterward. When her tomatoes and peppers came in, she donated bushels full to the food pantry for those less fortunate. In the winter, she read and knit and baked and watched her shows. Until recently, she had shoveled her very long driveway, but the past two years, she'd hired a plow service to do the job. Sometimes it was done before she even had her morning coffee. She was glad not to have to do it, but sometimes it seemed a bit too easy. There was something about facing an impossible task, breaking it down into small parts, and getting the job done that she found immensely satisfying.

And, of course, there was Samson, the pit bull mix who'd been her constant companion for the last eight years. He loved her so much that he got anxious if she was gone for more than two or three hours. She loved him so much that she sang to him and called him silly names, something she'd never done for any creature or person before, not even her child or husband. It was embarrassing how much she loved this dog. Taking Samson for a walk was a given, as much a part of her daily routine as brushing her teeth. And then there was his red ball, the thing he loved best. When he dropped the red ball at her feet and looked up at her pleadingly, she melted. A person would have to be pretty coldhearted not to drop everything and go outside for a rousing game of fetch. Sometimes the sight of that red ball sailing through the air and Samson leaping to catch it filled her with such joy, she felt like she might explode. Simple pleasures were often the best.

Generally she didn't concern herself with the neighbors, but today they were doing something out of the ordinary, setting something up in the backyard. Most of her land was covered in trees, what she thought of as the woods, but when this couple had the house built, they'd not only had trees removed where the house stood, they'd also created a large swath of backyard where they'd poured a patio and laid sod. Since her house was at the top of a slight incline, she had a good view of their backyard.

Joanne watched them now as they scurried back and forth, reminding her of ants carrying supplies back to the nest. She squinted, unable to figure out what they were doing and wishing she had binoculars. The man was carrying enormous metal pieces from around the side of the house, and the woman was pointing, instructing him on the placement of the pieces. The glint of the metal blinded her momentarily as the man positioned one of them on the ground. What in the world were they doing?

She thought hard, trying to remember their names. Paul and Laura. She was sure of their first names but fuzzy on the last name. Sutton, she thought. It was on their mailbox, but unfortunately they'd done it in black letters, which didn't provide much of a contrast against the metal. She'd look carefully the next time she went by and double-check, but she was fairly certain it was Sutton.

The woman, Laura, stood back, her hands on her hips, surveying what they had done. She and her husband exchanged a few words, nothing Joanne could hear from so far away, and then she dragged a large piece of metal over and moved it three feet. Eventually, the husband pulled something out of his pocket, a phone, she thought, and both of them studied the screen.

Joanne wondered if they were constructing a jungle gym or some other kind of playground equipment. Did they have children? It had been a year or so since they'd first bought the land and come up the hill to introduce themselves. The house had been built and completed more recently. Only a few months ago.

Joanne didn't remember seeing them with a baby or child, but maybe one of them had a child from a previous marriage? It was common enough. Families today were built differently than they used to be. Once, the owner of the local gas station had noticed her staring at some photos taped on the wall behind him. Joanne had said, "Your family?" and he had nodded and answered, "If you're wondering why we all look so different, it's because most of us are linked by love rather than blood."

Joanne loved that phrase: "linked by love." She'd answered, "A good-looking group."

Maybe her neighbors were anticipating a visit from a niece or nephew. It seemed unlikely someone would build a big play set for a short-term visitor, though. Well, she'd know more later on. Hopefully if there was a child, it wouldn't be the kind to wander over and tease her dog. The idea of someone being mean to Samson made her sick, but she pushed the thought away. Her husband used to say she had a tendency to borrow trouble, and as she got older, it became something she noticed more and more. More time on her hands meant more time to worry.

Down the hill, the woman dragged one of the pieces away from the rest and then leaned over to study it. The metal, Joanne saw now, was all wrong for a play set. The pieces were too wide, varied in width, and textured like brushed stainless steel. They were almost pretty. Wanting to get a better look, Joanne took a step closer, away from the shade of the garage, and craned her neck. Now she wasn't sure at all what this thing was. A sunshade? A grill? Something that would assemble into a pagoda or a gazebo? None of it was quite right for any of those things. Now that she saw all the pieces together, it looked like they were constructing a giant gyroscope. The idea was ridiculous, but that's what it looked like.

She pinched her fingers to her thumbs and put them up to her eyes, creating binoculars. She could see better now but still couldn't make out what was being built. She was just about to go into the house when the neighbor lady looked up and caught her staring. In a flash, Laura's arm raised into a friendly wave. Busted.

Embarrassed, Joanne had no choice but to wave in return before sheepishly backing into the security of the shade of her garage. Soon they'd think she was an old-lady busybody when nothing could be further from the truth. She was more curious than prying. Next time she'd be careful not to be seen.

CHAPTER FOUR

Logan took off running, not toward the gas station mini-mart, but down the road, away from the two men. They clearly weren't going to hurt him, but that didn't matter. He was afraid in general—fear-filled at having gotten himself into this predicament, so far from home and unable to communicate. A frantic knot gnawed at his stomach, the feeling that now he'd done it. There was no way out. If he could even find his way back, his father would be something way beyond furious. There was no way that would end well. And if he didn't go back home, to the apartment where he lived with Tia and her mother and his father, what would become of him? How would he live?

He stopped running when he got winded, slowed to a walk, and found himself leaning over and panting like a dog. That's when he realized he had the five-dollar bill clutched in one hand and a can of orange soda in the other. The soda was particularly troubling because it was stolen. The cola he'd consumed in the back of the truck had not been his property either. So that made two things he'd stolen. He would never consciously take something that didn't belong to him, so this blunder was completely out of character. Logan found consolation in the fact that the two men had to have seen the can in his hand, and neither one did anything about it. He had the feeling two sodas were not a big deal, considering everything that had happened.

There was no returning it now.

The road he was on was a two-lane highway bordered by tall grass. Beyond stood clusters of trees, mostly pines. He didn't see any houses or businesses, much less a police station or firehouse. How would a boy without a voice ask for help in a place like this?

He wasn't sure he wanted help.

Thoughts whirred through his mind as he put a plan into place. A right-now kind of plan. For the moment, he would take care of what was most necessary. He tucked the money into his pocket before stepping behind some trees and setting down the soda can. After unzipping his jeans, he relieved himself. When he was done, he zipped up, glad to feel the relief of a bladder unburdened. One thing accomplished.

He reclaimed the soda can and stepped out of the woods, looking back down the road toward the gas station. The truck he'd hid in was gone, no longer at the gas pump, and nowhere in sight. It would be safe to return. He took the money out of his pocket and did some quick calculations based on what he knew about the prices of gas station food. Five dollars would be enough to fill a hungry boy's stomach.

He took his time walking back, the duct tape wrapped around one sole making a *thwapping* noise against the asphalt road. Both big toes rubbed against the inside of his shoes, something that had angered his father when Tia's mother had pointed out the red spots on his feet, skin rubbed raw by the chafing. His father had exploded and yelled, "What the hell do you want me to do about it? I just bought him those shoes. The damn kid is going to drive me to the poorhouse." Tia's mother had cringed at the time and gone into the other room, where he'd heard stifled sobs. Logan had wished he could have told her not to worry, that it wasn't her fault for stirring up trouble.

She was new to his father's ways. She'd learn.

When Logan reached the drive leading into the mini-mart, he took care to enter from one side, hiding the unopened can in the bushes that lined a chain-link fence next to the parking lot.

In the front of the building was an empty wooden picnic table, the kind found in parks. He walked in behind a lady wearing a sundress and flip-flops; she held a curly-haired girl on one hip. The woman held the door open for him, and he smiled a shy thanks.

Inside was a feast second only to the Old Country Buffet he'd once gone to with Grandma Nan. In the center of the mini-mart was a setup that made his mouth water. Hot dogs spun on heated cylinders. Buns, condiments, and red-checkered cardboard holders were displayed alongside them, ready for customers to assemble their own. Premade sandwiches covered in plastic wrap were lined up in the cooler, next to a drink station that dispensed soft drinks and slush beverages. A reach-in freezer held Popsicles and ice-cream treats. Bags of salty foods were shelved next to individually wrapped containers of cookies and cupcakes. A napkin dispenser sat out in the open, along with paper plates and plastic forks and knives. Two older men were putting plates together, loading their hot dogs with pickle relish and mustard. One of them stepped away from the heated area and put his cup under a dispenser that shot out ice cubes in one noisy drop.

The woman who'd entered before him walked past, the little girl leaning out of her mother's arms and reaching for the cookies. "We'll get something *after* you go pee-pee," her mother said, yanking her upright and heading into the bathroom.

Logan took it all in, tabulating the costs of different combinations of food to determine how he'd get the most for his money. He finally settled on a prewrapped ham-and-cheese sandwich and a small bag of chips, then took it up to the counter to pay.

An old man sitting on a stool behind the counter watched a small television. A younger version of him—a man who resembled Logan's old gym teacher, Mr. Patel—stood in front of the register. It was this man who nodded when Logan set the food down on the counter. He'd been afraid someone would ask where his parents were, but neither man seemed to notice he was alone. As the man rang up his food, Logan quelled his anxiety by staring at the family photos taped to the back wall. The one that caught his eye had a large group posing in a parklike setting. At the center was an elderly couple; they were surrounded by numerous other adults, and mixed among them were at least a dozen children, including a baby in someone's arms. The group was comprised of people of different skin tones and body types, but the thing that most impressed him was the look on their faces. Every single one of them was smiling, seemingly overjoyed to be with each other. One man looked down and beamed at the little boy who stood next to him. A father and son, maybe? They looked like they wouldn't want to be anywhere else in the world. This was clearly a family who loved one another. If only.

"Your total comes to four dollars and two cents," the man said, interrupting his thoughts.

Logan pushed the five-dollar bill across the counter with one finger.

"Do you have the two cents?"

He shook his head no.

"That's okay. I've got you covered." Mr. Patel's look-alike plucked two pennies from a small ceramic bowl next to the register and added it to the till. "Have a good day, young man."

Logan had hoped he'd put his purchases in a bag, but the man hadn't, and since there was no way of asking, he picked up both items and quietly left the store. Outside, he paused and listened to the rush of the highway off in the distance. Next to the door was a newspaper box marked "FREE." Peering through the glass, he saw a stack of magazines titled *Central Wisconsin Vacation Homes for Sale*. Now he knew where he was! The truck had gone north from Chicago, and he was now in the middle of Wisconsin. Knowing this made him feel better. Everything he knew of Wisconsin was cheese, a football team called the Green Bay Packers, and a water park called Noah's Ark, which his father talked about taking him to but never did. That was one of the differences between his dad and Grandma Nan. She always kept her word. He almost never did.

He'd never heard anything bad about Wisconsin. It was a vacation place, or at least that's how it always sounded to him.

Logan retrieved the orange soda from its hiding spot and sat at the picnic table. He tried to eat the sandwich and chips slowly, sipping from the soda after every third bite. "Make it last." That was what his father always said when money was tight and there wasn't much food in the house. Which seemed to be all the time lately. They'd moved so many times since his mother had died. Sometimes they left in the night, leaving furniture behind. They went from apartment to apartment. Sometimes it was just the two of them, but more often they lived with other people, like Tia and her mom. Some things never changed, though, and he knew the routine. Keep quiet, make the food last, and don't cause trouble. If he did those things, he could get by without getting too much punishment.

Of course, it was getting harder and harder to get through a day without making his father angry. Lately, his father had been drinking more—because of his back pain, he said. "Damn car accident wrecked me," he'd say between swigs. The drinking made him mean. It was a simple cause and effect, like turning on a light switch. He'd never been a warm, cuddly father, but the drinking and meanness had gotten worse over time. Three moves ago, they'd lived in an apartment above a large Cuban family, and Logan had been shocked by how affectionate the father in that family had been toward his children. They ran to greet him when he came home from work, and he scooped up the little ones, kissing and hugging them with no sign of embarrassment. One boy had been older than Logan, and even he had hugged his father without a second thought. "Papi!" he'd call out, with unrestrained glee. Logan had wondered what that would be like. It was as alien an idea as eating tree bark.

When Logan was done eating the sandwich and chips, he crumpled up the wrappers and threw them into the garbage, keeping the can, which still had a little soda left. Buying the food and eating outdoors without being noticed gave him a boost of confidence, and he made a decision. He was not going back, at least not willingly. His father, Tia, Tia's mother—none of them would miss him, and he would not miss them either. Or at least he wouldn't miss the kind of life he led when he was with them.

And then there were the consequences of having left the apartment without permission. He'd heard how angry his father had been chasing him down the street and knew he would not come home to forgiveness. Instead, he'd be beaten or starved as punishment. Or maybe worse. Being lost and alone in Wisconsin was preferable to that.

A plan formed in Logan's mind, and this time it was a long-term plan. He'd hide for as long as possible. He thought he could do it for several days. He'd gone that long without food before. If he could find a house, there was a good chance of there being a water spigot outside where he could fill up his soda can without anyone noticing. And he still had a dollar left.

His father would never report him missing to the police. He was sure of that. He had too many outstanding warrants from the last place they'd lived. His father had been arrested for something called possession and drunken driving, and once for harassing a neighbor. He'd complained to anyone who would listen that he'd been unfairly targeted, but rather than appear in court, they'd moved again, and he'd gotten a job where he was paid in cash. That was when Tia and her mom had come into the picture too. Another new place with new people to get used to.

Because of his father's history with the police, it was a safe bet no one was looking for Logan. All he had to do was lie low for a few days or weeks, if he could manage it. As soon as he was discovered, he'd give the police a fake name and say he was from somewhere else. Or maybe he'd claim to have amnesia. He'd seen a movie once where that happened. The guy had no wallet on him when he was found unconscious, and when he woke up, he had no memory of who he was at all, like he knew nothing about himself, his life, or where he came from. If Logan was going to play the amnesia game, maybe he should become a total blank, not knowing anything at all. Or maybe just know his name but give them a fake one? He'd have to think about this some more and decide.

He knew what would happen next, after the police picked him up. They would then hand him over to social services, and the social worker would find a new family for him. A foster family. His father had threatened him with this so many times, but lately it hadn't seemed like too bad of a threat.

Maybe his foster family would have an older lady who could be a grandma to him. Logan thought about his grandma Nan. She had been awesome. Everything he did made her proud. Nothing made her angry. It had been so easy to be himself around her.

No one could take her place, but maybe he could feel that way again. That would be the best thing ever.

What a relief it would be to start over. He'd have to get used to a new place and new people, but he'd done that many times before. The idea of starting over wasn't as scary as going back to his father's rage.

CHAPTER FIVE

Laura Sutton stood at the sink, rinsing off dishes and putting them in the drying rack. Outside, the pieces from her mobile were laid out in exacting order; the glint of sun on the metal gave them a particular kind of beauty. But not the kind of beauty she imagined once it was assembled. It would be, she hoped, spectacular.

Paul came up behind her, wrapping his arms around her waist. He was so much taller and wider than she was, it was almost comical. She had trouble keeping weight on, while he had the opposite problem. Like Jack Sprat and his wife in reverse. So many times he'd said, "I will happily donate my extra pounds to you." It was a standing offer, he'd said.

Being hugged by Paul felt like being encircled in love. If his students could see their principal now, they'd be amazed to see his soft side. "Happy?" he asked. "You should be. It's been a long time coming."

She shrugged. "I won't be happy until it's installed, and everything works exactly the way it should."

"It'll work perfectly." He sounded confident. "The smaller one did, and the computer-generated one worked. All of your calculations are spot-on. What could go wrong?"

Laura knew he was right, in theory. She'd created the same mobile in miniature, and it worked perfectly, but there were variables in resizing, not to mention the installation. You never knew until the project was completed how things would work out. Everything had to be properly secured and perfectly balanced, which was easy in smaller mobiles but more challenging in a larger-scale version. This was her first big commission, and the hospital was paying $15,000 for this piece of artwork. Her biggest project yet. There were so many things to think about. First and foremost was safety. To ensure everything would be secure, employees at the hospital were going to help install the mobile in the indoor courtyard. Directly below the mobile was a garden area, and above, a circle of skylights. The garden area would be marked off-limits for all but the maintenance workers, so even if a piece of the mobile fell, there was almost no possibility of it striking a person. Still, the idea struck horror in her heart, and she was going to take extra care to make sure that never happened. She had no intention of becoming the artist whose work was deadly.

When Paul had been offered this job in a town she had jokingly called the middle of nowhere, she had been both relieved to quit the HR job she'd hated and excited to finally have time to be a full-time artist. But it hadn't quite worked out the way she'd anticipated. Building the house had been an exciting project that had both lasted too long and had been over too quickly. She'd loved helping design the house and creating a studio for herself, a designated place where she could leave her work and close the door when she was finished. She owned the mess, and it was part of her process.

Originally, she had envisioned building the house at the top of the small hill, farther back from the road, but when she and Paul had been walking the lot trying to determine where they would situate the house, she'd glanced over to see the old lady next door watching them with crossed arms and a scowl on her face. Laura had waved, and the old woman (later she learned her name was Joanne) had waved back. Friendly enough, but Laura had gotten the message. Joanne didn't like the idea of them building so close.

There was another plateau down the hill, closer to the road, and that's where they ultimately built. There was some upside to it. During the winter, the shorter driveway made snow clearance easier, and it was less of a hike to get the mail. Sometimes, though, she still thought about how nice it would be to look out the window and have the view from the top.

Paul broke into her thoughts. "Laura, it's brilliant. Everything is going to work out fine."

After twelve years of marriage and everything they'd been through together, he knew her need for reassurance. Of the two of them, he was the positive one, the practical one, the one prone to easy acceptance. They'd married so late in life that she knew getting pregnant would be a challenge, but she never dreamed it would be impossible. "Endometriosis," her doctor had told her after she had gone in for testing. "One of the most severe cases I've ever seen." He was shocked that her only symptoms were painful periods, based on how it presented. Some of that had abated after the laparoscopic surgery, but despite everything they'd tried medically, she'd never gotten pregnant, and with every passing year, their hopes eroded until reluctantly she'd agreed it was never going to happen.

She had never told Paul, but even after she'd claimed to be okay with it, she still hoped. Every month for nearly two years she'd secretly held out for a miracle. If her period was even one day late, she'd speculate as to what it would be like if she were somehow miraculously pregnant, and then counted forward to the month when that baby would be born. Lying in bed, she'd rest her hand on her stomach and imagine what it would be like to feel the first kick. And from there, she'd mentally project his entire childhood. How old she'd be when he started kindergarten. The first Christmas he'd be aware of the concept of Santa Claus. The age she and Paul would be when he graduated from high school. They'd definitely be the oldest parents at his graduation, but she wouldn't care. Miracle children didn't arrive when you wanted them, and they certainly didn't arrive in the conventional way, or they wouldn't be miracles.

In her mind, it was always a boy. She wasn't sure why. Maybe because the little boys she knew were unabashed in their love for their mothers. Her friend Sasha had a four-year-old son named Riley who said that if she died, he'd want to die at the same time because he didn't want to live without his mommy. A little morbid, especially from a preschooler, but so sweet. Who wouldn't want a child who loved you that much?

So she had hoped and prayed, and when her period arrived, as it always did, she grieved for a life that had never even begun.

At the end of several years of infertility, she had finally admitted, this time for good, that a pregnancy wasn't in their future. They had discussed adoption and surrogacy. Both required money they didn't have and had the potential for heartbreak, but Laura had still been open to either idea. Paul had said he couldn't wrap his head around the idea of surrogacy, but he was open to adoption. Except when it came time to borrow the money to adopt, they'd been in the process of selling one house and then building this new house. After that had come the big move into the new house. In between, they had rented an apartment, and he had started a new job. And when summer began, they'd had the concrete patio poured, which required patio furniture and the kind of grill Paul had always admired on their trips to Lowe's.

It was always something. And with each passing month, they got older. Lately, she got the impression he wasn't on board and was hoping she'd let it go.

Her craving for a child had been temporarily abated by the commission of this latest mobile. A major donor of the hospital had offered to pay for artwork for the indoor courtyard of the NICU and heard about her through her son, a former college friend of Paul's. They'd met privately, and Laura had shown Mrs. Lofgren her portfolio, along with images of the mobile as she imagined it. "It's abstract," she'd said, turning her laptop so the older woman could see the 3-D representation. She'd continued to explain. "The ends of the metal pieces represent the parents. The light shining through the prisms represent the babies. When the mobile rotates, the light reflects onto the metal pieces, connecting the two."

Laura had flipped through images showing it at several different angles. Mrs. Lofgren stared at the screen for the longest time, not saying a word. Laura had thought then that it was too abstract for someone of the older generation. Self-doubt crept in. Maybe she should have made it more realistic? Cherubs, maybe, or hands holding an infant? Oh, why did she go with abstract? "I can make changes if you don't like it," she'd said finally, to break the silence.

"Like it? I love it," Mrs. Lofgren had said, and when she turned toward her, Laura saw the tears in her eyes. Mrs. Lofgren removed her glasses and dabbed her eyes with a tissue she'd hastily retrieved from a pocket. "I lost a baby, you know. Thirty-two years ago. It's something you never get over." Laura hadn't known. "And your mobile is so perfect. The light can be interpreted so many ways, all of them uplifting. You've created something beautiful here. It reminds me of angels and miracles and hope." She'd sent the check earmarked for Laura's mobile to the hospital that day.

"I just don't want to screw this up," she said to Paul. "Mrs. Lofgren paid so much money for it, and she has such faith in me. I've never created anything this large."

"I have faith in you too."

"That should make me feel better, but instead I feel like I'll be letting multiple people down. This is so different from making something on my own and sitting in a booth at an art fair and waiting for buyers. This is big."

"I know, but you're up to it."

"Did I tell you they called and are creating a plaque? They wanted to know what name I wanted listed as the artist, and I had to give the mobile a name as well. It's like this official thing now."

He pulled away to look at her face. "When did this happen?"

"Yesterday."

"And you didn't mention it?"

"No, I . . ." She took a deep breath. "They caught me off guard, and I just blurted out the first thing that came to mind. Later, I thought it sounded stupid. I could still change it, I guess, if I get back to them soon, but I can't think of anything better."

"What did you pick?"

"I told them the artwork was named *This Thing Called Life.*"

Paul thought for a second. "Like from the Prince song?"

"Yeah." She looked a little sheepish. "Dumb, right?"

Paul shook his head. "I don't think it's dumb at all. I think it's perfect."

CHAPTER SIX

By the time the sun was lowering in the sky, Logan found the perfect sleeping spot. It was lucky the way he'd stumbled upon it. He'd been walking for what seemed like miles and had encountered a few houses along the way, but none had seemed quite right. He'd pause and consider each one in turn, but all of them looked so bare and wide open that he quickly discounted them.

As he walked, his strategy was to always have cover in sight; that way, if he heard a car come along, he could hide. It happened only once on the trek down the country road, and he'd darted behind some bushes before the truck came rumbling past. He'd waited another few minutes to see if it would slow down or turn around and breathed a sigh of relief when it was evident he hadn't been noticed.

In some ways, he thought, it was easier to hide in the city. There, no one would look twice at a random kid. Out here, seeing anyone was significant. A boy his size, walking alone, would be remembered.

He would have to make himself be invisible. Out of sight, out of mind, like Grandma Nan used to say. In the last few years, he'd gotten good at blending into the background.

By the end of the day, he was starting to wear down. It was around that time he spotted one more house up ahead. Closer to the road than some of the others, it sat in the base of a slanted piece of land surrounded by trees. This, he thought, was a good possibility. The house looked new, unlike the others he'd seen. It was slung low to the ground, all jutted-out angles and big windows. Modern. Even the driveway looked fancy: concrete instead of gravel or blacktop, with bricks lining both sides. Most of the houses he'd passed looked worn. This house was like a shiny brand-new toy just out of the package.

Logan saw no signs anyone was home, but still he was cautious. He circled around the perimeter of the house, taking cover in the trees. The trees were so close together that the glimpses of the sky above looked like blue shards of glass. He was invisible now, so he got a little bolder and edged closer to the house, checking to see signs of anyone around, but there was no one in view, just a back patio with some furniture and an enormous grill. On the grass behind the concrete slab, pieces of metal were laid out on the grass. Junk, maybe. Nothing that would interest him.

This house had an attached garage, and the door was closed, so he had no access to their trash cans. Logan knew from experience that garbage cans sitting unattended sometimes had food in them.

One time at school, a kid had taken one bite of an apple and then tossed it in the trash. Logan watched as it happened and knew he had to act quickly. He wasn't about to let something that good go to waste. When no one was looking, he plucked that apple off the top of the trash and stuck it in his pocket to wash off in the bathroom. It was a good apple too, a Honeycrisp. He was always on the lookout for signs of food being squandered. Sometimes there would be chips or pretzels in the bottoms of bags left behind on tabletops. If he acted quickly, he could score them for himself. Every now and then, a kid would open their lunch bag and groan at the sight of a liver sausage sandwich or sigh when they discovered their mom had packed green grapes instead of the red grapes they really wanted. And once in a great while, that kid, usually a kindhearted girl, would offer him the unwanted item, and he always took it, no matter what it was.

At his last school, his speech therapist, Ms. Tracey, noticed he didn't always bring his lunch, and she arranged for him to get free hot lunches. She didn't even call his house to set it up. If she had, his father would have told her that they had plenty of food, that Logan was just forgetful, and that going hungry would help him remember. But she didn't call, and there weren't any forms to fill out, just a plastic card that she told him to swipe up at the lunch counter when he got his food. It was like magic, having that card. He still missed Ms. Tracey, with her soft voice and understanding ways. She was the best, second only to Grandma Nan.

When Logan found out he had to go to speech therapy twice a week, he'd dreaded going, certain the therapist would try to force him to talk, something he found impossible. Unlike most things in life, his meeting with Ms. Tracey was actually better than he'd imagined ahead of time. The first day they sat across from each other at a round table in her small room, and she told him, "I want to help you communicate better. Most people communicate by talking, but I understand that's something you don't do."

He froze, but she just smiled sympathetically and kept going. "Do you ever talk when no one's around?"

When she got no response, she tried again, "According to your father, the doctor says there's nothing wrong with your vocal cords. The paperwork I got from your last school suggests that you have a form of mutism that is psychological in nature. Do you understand what that means?"

Logan stared at the table. Ms. Tracey was so pretty, with red wavy hair and tiny freckles sprinkled across her nose. Her voice was sweet too, like she was trying to be kind and wanted him to trust her. He knew where this was going. So many times adults thought they could force him to talk. His father had twisted his arm once, and the pain had been so horrible he'd almost passed out, but no sound had come out of his mouth even though he'd tried. The teachers he'd had at past schools threatened to fail him because he didn't participate in class discussions. Other kids had taunted him, trying to get him to speak.

Didn't they know he wanted to talk? He tried all the time, but his tongue froze in his mouth, and his throat convulsed. He wanted to talk more than anything, but he found it as impossible as trying to fly. Having no voice was a special kind of torture. He didn't choose this.

"Your teacher says you don't seem very happy. I'd like to help you if I can. Will you let me?"

He didn't answer that question either, but she was onto him now. "Okay," she said, her hands folded on the table. "How about this? I will never try to get you to talk against your will. I won't try to trick you into doing it, and you don't even have to answer me unless you want to."

Logan looked up from the table and managed a small smile.

"I have an idea," she said. "A special way of communicating, just between us. If I ask you a question, and you want to say yes, just give me a thumbs-up, like this." She did it with a smile, her teeth whiter than any he'd ever seen before. "And if you want to tell me no, touch your nose like this." She tapped the tip of her nose. "You'll remember because nose means no, and a thumbs-up is a yes. Do you think that would work out for you?"

Logan pulled his arm out from under the table and rested it on the surface. Slowly he clenched his hand into a fist and stuck his thumb upward.

Ms. Tracey nodded and said, "Okay, I'm glad we got that settled. Would you like to color? It's one of my favorite things to do." She got up from the table and pulled out large sheets of paper and two small buckets, one filled with crayons and one with markers. And that's how they started their session every single time they met. Ms. Tracey was a talker, filling the silence with stories about her miniature toy poodle and telling Logan about her family as they colored. Her voice twinkled like the keys on the quiet end of the piano.

She had a twin brother who, she said, "was also cursed with ugly red hair and freckles." If he could have talked and wasn't so afraid, Logan would have said he liked the way she looked. But instead he pointed to her hair and gave it a thumbs-up, and she said, "Well, thank you, Logan. I appreciate the compliment."

They colored a lot. One time he drew a picture of his grandmother and wrote, "Grandma Nan," across the top. He showed her wearing her sky-blue sweater, jeans, and the black shoes she called her flats.

Ms. Tracey said, "What a lovely picture. Does your grandmother live close by?"

He tapped his nose and then glanced downward, embarrassed when one lone tear dropped from his eye onto the paper, wrecking the drawing. He crumpled it up and threw it out, then started another one. Something different this time.

"Did she die?" she asked quietly.

He paused from coloring to raise one thumb just slightly, and then he looked back down at his picture.

"I'm sorry," Ms. Tracey said. "I didn't mean to upset you." They colored in silence then for the rest of the hour, and when the bell rang and it was time for him to go, she stopped him at the door and gave him a quick hug, even though grown-ups at school weren't supposed to hug students. Her hug helped make his sadness not quite as bad.

Sometimes she had him do speech therapy exercises that had nothing to do with talking. He practiced breathing, at first just blowing out air, sometimes using a bubble wand and liquid soap. The bubbles got all over the place, landing on the carpet and the furniture, but Ms. Tracey didn't care. "Don't worry about it," she said, shrugging. "I'll clean it up later."

Sometimes when he exhaled, a little noise came out afterward, and when that happened, she always looked so pleased. "Don't tell anyone," she said once, leaning across the table. "But I meet with a lot of students, and you are my favorite." She might have just been saying it, but he didn't think so. He definitely felt like her favorite.

"I know you're going through a difficult time now," she said. "But, believe me, things will get better for you, and you will speak again. I don't know when, but it will happen, and when it happens, it will be just like that." She snapped her fingers. "The words will come."

He must have looked skeptical because she added, "I promise you, Logan. Someday you will talk again. You have my word." She blinked and turned her head to look out the window. "I bet you have a beautiful voice."

Sometimes he imagined what it would be like if Ms. Tracey were his mom. He used to daydream that she'd go to his father saying that she'd gotten very fond of Logan and would it be okay if he came to live with her? In his imaginings, his father, relieved to have one less mouth to feed, said it was fine. There'd probably be some adoption papers his dad would have to sign, but he'd do it, no problem. And then after that, Logan would move in with Ms. Tracey and her little dog, Mimi, and they'd be a family. At night, she'd help him with his homework, and on weekends, they'd go grocery shopping, and he could carry the heavy stuff for her. At Christmastime, there would always be presents, and when he got sick, she'd take him to the doctor. When she was an old lady like Grandma Nan, he would take care of her and make sure she wasn't all alone when she died.

That would have been so perfect.

But it never happened, and then they moved, and now he was a fugitive, far from home and trying to find a place to stay hidden for at least a few days. He probably wouldn't see her ever again, until he was a grown man and went to find her.

Logan wondered if she would remember him.

He found himself climbing up a hill. It was better in the shade, out of the heat where he was shielded from the road. There were enough pine needles and leaves on the ground that he thought he might be able to make a pile to sleep on. It wouldn't be ideal, but it might work.

Logan kept exploring. He trudged upward, the duct tape on his shoe the only thing that kept him from being completely silent. At the crest of the hill, he heard the sound of rushing water on the other side of the ridge. It was so unexpected that at first he thought he was hearing things, so he paused to listen. Yes! There was water, and the sound of birds too, up in the trees.

Going down a small incline, the ground flattened out, and it was there he found a small creek, maybe five or six feet across. It was shallow, no more than knee-deep, but it flowed steadily, burbling through the streambed as if in a hurry to get somewhere. A few of the trees grew close enough to have one root in, like sticking a toe in the water. Logan sat down and took off his shoes, peeled off his socks, and rolled his jeans up to his knees. When he was done, he set down the empty soda can and stepped in, feeling the rushing coolness of the water and the soft muck between his toes. *Ahh*. What a relief to his tired feet.

He knew from watching *National Geographic* that moving water was usually safe to drink, so he took a chance and scooped it up with cupped hands and slurped it into his mouth. Then he did it again, this time letting the water run over his head and down the back of his neck.

It felt so good that he kicked up some water, delighting in how it sprayed in the air. Alone, standing in the creek, he felt like the pioneers must have when they'd discovered something new. If you found it, you could name it, according to his grandmother. Which made sense to him now that he stood in Logan's Creek, a body of water that wove its way through a piece of land that would someday be known as Logan's Escape.

The thought made him smile.

He did a ninja kick and then another one, spinning in circles as he went, and that's when he spotted the tree house located in the uppermost branches of an adjacent tree. It was as large as a garden shed and partly camouflaged by leafy branches. Logan got out of the creek and stood below it. He wondered if it belonged to some kid who might be up there right now, reading comic books, or worse yet, spying on him. He set his shoes, socks, and soda can at the base of the tree and gave it some thought. It could be a tree stand, the kind hunters used when deer hunting. That was possible, but it didn't look like a tree stand, and anyway, it wasn't deer-hunting season just yet. That, he knew, happened closer to Thanksgiving.

A ladder leaning against the tree was attached to what looked like a platform on top. Before he could chicken out, he went ahead and started to climb. Hand over hand, he made his way, careful not to look down. When he got all the way up, he saw that the platform was an actual deck, covered in several layers of matted dead leaves. The shingled roof was beat up and covered with moss. After getting up to a stand, he got a close view of the cedar-sided miniature tree house with the shingled roof. The platform had railings all around to ensure no one would topple off. He tried the knob on the front door, and it turned easily, swinging open.

Inside, it was the size of a small bedroom. Two padded chairs were on either side of a wicker table that had been set for a tea party. The plastic teapot had tipped over, but two plastic cups sat on saucers as if waiting for someone to return. Plastic cutlery sat next to each cup. In the middle of the room, he could stand upright without hitting his head. The windows on three sides were covered in curtains. When he pushed the curtains aside, he saw that the windows were actual windows, the kind that could be pushed up to expose screens.

Logan ran his finger over the window ledge and looked at his now-dusty finger. He went from window to window, pushing up each sash to let the breeze drive out the stale, hot air. Between the leaf-covered platform and the dust inside, it was clear that no one had been there for a long time, which made it the ideal place for Logan to sleep that night.

A place where no one would find him and no one could bother him. Where he'd be safe for now. Logan's own little home.

CHAPTER SEVEN

Ms. Tracey stepped back to see if the poster was positioned evenly on the wall, decided it was, and began stapling the scalloped trim around the edges. School wouldn't start for another two weeks, but she wanted to have her room finished ahead of time. Very often she was assigned kids at the last minute. And if that happened, just getting up to speed with the newly assigned students would be enough to keep her busy. If she waited until the last minute to get the room ready, the walls would never get decorated.

When she'd first arrived that morning, storage bin in hand, the school assistant, Jenny Barnes, had buzzed her in. In the hallway, she'd spotted the maintenance guy, Trey, up on a ladder replacing florescent light bulbs. The floors had just been cleaned and smelled of disinfectant. There had been a few teachers coming and going, and more of them would be filtering in next week.

Her small room at the end of the hallway had originally been a walk-in storage closet. When they had decided to use it for speech therapy, they'd added a window, but only because it was required by law. Fire code and all that. So she had a window, and they'd given her a small table and two chairs, all of them the right size for grade-school kids, but teeny for her. The bookcase and storage cubbies she'd bought from Ikea and assembled herself at school, and the posters had been ordered from Amazon. All of it using her own money.

At one time, she'd had a bulletin board where she'd posted some of her kids' drawings, but the principal had made a snide comment about this display, something about this not being art class but speech therapy. She'd had to keep her lips clamped together to keep the peace. She could have explained her philosophy about artwork being a means to gain the kids' trust and that their pictures often gave her insights into their home life, but she'd had a feeling it would have been just so many words to him. He was all about the rules. So after he'd left, she took the drawings down and replaced them with inspirational sayings. *You can do it! Believe in yourself! Failing is the first step to succeeding!*

As jobs went, she couldn't complain too much. Except for the crack about the artwork, her principal was easygoing. As long as her paperwork was in order, her students were making progress, and no parents complained, she was free to do what she wanted. She knew the classroom teachers thought she had an easy gig, and in a way, she knew they were right. But if they really wanted her job, they could get their master's degree in speech-language pathology. Then they too could work in a room so small that keeping the door ajar was required to stave off claustrophobia.

Ms. Tracey was rummaging through the bin of decorations when there was a knock on the partially opened door. "Yes?"

An older woman stood in the doorway wringing her hands. "You're the speech therapist? Ms. Tracey?"

"Yes. Can I help you?"

"I'm looking for my grandson."

Now she saw that the woman had been crying—was still crying, in fact. She had a crumpled tissue in one hand, which she now dabbed under her nose.

"I'm sorry, but there aren't any students here today. School doesn't start for two weeks."

"I know, but the lady in the front office said Logan used to come to you for speech therapy last year. She said you knew him." She rummaged through her big handbag and pulled out a photo. "Did you know him? Logan?" She thrust out the picture, but Ms. Tracey didn't even have to look.

"Logan Weber?"

The woman nodded. "I'm his grandmother, Nancy Shaw."

"Grandma Nan?"

Her face brightened. "So Logan mentioned me? Do you know where they moved to?"

"No, I don't know where he is. I wish I did," she said softly. "Why don't you sit down and we can start from the beginning? You fill me in, and I'll tell you what I know."

Both of them took a seat, their knees up against the edge of the table. Grandma Nan said, "You probably already know that my daughter, Amber, Logan's mother, died three years ago. Before that, they lived right down the block from me, and I used to babysit for Logan every day while they were at work." She paused to blow her nose. "I adore that little boy. Amber was an only child, and Logan is all I have left. He's my world."

"He really is a special kid." Ms. Tracey nodded.

"After Amber died, Logan stopped talking. Just stopped. We all assumed it was from the grief of losing his mom, but after a few weeks, I was really alarmed. I kept telling Robert—that's Logan's dad—that he needed to take him to see someone, a doctor or therapist, but he wouldn't listen. I tried talking to Logan about it, but . . ." Her voice faltered, and her gaze wandered to the window. "Well, I didn't get anywhere. He just seemed so miserable and not himself."

"I know. I got the impression he didn't have a happy home life."

"Did you get him to talk? It's been three years."

"No, he never spoke, at least not to anyone here. I felt like I was on the verge of making progress when he stopped coming to school. I was worried so I went to the home address that was listed, and the landlord said they'd moved. No notice or anything. Just left one night. Gone." This happened within days of Ms. Tracey reporting her concerns about Logan's inappropriate clothing and lack of hygiene to child protective services. She didn't think it was a coincidence.

Grandma Nan didn't look surprised. "That's been Robert's pattern for the last three years. I can't even tell you how many times they've moved. We're from Nebraska, and when he moved to Indiana for a summer job a few months after Amber died, I begged him to leave Logan with me, but he wouldn't."

The rest of the details spilled out then, how Robert and Logan seemed to move every few months, that her attempts to visit were always discouraged, although she did manage to do it two different times when they were in Southern Illinois. How Robert eventually stopped giving her their new address when they moved but would let her talk to Logan on the phone. Which didn't mean much because Logan could only listen, so she had no way of knowing if her grandson was even there.

"Robert's punishing me," she said. "Because I called social services after the last time I visited. Logan was so skinny, and his clothing was dirty and didn't fit him well. It broke my heart. I begged social services not to tell them I was the one who reported him, but he must have guessed because after that he changed his cell number and cut me off."

Grandma Nan said she had tried filing a police report, but the police had said since Logan was with his father, his legal guardian, he wasn't officially missing. Finally, after trying everything she could think of and failing, she'd hired a private investigator. The trail the man followed ended at Logan's last apartment complex. The management company for the apartment didn't know where they'd gone. She thought of checking with the local public school herself to see if anyone there had information. "And the secretary said you and Logan were close. She thought you might know something that could help me."

"We were never officially notified that they were pulling the kids out of school," Ms. Tracey said. "Logan and Tia just stopped coming."

Grandma Nan sat upright, a startled look on her face. "Who's Tia?"

"You don't know Tia?"

"No."

"She was another third grader in Logan's class. She and her mother lived with Logan and his father." She watched as the woman registered this new information.

Grandma Nan spoke quietly. "Were they married?"

"I don't think so. The kids' teacher told me once . . ." Here, she hesitated. This woman was obviously in pain. Ms. Tracey wanted to help, but how helpful would it be to pass on gossip?

"What?" She leaned over the table. "What did she say?"

"Apparently Tia told her teacher that she and her mother were living in a homeless shelter before they went to live with Logan and his dad. I got the impression Mr. Weber was there volunteering, which is how they met."

"Pffft." She exhaled in disgust. "Volunteering. That's rich. More like trolling for a girlfriend."

"Well, I can't speak to that," Ms. Tracey said, coming to the realization that perhaps she'd said too much. There were so many rules about students' privacy. She knew of one instance where a teacher had recommended that a parent discourage a friendship between their son and another boy because the two weren't a good combination. The other kid's parents got wind of this and threatened to sue. Grandma Nan didn't seem like the litigating type, but you never knew. "Mr. Weber never came to any school functions, and the cell phone number on Logan's school paperwork didn't work. And then, Logan was very guarded."

Grandma Nan said, "I guess I'm not surprised."

"There's one thing I've been wondering about. I often give the kids snacks during our time together. The students like it, and sometimes I incorporate it into our speech work—we'll count the chips or arrange them in patterns, things like that." She paused, then plunged forward. It was going to sound odd, but she had to know. "Did Logan ever have a bad experience with Teddy Grahams?"

The older woman had a blank look on her face. "Teddy Grahams?"

"Yes. Did he choke on them when he was little or something?"

"Not that I know of."

"I only ask because when I tried to give him some, he refused them, not even wanting to look at them." Ms. Tracey remembered the way he'd turned pale, a horrified look on his face as he put his hand to his mouth as if to keep from vomiting. She'd reacted quickly, scooping up the paper plate of Teddy Grahams and putting it out of sight, but he'd been an emotional mess for the rest of the session, trembling and distracted. She'd asked him about it the next time they'd met, but he'd just shaken his head. Clearly he didn't want to go into it.

Grandma Nan leaned across the table. "Do you know anything else about Logan? Did he seem to be taken care of? Did he have warm clothes this winter?"

"Yes, he had a nice warm winter jacket, and he had a hat and gloves and boots." She knew this because the teachers had cobbled together the whole set from extras their own kids had outgrown. She herself had sewn a label with his name into each item. "And he took hot lunch." Something she'd arranged.

Grandma Nan exhaled in relief. "I'm glad to hear that. Did he seem happy?"

How to answer that honestly? "I could usually get a smile out of him. He was one of my favorites." Before Logan's grandmother could delve further, she asked, "Would you like to see the drawings Logan made during our sessions?"

"Yes, I would."

Ms. Tracey got up and went to the bookcase, returning with a blue folder with Logan's name on the front. "I was encouraging him to communicate through his drawings. I had wanted him to write sentences about his life, but he shut down pretty quickly, so I backed off. We were working on breathing exercises, and occasionally when he exhaled, he'd manage a little sound. With more time, I think we could have made more progress." She slid the folder across the table.

Grandma Nan opened it with a sense of wonder, looking at each page carefully before going on to the next. "Oh! He writes his name like a big kid now. He must have changed so much since the last time I saw him. Do you have any photos of him?"

"No. I'm sorry. You can ask at the office on your way out. If he was at school on picture day, Jenny would have a copy of his class photo."

The room was quiet, just the shuffle of paper as Grandma Nan went through the stack. When she got to the last one, her eyebrows knit together. She looked up at Ms. Tracey. "He drew a picture of me, but why is it all crumpled?" She held it up, pulling it taut. Even stretched like that, the wrinkles and blotches were evident.

"Logan did that," Ms. Tracey said, suddenly remembering. "It was my fault, I'm afraid. After he finished the drawing, I asked him about you, and it made him sad." She recalled the boy's downcast head, the fat tear that had plopped onto the paper, and the anguished way he had crushed the paper and thrown it into the wastebasket. After he'd left the room, she'd retrieved it and smoothed it out. She had meant to ask Mr. Weber about the grandmother's death when they met during Logan's teacher's conference, but that had never happened, of course.

"Did you get the feeling that he missed me?" Grandma Nan asked eagerly. "Is that why he was upset?"

Ms. Tracey weighed all the possible answers to this question: *maybe; I can't say; it's possible; I don't remember; he wouldn't tell me.* Any of them would work, but it didn't feel right to lie to Logan's grandmother, so she settled on the truth. "I got the impression he'd been told you'd died."

CHAPTER EIGHT

When Grandma Nan stopped in at the office on her way out of the elementary school, she caught the school assistant, Jenny, eating lunch at her desk. "Sorry about that," the younger woman said, wiping her mouth with a napkin. "Did you find Ms. Tracey?" Jenny smiled in a friendly way, making Grandma Nan think of how welcoming this woman must be to those who came seeking comfort from playground injuries.

"I did, thank you." Grandma Nan rested her palms on the counter. "She said you might have Logan's class photo? If you do, I would really like to see it. I haven't seen Logan in more than two years."

"Two years?" Jenny pushed back from her desk, a sympathetic look on her face. "That's so sad. I bet you miss him something awful."

Grandma Nan had mentioned that she'd lost touch with Logan's family when she had first stopped in at the office, but she hadn't gone into the particulars. Somehow it had seemed a little bit shameful. What kind of grandmother didn't keep up with her own grandson? It was hard to convey that none of it was her fault. When her daughter, Amber, was alive, she'd seen Logan nearly every day. She'd had a good relationship with Robert too, although she never did love the guy. There was something about him—something a little smarmy. He could be charming, oh so charming, but all you had to do was say something he'd take the wrong way (and you never knew what that might be), and he'd become hurt and angry, saying things like, *You're out of line*, or *I don't need to take that from you.* Just to keep the peace, she always apologized, and that seemed to calm him.

Afterward, Amber made excuses for him. He'd had a stressful day at work. He hadn't slept well the night before. Anyone else might have accepted the excuses, but Grandma Nan knew better. This was not normal behavior; in fact, it was alarming. If the wrong word could set him off, what more was he capable of? Far worse, she suspected.

Robert was a drinker in a way that exceeded what she thought was normal social drinking. He was a beer and Scotch-whiskey man. She'd never seen him drunk, but the sheer volume of what he consumed, even considering his size, was alarming.

When Robert and Amber had first started going out, she'd had her misgivings. "Sometimes when you think you're falling in love with someone, you're really falling in love with the way they make you feel," she'd told her daughter. "If he's not someone you'd want as a friend, he probably isn't someone you'd want as a partner." Amber had nodded as if agreeing, but nothing changed. Amber was good at that—agreeing to her face but disregarding her advice. That girl had a mind of her own.

Usually she didn't share her family woes with other people. But if she was going to find Logan, she needed information, and if divulging some family secrets would lead her to her grandson, that was what she would do.

"I miss him terribly," Grandma Nan said, getting back to the topic of the class photo. "Seeing a recent picture would mean so much to me."

Jenny leaned across the counter and whispered conspiratorially. "I can show you the picture, but we have to make it quick. I shouldn't have even let you go back to talk to Ms. Tracey. It's against school policy for me to share student information."

Grandma Nan nodded. "I understand. I won't get you in trouble."

Jenny nodded and went over to a filing cabinet in the corner. She came back with the classroom picture and handed it to her.

Grandma Nan set it on the counter and studied it carefully. At the top was the name of the elementary school, and above the picture of the classroom teacher, Mrs. Park, were the words *Grade Three*. Below were color pictures of all the kids, along with their names.

"Oh," she said, putting her hand to her heart. Seeing Logan's face made her almost dizzy. She leaned against the counter, taking it all in. She would've known her grandson anywhere, but this was a different version of the Logan she knew. Older, of course, but his face was thinner and his hair shaggier. Amber would never have let his hair get so long. He had a pinched look too, and he lacked the joyful smile she remembered. Instead, his lip stretched into one thin line, as if the photographer had told him to smile and that was the best he could muster. Some of the boys wore shirts with a collar, but Logan had on a gray T-shirt, as if class-picture day had snuck up on him. Without a mother, so much got missed.

"He looks so grown up," she said. "Did you know him? I mean, I know there are a lot of kids at this school, but do you remember seeing him around?" She was grasping at straws, she knew, but she was hungry for details about the life he was leading without her. It was impossible to think of him being out in the world and out of her reach, not knowing anything about what was going on in his life. The gaping hole that was left by his absence was almost as bad as her daughter's death. She had cried every day after Amber's funeral but had always managed to pull herself together when it came time to babysit for Logan. She had wiped her eyes and made herself smile.

The emotional trauma that came with her daughter's death was the worst thing she'd ever endured, and it was ongoing, her grief raw and unyielding. If not for Logan, she doubted she would have survived the pain. He was the other half of her heart, and now he was gone.

"I knew who he was," Jenny said quietly. "I remember Mrs. Park saying he was a good student and no trouble."

Grandma Nan turned her attention back to the photo and ran her finger under each line of kids, searching. "There was another child in his class? A girl named Tia? I don't see her here."

"Let me see."

Grandma Nan turned the photo around.

"Here she is. Satira Zafiris." Jenny pointed to a little girl with a wide grin and a glossy black head of hair. "She has the same name as her mother, so they call her Tia as a nickname. Isn't that cute?"

Grandma Nan nodded in agreement. "What did you know about her?"

"Now her, I remember," Jenny said, still keeping her voice low. "A real character. She was what we call a frequent flier in the health room. Always coming in with some ailment, always angling to go home."

"So did she go home, then?"

"Not so much that I remember. Her mother worked as a cashier at Aldi, and we almost never could reach her. Usually we just let Tia rest on the cot for a few minutes before sending her back to her classroom. A lot of kids are like that. They just want a little bit of attention."

Grandma Nan looked at the photo again. Tia's face beamed up at her like a flower to the sun. What a stark contrast to Logan's serious expression. Were the two of them friends? She tried to imagine them doing homework together at the kitchen table. Logan was a good student and would have helped her if she needed it. Did the presence of Tia and her mom in the household provide a buffer for Robert's emotional outbursts? Or maybe eliminate them altogether? You'd think a grown man would be embarrassed to carry on the way he did, getting irate over the littlest things. It was the drinking that did this to him. He'd been balancing on a fulcrum, and the alcohol put him off-kilter and made him crazy.

A wave of emotion came over Grandma Nan. *Oh, Logan, where did you go?* She held the photo up and asked, "Is there any way I can get a copy of this?"

Jenny hesitated.

"Off the record?" Grandma Nan pleaded.

"That's probably not a good idea," Jenny said, her gaze on the photo. "I can tell you're really going through something terrible, but if anyone found out, I'd be in big trouble." She deliberated for a moment and then plucked the photo from Grandma Nan's grasp. "Wait here," she said, and disappeared through a doorway.

When she returned, she had two copies: a classroom photo and a larger one of just Logan. She stuck them into an envelope and said, "You didn't get these from me."

Grandma Nan said, "You have no idea how much I appreciate this."

CHAPTER NINE

Logan stood on the deck of the tree house watching over the land below him. The trees seemed to go on and on. He imagined that this land belonged to him, that he was the king of all he surveyed. If he were a king, he'd be the sort of leader who'd be kind to his people. They'd come to him with their problems and seek his wise counsel, and he would always have the right answers. No one in his kingdom would ever go hungry or thirsty. Those who were sick or injured would always be able to see a healer, and they wouldn't even need money to pay for it.

In his kingdom, there would be a special book they'd call *The Book of Logan* where one could find answers to every question and solutions for every problem. He imagined standing on a balcony, his humble servants clustered below, so many they could fill a football stadium. The crowd would go back as far as the eye could see. He'd give speeches that would be lauded by all who heard them, and his words would be repeated for generations. He would outlaw physical punishment for children. Instead, parents would know to speak kindly to their kids, correcting them gently and teaching them a better way. He could see it all in his mind's eye.

A passing breeze made the leaves rustle. On all sides, birds sang random notes as if acknowledging his presence among them. He leaned on his elbows, not even caring that the wood on the railing wasn't all that clean. Staring through the trees, he noticed something he hadn't seen before. A house. Not the house down the hill, the modern one with the patio, grill, and metal pieces strewn in the yard. This house was closer. Close enough that if he yelled very loudly, a person standing in the backyard might be able to hear. So close.

Too close. He would have to be particularly careful if he decided the tree house was his home base for now.

Curiosity got the better of him, and he decided to check it out. He left the empty soda can on the table next to the plastic teacups and silverware, then climbed down the ladder and made his way toward the house. When he got to the edge of the woods, he stopped, peering out from behind a shrub. There was the house, right in front of him. More of a cottage, really. It had wood siding, dark-green shutters, and windows divided by crisscross grids. The back patio was covered with an overhang, a piece of metal ridged like a potato chip and held up by decorative wrought iron posts. The posts' decorative scrollwork reminded Logan of the letter S. There was a concrete stoop by the back door, and next to the stoop, underneath the window, there was a bench holding dog toys and a watering can.

To the right of the patio was a good-size garden surrounded by stakes wrapped in chicken wire, presumably to keep out rabbits and other wild animals. The plants were tall and lush and green. He saw the red of nearly ripened tomatoes, and his mouth salivated. The sandwich and chips of earlier were now just a memory, and his stomach was ready for more food. And what else did he see? Were those bell peppers? He craned his neck but couldn't be sure. In one corner, he recognized cornstalks. Next to the garden, laundry hung to dry, flapping in the breeze.

Logan took in this unexpected bounty of food and thought hard. His grandmother had always impressed upon him the importance of honesty. One time, she had knelt down and put her hands on each side of his face, making him promise that he would never lie to her. Another time, she had explained to him the idea of karma, that what you put out into the world comes back to you. That it's not always readily apparent, but doing the right thing was *always* the right thing. He had told her that he would never steal—promised, in fact. Grandma Nan had kissed him then and said, "I know you never would. You're a good boy."

He thought about that every time he felt like bending the truth or taking something that didn't belong to him. Even considering such things made him uneasy, like he was letting her down. But the food was right there, out in the open. It looked like more than one family could eat. His mind whirled with thoughts. Was it stealing if the person didn't miss it? Was it stealing if one person had more than enough and someone else had too little? He knew the answer to both questions. There was no such thing as a little stealing or not quite stealing. Stealing was stealing.

He remembered taking the apple that had been thrown away in the cafeteria. That had not been stealing because the boy had discarded it. If there were vegetables on the ground, nibbled on by animals or starting to go bad, he had a feeling that it would be okay for him to take it. It would be the equivalent of garbage. He would be helping the gardener by cleaning up the area.

It was dusk now, though still light enough for him to see. The back porch light wasn't on, so it would be difficult for someone to spot him through the window. If he found some vegetables now, he could take them back to the tree house and then would have them for tomorrow. He still had the dollar too. Tomorrow he could walk back to the gas station mini-mart and buy something else to eat.

He walked out across the yard, past the patio, and right to the enclosed garden. Now he was close enough to see the hinged door that accessed the garden. The chicken-wire barrier was as high as his neck. Whoever had planted these vegetables took protecting them very seriously.

Glancing nervously at the house, Logan was relieved to see that the lights were still out. The garden gate was secured by a hook and eye.

He popped up the hook and stepped in, quickly assessing each row of plants. Sure enough, on the ground near one of the plants, a bright-red tomato sat in the dirt, as if waiting for him. Logan picked it up and rubbed it on his shirt. What a beauty. He'd eat it like an apple when he got back to the tree house.

He left the garden as quickly as he'd entered, latching the gate behind him. The rustle of the fabric drying on the clothesline caught his attention, and he saw two striped bath towels lined up neatly alongside a few hand towels and washcloths.

He went over and felt the fabric. It was thicker and softer than any towels his dad owned, and he thought about how nice it would be to have one of those towels at night. He never slept well without a cover. Having a towel over him would help him sleep, and in the morning, he could bathe in the creek and use the towel to dry himself. Would it be stealing if he took one now and returned it later on? Something niggled at his brain and told him the homeowner would be unhappy to discover one of the towels missing. But think how happy they'd be when he brought it back! This, he knew, was playing fast and loose with the rules, but his desire got the better of him. In an instant, he decided he'd borrow a towel.

Standing on tiptoe, he was just able to pinch the clothespins apart and pull one of the striped towels off the line. He was heading back, past the garden and over the patio, a towel over one arm and the tomato in hand, when everything went wrong.

Seemingly all at once, the back porch light went on, and the door opened, releasing an enormous, bigheaded dog. Logan froze for just a second, and then the dog barked loudly while a woman standing in the doorway yelled, "Hey, there!" And then, his brain gave his legs permission to run. "Get back here. Stop, thief!" The dog was following him now and threatening to close the gap when he reached the edge of the woods. Instinctively, he threw the tomato behind him, and then he ran faster than he'd ever run before, branches hitting him in the face as he plowed right through.

When he made it to the tree house, he scrambled up the ladder, went inside, and closed the door behind him, wishing there was a lock. He heard the dog's deep-throated bark, not menacing, but still scary, reverberating off in the distance until finally he heard the woman call, "Samson. Samson! Get back here."

He dropped into a crouch on the floor of the tree house and rocked back and forth. His heart raged, and Logan gasped for air, a horrible but familiar feeling that he was being squeezed in the middle. The first time this had happened, he'd been a much younger kid, and he'd thought he was having a heart attack and would die soon, but the sensation had passed that time and every time since, and it hadn't killed him yet. Knowing he'd get through it didn't make it any easier. He'd almost been discovered stealing food and a towel. That was against the law. This was serious.

Well, he still had the towel, so if he was discovered now, they'd know he was a thief. He'd trespassed and stolen property. That woman would surely call the police and have him taken away. He dropped to his butt and pulled the towel around him so that only his eyes and the top of his head stuck out. The towel was thicker and fluffier than he was used to, and it smelled good too, like a sunny breeze. He inhaled, trying to will his heart to slow down, to keep it from pounding straight through his chest.

When he'd had these mini heart attacks at home, his father had no sympathy. He had been, in fact, disgusted with him. "You're a disappointment to me," he'd said more than once. His father had wanted a son who was tough like he was, one who was good at sports and arm wrestling. One who was loud and confident. But that wasn't Logan. That wasn't Logan at all. He was never sure of himself. Life was loud and confusing and scary. Having these attacks made it worse because he never knew when they would happen.

But what he did know was how they had started. It was right after the worst thing that had ever happened to him. Logan had been there when it occurred, although later the police were told he was in bed asleep at the time. That had been a lie. He'd been a witness, and even now, years later, the evening's end replayed in his memory in one horrible loop.

It had started with raised angry voices and finished in a sight so devastating even thinking about it now made him want to cry. When it finally ended, his father had stood over him and said, "Not a word about this, do you understand? Not a word. Tell anyone and you'll be sorry."

He'd never told anyone what he'd seen. There was no point in telling. It wouldn't change things.

CHAPTER TEN

The area Joanne lived in was so rural that she rarely saw cars going down the road, much less a person showing up unexpectedly in her backyard. So it was a shock to open the back door to let Samson out to do his business and see a dark figure moving stealthily across the yard. Even in the dim light, she could see it was too small to be an adult. It was a boy. A young boy, and he had one of her striped towels draped over his arm.

It all happened at once then. Samson caught sight of the boy at the same time she did and went into protective mode, barking as he charged forth. She yelled something then, scaring the boy and causing him to run out of the yard and into the woods, Samson right on his heels. When a moment or two passed, she called the dog back, worried that the child would somehow retaliate, maybe kick at the dog or hit him with a stick. She cringed at the thought. Samson was a large dog with a loud bark, but he was a big baby at heart. Glenn had been concerned when he found out that she had adopted a pit bull mix from the Humane Society, but she'd never been worried. From the day she'd brought him home, he'd been nothing but gentle and solicitous, following her around like her own canine guardian angel. When she left him alone in the house and she was gone longer than usual, he greeted her at the door with more enthusiasm than she deserved. More than any living person had ever greeted her with, come to think of it.

Samson returned, bounding back to her with his usual enthusiasm. As he came into view of the back porch light, she noticed something red and mushy around his mouth, and for a split second, she wondered if he'd bitten into something—the boy's leg or a dead animal in the woods. But on closer inspection, she realized it was a tomato. In an instant, all the pieces came together in her mind. The boy who'd been in her yard had thrown a tomato at Samson, and Samson, always a pro at catching the red ball in midair, had responded instinctively, catching it in his mouth.

Joanne rubbed his head. "Aren't you a good boy, going after the intruder?" she cooed. "Yes, you are the best boy. Now go on and do your business." She waved a hand to the far side of the yard, a gesture the dog knew well. She didn't know why her voice went up an octave whenever she spoke to Samson, but it always did. She glanced toward the woods, focusing on the spot where the child had disappeared, but there was no sign anyone had gone that way. If it hadn't been for the fact that Samson had seen him too, she'd have wondered if her old eyes were playing tricks on her.

Seeing a stranger, even a small one, gave her an uneasy feeling. Her yard had always felt sacrosanct to her, as secure as being behind locked doors. Having someone trespass on her property and steal from her was an affront. And to make matters worse, the towel the boy had taken had been one of the two she used to wipe down Samson on bath day, which made it seem even more personal.

She gave it more thought while Samson sniffed around the yard, searching for just the right spot. Was it worth getting the police involved? Maybe. It was just a towel, but it felt like more than that to her. The boy had stolen from her. Worse yet, he'd trespassed and thrown a tomato at Samson. And who's to say he wouldn't have done worse if she hadn't come out just then? Maybe he would have broken into the garage or the house. And she had an even more terrible thought—what if he'd thrown a rock instead of a tomato? Samson could have been seriously hurt.

In the kitchen a few minutes later, she held Samson's snout and wiped away the tomato residue with a clean dishcloth. As she looked at the cloth, it was easy to confirm that it absolutely had been a tomato. Probably one from her own garden. Where could that kid have come from? Her house was miles from town, and except for Laura and Paul down the hill, the neighboring houses were a fair trek away. "I think," she said to the dog, "I need to go talk to them." Laura and Paul needed to be aware there was a thief in the area. Or maybe they would know who the boy was. Perhaps it was even their child or someone who was visiting them. If that were the case, they'd certainly want to hear what had happened.

She locked up the house and grabbed her keys on the way out the door. The quickest way to their house was through the woods, but she wasn't going to do that, not knowing who was out there. "I'll be right back," she called out to the dog as the door shut behind her.

Her long driveway was another one of Glenn's objections to her staying in the house: too much maintenance, too icy in the winter, so far to go for the mail, and so on. He did have a point, she thought, as she carefully stepped down the incline. She'd gotten so used to driving up and down it that it had always seemed manageable. When she got down to the street, she checked her mailbox out of habit even though she'd already gotten the mail that day. It was empty, but she was able to confirm that the mailbox next to it had the name "Sutton" above the mailing address. She continued on to the bottom of her neighbors' driveway and then worked her way to their house.

She'd never seen her neighbor's house so close up and was amazed by all the windows—a wall of glass that wrapped itself around all sides. More surprising yet was the lack of window coverings. A person could look right in. The house was brightly lit, and she felt like she was viewing a museum exhibit through the glass. It would be labeled something like "Modern Couple's Living Room" and would showcase Scandinavian design furniture, hanging light fixtures reminiscent of paper lanterns, and a television screen the size of a grade-school classroom's world map. Such a contrast to her plaid couch, tan recliner, and phone still mounted on the wall in the kitchen. Her granddaughters had gotten a good laugh out of that one, pretending they were on the phone and walking away but getting boomeranged back when they reached the end of the cord. It was rather funny, but she still wasn't getting a new phone. The one she had served her purposes just fine, thank you very much.

Joanne knocked on Paul and Laura's door a few times, and when there was no response, she pressed the doorbell.

CHAPTER ELEVEN

They'd been just cleaning up the dinner dishes when the doorbell rang. Paul and Laura exchanged a quizzical look. "That better not be your mother," Laura said, only half joking. Unlikely, since his parents lived three hours away, and they were not known to drop by without notice. Also unlikely because he'd talked to his mother for an hour on the phone earlier today while Laura was at the grocery store. Their long conversation meant that they were, for all purposes, caught up on all the details of their respective lives. His mother, a woman who could be abrupt at times, actually closed by saying, "Well, I think we're caught up now. Give my love to Laura."

When Paul opened the door, he didn't recognize the older woman at first. "Can I help you?" he asked, aware of his wife hovering right behind his left shoulder.

"Yes, I'm your neighbor from up the hill. Joanne Dembiec?"

Of course. They'd met once before just to exchange introductions and often waved to each other when passing in the car. Her son had handled most of the details of the sale of the land and said his mother was happy to be gaining a close neighbor, but that wasn't the impression Paul had gotten. "Please. Come in." He stepped back and held the door open for her.

"I hate to intrude," she began, stepping through the doorway, "but I wondered, do you have a child? A little boy?"

Paul felt Laura's hand tighten on his shoulder. He said, "We don't have any children. It's just us."

Joanne continued. "So you don't have anyone visiting you?"

"No."

"I only ask because a few minutes ago I caught a kid in my yard. He stole a towel off my clothesline and threw a tomato at my dog. Then he disappeared into the woods. I'm not sure where he came from, but I thought you should know. You might want to watch your property and bring in any valuables."

"Did you call the police?" Paul asked.

"Not yet," Joanne said. "This just happened a few minutes ago, and I didn't get a good look at the boy, so I can't imagine there's much they can do about it. I thought you should be informed because you're so close by." Her voice quavered at the end. Paul took this is as a sign she was more rattled by the incident than she'd first appeared.

Laura was by his side now. Her expression was one Paul knew well. "Why don't you come in and sit down," she said gently, gesturing toward the living room. "You can tell us exactly what happened right from the beginning."

Joanne nodded, letting Laura lead her to the couch.

"Can I get you something to drink?" Laura asked. "A soft drink or a glass of water?"

"Or wine?" Paul added. "We just opened a bottle of Riesling."

Joanne nodded. "Riesling sounds nice. Maybe just half a glass?"

Paul went into the kitchen to get the wine and listened as he heard the two women talking, Joanne saying what a shock it was to see a stranger in the dark in her yard, and Laura murmuring a sympathetic response. Laura had a knack for drawing people out. It was like she cast spells wherever she went. People on elevators talked to her. Cashiers told her their troubles. Babies stopped crying when she talked to them.

He'd tried to figure out what exactly it was about her that made her so approachable, and all he could come up with was that she exuded empathy. With just a nod and a tilt of the head, it was apparent she cared.

Paul whistled as he got out three wineglasses and lined them up on the kitchen counter. The patio light was on, and through the window above the sink, he could see the pieces of Laura's mobile still laid out on the grass. It was unlikely someone would steal them, but he'd still bring them in. Better safe than sorry. As he poured the wine, he thought about the phone conversation he'd had with his mother earlier. It was rare for them to talk for so long. Usually they exchanged a few pleasantries before he handed the phone over to Laura, the one she really wanted to talk to. This time it was different, though. For some reason, he had blurted out the one unresolved issue in his marriage. Children. Or one child, really. Laura had a sort of desperate need, a craving, almost, to love and raise a child. Since they had discovered a pregnancy was impossible, other options had come up. They'd ruled out surrogacy, or actually, he'd ruled it out. He had trouble wrapping his head around the idea, and the cost was outrageous.

Laura had conceded that point but said she didn't care if the child was related to them; she was open to anything. She had suggested doing foster care with an eye toward adoption. In her mind, there was a child out there waiting for them, and the longer he delayed the process by endlessly thinking about it, the longer that child waited.

"So what's wrong with that idea?" his mother said. "You don't want to do foster care?"

Paul sighed. "It's not that I don't *want* to do it. It's just that I don't think she's thought it through. She doesn't seem to realize she might be setting herself up for heartbreak. Who knows what these kids have been through? I'm with kids all day, and believe me, there's a range. Laura wants a child to love, but I don't think she fully realizes you never know what you're going to get."

His mother laughed. "Paul, even when you have your own, you never know what you're going to get. I gave birth to all three of you, and you and your brother and sister couldn't be more different."

"I know that," he said, a little impatient. "I'm talking about the possibility of getting a child with a severe mental illness or an outrageous behavioral problem." Something that could ruin a marriage. He didn't say it, but it was his main objection.

"We have that in our family too." She was almost giddy now, happy to refute all his objections. "Remember Uncle Dave at the last family wedding?"

Paul wasn't going there. He said, "And even if the foster kid is well adjusted and doesn't have a behavioral problem, what if you get attached and want to add them to your family, but the birth parents get their act together and want them back? How devastating would that be for Laura? I'm just trying to protect her."

Now his mother was quiet on the other end of the line. "I know you love Laura and want to protect her, but I'll tell you what I'm really hearing—*you're* the one who is worried about all these things. Laura sounds like she's willing to take on the risks. You know that there's no compromise on this kind of issue. You can't have half a child. You're either in or you're out. Laura's always been there for you. Don't you want her to be happy?"

"She is happy," he said with a heavy emphasis on *happy*. "She finally has time to work on her artwork, and she just got that big commission. And we're planning to go to Spain next summer." It seemed to him like that should have been enough. "I think if she continues to have success in the art world, this will fade. She'll be too busy to even think about it."

"I don't see that happening, Paul."

"We'll see, I guess."

"I know you didn't ask for my advice . . ."

"But that's not going to stop you."

His mother laughed. "You always were a smart boy. Anyway, this is what I do when I have a difficult decision and I don't know what to do. I don't do anything at first. I just listen."

"You listen?"

"I listen, and sooner or later, I get a sign that points me in the right direction. It's not always an actual physical sign. Sometimes it's just a still, small voice inside of me, but every single time, I get a sign. Once it happens, the answer to my dilemma becomes very clear to me. Now I'm not saying this is the only way to go about it, but it works for me, so you might want to take a pause and listen, then see what happens."

"Okay, Mom, I'll give that a try."

They both realized he was humoring her, but he knew better than to argue with his mother. When he was growing up, the family motto was "Mother knows best." He hadn't checked lately, but he believed it was still in effect.

Now he recorked the bottle, put it back in the fridge, and carried all three glasses into the living room. The two women barely gave him a glance as they took a glass and kept talking.

"Fascinating," Joanne said. "I can't believe I live right next door to an artist."

Paul took a seat opposite them and watched as they chatted like old friends. Laura got out her laptop and showed Joanne the images of the finished mobile. "It's going to hang in an indoor courtyard at the NICU in a hospital in Milwaukee," she explained.

"NICU?"

"Neonatal Intensive Care Unit. It's where the preemie babies stay until they're healthy enough to go home."

Laura explained how the spotlights below would hit the prism, resulting in beams of light that would connect with the metal pieces as they moved, and Joanne marveled at the ingenuity of it all. "You're part artist, part inventor, part magician," she exclaimed.

"Oh, I don't know about that," Laura said, her cheeks flushed from the praise.

Joanne looked straight at Paul. "You must feel so lucky to be married to such a talented woman."

"Believe me I do. I won the wife lottery."

"Oh, stop." Laura waved a hand in his direction, trying to fend off his words, but it was clear she was pleased. Compliments made her so happy; he really needed to pay them more often.

There really was nothing Paul *didn't* love about his wife. The first time he'd spotted her, both of them had been taking night classes toward a master's degree. She'd been filling a water bottle at the drinking fountain and humming to herself. The halls were filled with other students coming and going, but once she'd caught his eye, it was like a spotlight had clicked on, casting a cone of illumination over her. She was pretty, it was true, but the campus was filled with pretty young women. None like her, though. That day, she'd had her hair braided and wrapped around her head, a style that might have looked odd on anyone else, but on her it had worked. As she'd filled her water bottle, she noticed him staring and said, "Sorry for taking so long. Almost done." And then, as she screwed the cap on and stepped back, she'd said, "Important to keep hydrated, you know."

When he saw her later sitting on a bench outside, he took the seat next to her and said, "Still keeping hydrated?" He'd thought it was a good line and pretty slick on his part, but she had no recollection of what she'd said earlier and gave him a blank look. Paul had to explain why he'd randomly said this weird thing, and instead of it being awkward, she'd thought it was hilariously funny. They'd started talking then and never stopped. Now the bit about keeping hydrated was one of their catchphrases, a private joke between them.

He loved everything about Laura. If he could have given her a baby, it would have made her supremely happy and him too. That it didn't work out was his biggest regret.

Paul sipped his wine and let the two women talk. Joanne's son lived in Seattle, a city Paul and Laura had visited recently, so they compared notes. They also discussed the library in their own small town and the café on Main Street. "We'll have to go to lunch sometime," Laura said. Joanne looked pleased, and in that instant, it was clear his wife had made a friend. After they'd chatted for an hour, Joanne said something about hiking up the hill toward home, and Laura said, "You shouldn't walk in the dark. Especially with a stranger lurking out there."

Paul knew his cue when he heard it. "I'll drive you," he said, standing up.

"But it's so close," Joanne protested. "I hate to put you to the trouble."

"Yes, but it's dark, and the hill might be slippery," Laura said. "Just let Paul give you a ride. Please? I would worry otherwise."

"It's no trouble at all," Paul said. "I'll get the keys."

CHAPTER TWELVE

Back in the tree house, Logan tried to relax his racing heart using a trick he'd come up with long ago. He'd discovered that if he tried to ignore the rapid pounding and concentrated on something else instead, it helped. It was almost as if his heart lost interest in being afraid.

In the dark tree house, he took the dollar bill out of his pocket, sat down on one of the cushioned chairs, and laid it flat on the table, smoothing out the wrinkles with his fingertips. One dollar. All the money he had in the world. He would have to be very careful. He had just enough to buy a little something at the gas station tomorrow, and after that, he'd be out of luck. SOL, his father used to say. The letters stood for something Logan knew not to say aloud. Grandma Nan hated profanity and said that cursing was a lazy way of speaking, that an intelligent person could come up with all different kinds of words to describe things. "Keep expanding your mind, Logan," she'd say. "A smart boy like you will go far in this world."

Grandma Nan loved to learn, and she especially liked to share interesting ideas with Logan. She always carried a book in her purse, so she'd have something to read if she had to wait somewhere. The last book he remembered seeing her read was about some guy named Genghis Khan. She'd said it was fascinating. Sometimes she read mysteries or thrillers too, but only if they weren't too gory. Her favorites were about real-life people or nonfiction books about scientific discoveries. She would say things like, "The more I learn, the more I realize how little I know."

Another good thing about Grandma Nan? If she told him she was going to do something—take him to the park or bake cookies together or build a snowman, it always happened. Grandma always kept her word. She'd say, "A promise is a promise," which was puzzling, because what else could a promise be?

Sometimes she told him stories about his mother when she was a little girl, and the stories brought her to life in his mind. Amber was his mother's name. Grandma Nan made her childhood sound wonderful. His mother had lived in the same house from the time she was a little baby. Same school too. He could only imagine what that would be like.

He did some deep breathing and closed his eyes for a moment, happy to realize his attack had passed. Preparing for sleep, he pushed the furniture against the wall and took the cushions off the chairs. When he lined them up on the floor, he'd created a makeshift mattress. He settled down on the cushions, pulling the towel over him. Not as good as a blanket, since it only covered his feet to his midchest, but at least it was something.

Logan lay there for minutes that felt like hours. He blinked, and the view with his eyes open was the same as with them closed. The wind in the trees became eerie voices, the whispers of little kids telling each other ghost stories.

He thought he'd feel more secure sleeping with the towel covering him, but now the guilt of having taken something that wasn't his weighed heavily on him. He could almost hear Grandma Nan's voice speaking to him about honesty and the importance of telling the truth and how karma worked. All the good and all the bad, it all came back to you, was how she put it. She would be ashamed, knowing what he'd done. Maybe she knew, even now, watching over him from heaven.

For a year or so after they'd first moved, he'd heard from his grandmother on a regular basis. On two different occasions, his father had even allowed her to visit. She'd sent packages and cards filled with five-dollar bills almost every week. His father had usually taken the money for household expenses, but one time, he'd let Logan keep it, and he'd bought candy at the corner store. Grandma Nan had called often, never expecting him to talk. Instead, she'd fill the silence herself with updates on her life, talk of how much she missed him, and promises that he could come and visit her in the future if his father agreed.

That all changed one night shortly after they'd moved into an apartment with his father's new girlfriend at the time. Her name was Alicia.

Alicia was not nearly as nice as Tia's mother, but she had kept the place clean, and she had cooked too. Like his father, Alicia was a beer drinker, and man, could she drink a lot! As much as his dad, even. When Alicia and his dad were drunk, neither of them seemed to want Logan around. That was when he first perfected the art of being invisible. If he kept out of sight and didn't create any mess and didn't ask them for anything, they would forget he was there, which clearly was the best thing for everyone.

One evening shortly after he'd gone to bed, he overheard Alicia ask his father if there were some other relatives who could take Logan off their hands. Logan had often wondered this himself, knowing that Grandma Nan had offered to let him live with her, but that his father had said no. His refusal had been somehow connected to something called a Social Security check. He knew this because he once overheard Grandma Nan on the phone telling her sister that Robert was only keeping Logan for the Social Security check. "He can keep the money, as far as I'm concerned," she had said. "I just want Logan." But that never happened, and now Alicia had brought up the subject again. Logan's ears perked up, waiting to see what his father would say.

"The boy only has me," his father had bellowed, his words slurred. Logan could picture the two of them in the kitchen, drinking beer, numerous empty cans pushed off to one side of the table. "All his mother's people are dead."

Alicia had said, "All of them?"

Logan had gotten out of bed and tiptoed to the door to listen more closely.

"Any of 'em who'd take him," his father had said.

Overriding the urge to be invisible, Logan had gone into the kitchen and scrawled a note on a receipt he'd found on the counter: *Is Grandma Nan dead?* He pushed it toward his father and held his breath. He had to know the truth even as he dreaded finding out.

His father took a swig of beer before looking at Logan's note and nodding a yes. "Old people die, son. That's a fact of life. You gotta get used to it. Now get back to bed."

Logan had cried that night, silent sobs into his pillow. When he'd woken up the next morning, his eyes were swollen and red. He'd looked and felt awful, but no one seemed to notice. It had occurred to him that his father didn't always tell the truth, but when he hadn't heard from his grandmother for days and then weeks, he had to face facts.

She was gone. If she were alive, she would've called and sent cards and packages. There was no way she would've forgotten about him. If he thought about it too much, the grief became fresh, and he'd start crying all over again. There was no point to that.

He could imagine what Grandma Nan would say about taking the towel and the tomato and trespassing on that lady's yard. She would not be proud of him. Knowing how disappointed she'd be made him disappointed in himself.

He knew what he had to do.

Moments later, he was climbing down the ladder, the towel over his shoulder. After his feet hit the ground, he headed toward the lady's house, guided through the trees by the light in the windows. He stepped carefully, pausing for just a second when he heard a rustling nearby. The wind or some animal? It was best not to think about it, or he'd freak himself out.

When he finally got to the patio, he stopped and folded the towel into one neat square. The back porch light wasn't on, but the interior was lit in a friendly way, making him vaguely homesick for a home he remembered from long ago, before his mother had died and life became complicated and harsh.

He climbed up on the bench next to the concrete stoop and peered in through the kitchen window. No one was in the kitchen, but through an arched opening into the living room, he caught sight of the woman sitting in a recliner, her eyes closed. Her dog was at her feet, his head resting on her shoes, his paws on either side. Both looked comfortable and relaxed. He got a good look at her now, the lady who'd chased him off her property. She didn't look scary now—just old—with gray hair chopped off at chin length and wire-rim glasses. Even though it was summertime, she wore a cardigan sweater and long pants.

Logan slowly got down off the bench, placed the folded towel on the back stoop, and knocked on the screen door twice. When he heard the dog bark, he took off like a cannonball, out of her yard and into the woods, back into the void, heading for the safety of the tree house.

~

Joanne had been resting her eyes when Samson suddenly howled and bolted to the back door. "What is it, boy?" She followed him into the kitchen and found him stationed by the door, barking continuously.

"Quiet, Samson," she said, ordering him to sit and stay. The dog sat on its haunches and whined, his tail twitching slightly.

Tentatively, she switched on the back porch light and opened the door. "Who's there?" she called out into the humid night air. Hearing nothing, she leaned forward through the doorframe and spotted the towel on the stoop.

She picked it up and found it neatly folded. So odd to have it returned to her like that. The boy had returned it in perfect condition, late at night, and then slipped back into the forest before she could get out of her chair and to the door. Either someone had told him to give it back or his conscience had been bothering him. She stared at the trees surrounding her yard and imagined what it would take for a child to dive back into its dark depths. "Thank you," she called out, then went back into the house, the screen door shutting behind her.

CHAPTER THIRTEEN

Grandma Nan sat in her car with the windows open, staring at the photo of Logan. He'd been at this school only a few months ago. If she hadn't waited so long to hire the private investigator, she would have found him. She tried to picture him walking the halls, carrying his hot lunch on a tray across the cafeteria, and sitting at Ms. Tracey's table in the tiny speech therapy room, but it was hard. In her mind, he was a much smaller boy, and now she had to replace that image with this big kid, the child he'd become in her absence.

When she'd left the speech room, Ms. Tracey had asked if she wanted Logan's artwork. Gratefully, she'd said yes. She'd walked away with the envelope clutched to her chest, the contents as precious as anything she'd ever owned.

It comforted her to have something he'd done recently, although the idea that he thought she was dead wrung her out and broke her heart. It would make sense, though, to a boy of nine. How else to explain the lapse of a devoted grandmother who'd sent cards and packages every week? It was Robert who'd cut her off, and he would have been the one saying she was dead. Death. An easy way to shake off unwanted attachments. Such cruelty, and why? Knowing how touchy Robert could be, she'd never been anything but nice to him.

When Robert and Logan had stopped answering the phone, she'd been alarmed, and when the first package had been returned marked "Not Deliverable as Addressed, Unable to Forward" she'd become nearly frantic. A dozen scenarios had played out in her head. They'd gone on a trip or were visiting some of those dysfunctional relatives on Robert's side. Or maybe they'd been evicted and just hadn't gotten around to giving her their new address. As the weeks went on, her mind had created reasons too terrible to even think about. They had both been murdered. One or both of them had been abducted. Robert had abandoned Logan and taken off with a new girlfriend, and now Logan was wandering the streets alone.

She'd joined Facebook, and once she figured out how to message, she'd contacted everyone who had a connection to Amber or Robert, including Robert's sister-in-law, a woman named Yvonne who was married to Robert's older brother, Neal. Neal was another winner, in and out of jail like it was a revolving door. None of the charges were valid, according to him. The local police hated him and targeted him.

No one Grandma Nan had messaged knew how to find Logan and Robert, although Yvonne had said Robert had a new phone number, but she couldn't give it to her. "I'll let him know you're looking for him," she'd said.

Grandma Nan had been hopeful after that, but as the days and weeks went on with no call, hope had died out, like a fire turned to ash. And then Yvonne had blocked her, and that was that.

Months went by and then a year, and then more months, each day a marker of what she'd lost. She did Internet searches and some investigating on her own, going to bars Robert used to frequent and talking to his former coworkers. None of it led to anything. The police had been sympathetic but not helpful. Eventually she hired a private eye, an ex-cop named Granger Finch. "Everyone calls me Grinch," he'd said the first time she visited his office. Grinch. She was putting all her faith and hopes in a guy named after a heartless picture-book character.

Grinch had an office in the lower level of a complex where each room housed a different business; they all shared a bathroom out in the hallway. His room was sparse: a desk fronted by a chair, a computer, and an upholstered armchair in one corner. He looked like an eighties sitcom grandpa: thinning hair combed over the top of his pink scalp, thick-lensed glass, and a striped button-down shirt with a gray sweater vest over it.

"Most people contact me by phone," he'd said apologetically before getting up to move the chair closer to his desk. She told him her story, and he'd nodded as she talked. He asked a lot of questions, took notes, told her his fees, and said he'd be in touch.

He'd somehow traced Robert to this town in Illinois and got the address to their apartment. Once she had the address in hand, she immediately packed, got into her car, and drove, only stopping for bathroom breaks. When she arrived at the apartment and found out they'd moved, she came up with the idea of visiting Logan's former elementary school to see what she could find out.

The class picture and folder of artwork were proof of her grandson's recent existence. She was glad to have it, but it was not enough. Not nearly enough. Not even close.

She shuffled through the artwork one more time, and as she flipped over one of the papers, she noticed something she hadn't seen before—a sticky note with delicate writing in blue ink. She peeled it off and read it: *Logan is visibly distressed when questioned about his mother's death. I suspect he may have witnessed this traumatic event.* The note had to be written by the speech therapist. Somehow it had gotten mixed into his artwork folder.

I suspect he may have witnessed this traumatic event.

But that didn't make any sense. There had to be some kind of mistake. Logan had been asleep during Amber's accident and had only woken up after the police had arrived. And his father hadn't even been home at the time. It was in the police report, and when she'd asked Logan if that's how it happened, his nod had confirmed it.

Studying the class photo, it dawned on her that it gave her more information than she'd had before.

Tia's mother.

Jenny had said the girl and her mother had the same name and that the mom had worked at the Aldi grocery store. Should she call Grinch with this new development? Perhaps the manager at Aldi would have Tia's mother's forwarding address, and she could track Logan that way.

She'd driven all the way from Nebraska to find him, and she wasn't going home until she could wrap that little boy in her arms and hold him close. She'd stay in Illinois forever if necessary.

CHAPTER FOURTEEN

Logan woke up to the sound of birds singing. Loudly. Very loudly. He didn't know birds could make that much noise—chirping and squawking as if they were right in the room with him. He rubbed his eyes and stared upward, pinpricks of daylight coming through tiny holes in the ceiling of the tree house. It took him a split second to realize where he was—to remember the events of the last twenty-four hours: throwing up on his father, running in terror, and being accidentally trucked to Wisconsin, where he found this tree house.

The room began to take shape around him as he focused on the details, the tiny specks of dust that whirled in the sunlight, not in any hurry to find the floor. The squared windows covered by the plain strips of fabric that served as curtains. The underside of the table where the wood wasn't finished and someone had marked the number thirty-six in black marker.

The cushions he'd been sleeping on had shifted during the night, and there was now a gap between his butt and legs. He sat up and blinked, then rubbed at his eyes again. The thin curtains fluttering with the breeze didn't do much to block the light, and he saw the inside of the room in a whole new way. Dust covered most of the floor, and even the cushions looked water-spotted and grungy. Clearly no one except him had been up here in a long time.

Logan got up and pushed the curtains aside to look out but couldn't see much beyond the leafy branches right outside the window. He opened the door, scaring a bunch of birds that had been roosting on the deck. The birds couldn't have been that frightened, though, because a moment later, he heard them settle in a nearby tree, cheeping and chirping as annoyingly as they had when they'd first woken him up.

Stupid birds.

He assessed his situation and listed off his needs in order. Bathroom break first. That one was easy. Then water and then food. His stomach growled, reminding him that yesterday's sandwich was only a memory. That dollar would have to stretch as far as possible. He wondered if the gas station would be open this early, then decided it probably would. After getting his shoes on and grabbing the empty soda can, he made his way down the ladder and hoped he wouldn't encounter that big dog again. What was his name? Oh, yes, Samson. The dog hadn't growled at him, but that didn't mean anything. A dog protecting his property could attack, and he could certainly outrun Logan. If he hadn't been distracted by the sight of the tomato flying through the air, Samson would have caught up to him, no problem. And who knows what would have happened then?

After filling the can in the stream and sipping from the cool water and pouring some over his head, he headed to the gas station. It was going to be a hot day, and he wanted to get this over with.

He passed only one vehicle on the way, and he had plenty of time to duck for cover. Once the car went by, he waited until it was out of sight before leaving the bushes and walking on the road again. The soda can had been purposely left behind, but he had the dollar in his pocket and kept checking to make sure it was there. He thought about the money he'd hidden in his sock drawer at home. After Tia had taken money from his stash, he had gotten smart about it and moved it into one of his socks, a pair he then mixed in with the others in his underwear drawer. Even Tia wouldn't mess around with his briefs, so it had been safe after that.

Six dollars and thirty-seven cents was how much he had saved up. Money he'd gotten in change after buying candy with one of Grandma Nan's five-dollar bills, combined with a few dollars Mrs. Smith, a neighbor at the apartment complex, had given him after he'd helped her carry some heavy groceries from the neighborhood store. She'd done a magic trick, pretending to shake his hand, then grinning at his expression when he'd realized she'd slipped him some money. He'd tried to give it back, but she had been firm, closing his fingers around the dollars. "I insist," she'd said. "I want you to have it."

If he'd had that money with him when he hid in the truck, he could buy lots of food today. Well, there was no point in thinking about it too much. It's not like he'd ever see that money again.

By the time he arrived at the gas station, the day was beginning to heat up, and he was glad to get into the air-conditioning. Outside, almost all the pumps were occupied, and indoors, a small line led up to the counter. Twin girls about his age hovered near a display of doughnuts by the coffee station, while their mother stood nearby, adding creamer to her tall to-go cup. "Remember, one each, girls," she said, glancing their way.

He darted into the bathroom to use the facilities, glad it was a room that only one person could use at a time. He washed his face, hands, and neck, then dried off with the brown paper towels. It occurred to him, as he pulled out the third and fourth paper towels, that the supply of paper towels was free and endless, so when he was done washing up, he took several more, folding them into his pocket for later.

At the food area, Logan scanned all his choices, his heart sinking when he realized his dollar wouldn't buy anything too substantial. He walked listlessly around the store, ruling out sandwiches, hot dogs, and chips. A candy bar was a possibility. A few were discounted and listed at eighty-nine cents. But as delicious as candy was, he knew it wouldn't stick with him through the day. He could get an ice-cream sandwich, but that too would not keep his belly full for very long.

He meandered away from the food area, and that's when he saw a basket of bananas sitting on the counter near the register. A sign said they were forty-nine cents each. It was his lucky day. He could afford to buy two. Logan grabbed the two largest bananas in the basket and got into line, his dollar bill in hand. He waited as the line inched forward, listening as other customers made small talk.

"Did you hear about the big storm that's coming?" a man with a trucker hat asked as he handed his credit card over the counter.

"But it's so sunny," an old lady right in front of Logan said. "Are you sure?"

The man turned and told her, "It's not today. It's later on. A huge front is moving in. Make sure your windows are closed."

"They're already closed," she said. "We've had the air-conditioning on since June."

It always puzzled Logan how adults could go on and on talking about the weather. Who cared? It was just weather. It came and it went. Sometimes it snowed, sometimes it rained, and sometimes the wind blew. Talking about it didn't change anything, and it wasn't all that interesting to begin with. The only time he really took notice of the weather was last winter when it had gotten so cold and he only had a sweatshirt jacket. It had gotten to be kind of embarrassing. When the snow had started to fly, even some of the kids started asking why he wasn't wearing a winter coat. He'd just shrugged like he didn't feel the cold at all, but really he was freezing, and it was tiresome having to keep his hands in his pockets when he was outside. Plus, his shoes had filled with slush, and his feet had been frozen half the time.

One day his teacher, Mrs. Park, told him to stay after class. He'd been worried he'd done something wrong, especially because she'd waited until all the other kids had left, even ducking her head out the door to make sure no one was in the hallway. After that, she took a large plastic bag out of her closet, pulled out a jacket, hat, gloves, and boots, and laid them across the table in the back of the room. "These are yours," she had said, and then clarified further. "For you to keep. Extras that the school had."

He pulled them on eagerly and mouthed the words "Thank you." She'd said, "You're welcome, Logan. Stay warm."

Later, he noticed that each item had a small cloth label with his name on it stitched right into the fabric. He'd thought his father would make a big deal out of the free clothing, but if he noticed, he didn't say anything.

The rest of the winter on the playground had been much nicer since he no longer had to fight chattering teeth and worry about frozen feet. It had been kind of Mrs. Park to notice and give him what he'd needed without the other kids finding out.

There were so many good people in the world, but it always seemed like there were more bad people because they made more noise.

The man in the front of the line was still talking about the weather, even as he was punching in the code for his debit card. "I'm gonna make sure I batten down the hatches. Last time I lost a folding chair when it blew off my patio. We looked everywhere and never did find it."

Logan was so hungry he could almost taste the bananas in his hand. Hurry up, hurry up, hurry up! Why was this line moving so slowly?

Eventually, the man with the trucker hat left, the door jangling as he exited. After the lady in front of Logan finished paying for her gas and gum, it was his turn. After putting the two bananas on the counter in front of him, he held the dollar out to the man behind the register, the one who'd reminded him of his old gym teacher, Mr. Patel. Today, though, he was alone. The elderly man who'd been watching TV the day before was nowhere in sight. It had been only yesterday that Logan had been here, but it seemed like a long time ago.

"Ah, so you've returned," the man said, a smile spreading across his face. "Good morning to you."

Logan felt himself stiffen, surprised at being remembered. He felt a wave of panic rise up in his chest. It was never good when people talked to you and you couldn't talk back. What if this man asked why he was always alone? Even if his voice worked, there was no sensible explanation.

The man continued. "There's actually a sale on bananas today. Buy two get one free. Go ahead and take one more, if you'd like."

Logan felt worry lift off his shoulders like a helium balloon. He reached over and grabbed a banana, picking it out without even looking because he didn't want to lose his place in line.

"That will be ninety-eight cents," the man announced as the cash register whirred. Logan handed over his dollar and got two pennies in exchange. The man put the bananas in a plastic bag with a handle and lifted it over the counter. "Have a good day, young man."

Logan grinned as he walked out the door. He now had three bananas and a plastic bag. His day had just gotten a whole lot better.

CHAPTER FIFTEEN

Sitting at the kitchen table, Laura took a sip of coffee and pondered what Joanne had told them the night before about catching the boy in the act of stealing. Joanne had been so upset to encounter someone in her backyard that it seemed to Laura she'd put an unnecessarily threatening spin on the story. A child taking a towel and a tomato sounded more sad than menacing to her.

Paul had told her that a lot of the kids in his high school came from families with financial problems. She noticed that anytime they went to a business in the area—the A&W for burgers, the local grocery store, even the roadside strawberry stand—the teenagers who worked there saw Paul and called out, "Hey, Mr. Sutton!" Paul said the ones who had jobs were the lucky ones because there weren't a lot of opportunities in the area.

One of the boys at the strawberry farm had said the kids rotated between picking strawberries in the field and working the stand. He'd said it was hot in the field and hard work too, but high school students got paid by the amount they picked. They could make a lot of money in a few weeks if they were willing to put in the time and effort.

She wondered what the boy considered to be a lot of money. Probably not much, by some people's standards, but it might make the difference between paying for gas and going out with friends or getting new school clothes at the beginning of the year.

If life was tough for teenagers, what about the younger children? Specifically, what kind of kid steals a towel and a tomato? Maybe a hungry, wet one?

The idea made her sad, but she consoled herself by thinking that there really was no way of knowing this kid's motivation. It might just have been tomfoolery, as Joanne suspected, but any child who lived around here would have to walk a long way to pull off a stunt like that. And for what? It wasn't much of a joke, and the payoff of a towel wasn't great. It seemed unlikely that a child would go out of his way for a tomato and towel solely as a lark.

Laura got up and refilled her coffee cup. She was admiring the view of the woods when she caught a glimpse of someone moving between the trees heading uphill. There it was again, a smudge of color. She squinted and saw a flash of movement through the trees—a boy walking, swinging something white as he went. Maybe a plastic shopping bag? She blinked, and he was out of sight, but she was sure of what she'd seen. Too bad Paul had gone into school for the day, or there would have been two of them there to witness it.

She set down her mug and went to the refrigerator. A few moments later, she'd made a ham sandwich, which she put into a paper lunch bag, along with a large oatmeal chocolate chip cookie. Then she was out the back door and on her way to follow the kid's trail. Laura didn't even stop to lock up the house. She just listened for the screen door to click shut, then walked as quietly as she could, out of her yard, and into the woods.

Laura and Paul had hiked through these woods many times, and she knew it well. If she kept going forward, she'd reach the top of the ridge. At the top of the small incline, the land flattened out. A little bit beyond that was the creek. It was picturesque, but Paul had lost interest as soon as he had found out it was too shallow for kayaking and a total bust for fishing.

Across the street was a farmer's field. As long as that held true, Joanne would remain their only neighbor.

Laura paused to listen and caught the faintest shuffle of small feet walking just ahead. *Yes.* Her imagination hadn't played tricks on her. He was still there, just ahead of her. She concentrated intently, her eyes searching for visuals but finding none. Taking a few steps at a time, she followed.

Walking without making any noise was nearly impossible. She'd hoped to sneak up on the child but not to scare him. In fact, what she wanted was just the opposite. Her idea was to just wander into view, like she'd been taking a walk and happened upon him, then strike up a conversation and ask where he lived. Offering him the food was a dicey proposition. What child would take a sandwich from a stranger? Maybe if he was really hungry, he'd accept.

If nothing else, she could get a handle on who he was and what was going on. It was a good idea in theory, a bad one in practice. He was going to hear her coming. It was too quiet here, and she was not practiced in the art of silently trailing another person.

She gave up on her initial plan and hurried, hoping that by picking up the pace she could catch up to him. Joanne had said the kid looked small, grade-school age. Certainly she could outrun him. She charged forward and then halted. From the sound of things, the kid had started running too. He'd heard her and taken off, thinking she was a threat. She stopped and cupped her hands around her mouth. "Wait!" she called out, trying to keep her voice friendly. "I just want to talk to you. It's okay. I don't mind that you're here. I'm just not used to seeing people around here that often."

Beginning to walk again, she yelled out, "My name is Laura. I'm not scary at all. I'm very friendly." It struck her that what she wanted to say was, *I love kids. I'm a mom. I want to help you.* The word *mom* popped into her brain. From where, she hadn't a clue. Didn't all kids respond to knowing a woman was a mom? It made them think of their own mothers. Someone caring, someone kind. But she wasn't anyone's mother, and yelling out that she was a woman in her forties didn't quite convey the same thing.

"Please? Won't you come out and talk to me? I promise I'm a nice person." Which was probably the kind of thing serial killers said, she realized ruefully.

When she reached the top of the incline and still didn't see him, she realized he was gone, nowhere in sight. Somehow he'd slipped away. The creek was down below, and beyond that, more woods. He could have circled back. It was even possible that he'd passed her. The trees were thick enough that she might not have seen him.

She tried one more time. "If you're in trouble or need something, I live in the house at the bottom of the hill. My name is Laura, and I want to help." The sound of the rushing water and the caw of a crow were the only responses. She waited a few more minutes. "I have a ham sandwich and a cookie in this bag. I'm just going to leave it here for you, okay?" She set it down at the base of the tree and listened, but there was no response. Finally, she gave up, turned around, and went home. There was a cup of coffee waiting for her. It would need to be microwaved by now. She was certain of that.

~

In the tree house, Logan sat on the floor, hugging his knees to his chest. She'd almost caught up to him, and then what? He wasn't ready to be found just yet. A few more days, and if there wasn't an AMBER Alert out on him, he could write down any name he wanted, and the police wouldn't know any different. Then he could start somewhere fresh, somewhere less scary. Maybe Ms. Tracey's prediction would come true, and he would begin to talk then. He sat with his head against his knees for a very long time, not wanting to move in case that woman, Laura, was still around. Finally, he got up and peeked out the window. Seeing nothing but trees, he felt comfortable moving around in the tree house.

Eventually, when he thought it was safe, he climbed down the ladder to retrieve the food Laura had left for him. Later, eating from the paper bag up in the tree house, he decided a ham sandwich and oatmeal chocolate chip cookie had never tasted so good.

CHAPTER SIXTEEN

Grandma Nan pulled into the parking lot of an Aldi grocery store. She never thought she'd spend her retirement years working as her own personal private investigator, but she'd go to any lengths to find Logan. She wasn't giving up until she found him.

She'd tried calling Granger Finch while she was still in the car at the elementary school and had no luck reaching him. She'd gotten his answering machine, of all things. The recorded message said, "You've reached the office of private investigator Granger Finch, otherwise known as Grinch. I'm not available at the moment. Please leave a message at the beep." Unbelievably annoying. Why wasn't he available? She was older than he was, and even she had a cell phone and could be reached at any given moment. In his line of work, you'd think being easily accessible would be imperative. She didn't even bother to leave a message. There was no way she could wait for him to call her back. She'd have to do this herself.

The office lady had said Tia's mother worked at a grocery store called Aldi. It didn't take much sleuthing, just a minute on her phone, actually, to figure out that there were two Aldis in town. She visited the one closest to Robert's apartment, thinking that would be the most logical choice, but the manager there said they'd never had an employee named Satira Zafiris.

Undeterred, she got back in her car and headed to the second store. "Here goes nothing," she muttered to herself as she crossed the parking lot. She patted her purse, which contained the photos. Heading inside, she knew just where to go. It had an identical layout to the other store, and probably all the Aldi stores as well. She snaked around the candy aisle and went past the produce, heading to the front of the store. She bypassed the checkout line, went up to a cashier, and asked if she could speak to a manager. The cashier, a woman whose name tag identified her as Marjorie, continued scanning items, the beep beep beep coming at a regular pace. Without even looking in Grandma Nan's direction, she called out, "Carlos, this lady would like to speak to you."

Carlos trotted over in a way that made her think he was going to be accommodating, but as it turned out, he was no help at all.

So as not to block the line of customers, Grandma Nan stepped away from where Marjorie worked, and smiled. "I was hoping you could help me. I have a few questions about one of your employees," she began. "A woman named Satira Zafiris? Did she work here?"

Carlos frowned. "What is this regarding?"

"I just want to confirm that she worked here."

He shook his head slowly. "I can't give out employee information."

"But she's not an employee anymore, right? I'm not trying to get her in trouble. It's just that my grandson lives with her, and I'm trying to track him down."

"Sorry, I can't help you." He started to turn away, and she grabbed his sleeve.

"Please, just listen. Just for a minute," she pleaded. When he paused, she let go of his sleeve and fumbled through her purse. With shaking hands, she pulled out the photo of Logan. "His name is Logan. He's my only grandchild. He's nine years old, and I haven't seen him in more than two years. Two years. I'm about out of my mind. If you have children, you can imagine what I'm going through," she said, trying to appeal to this man's sympathy. Anyone could see that she was desperate.

"Can't you please help me? I just want to know if you have a forwarding address for Satira. I promise I won't tell anyone that you gave it to me."

Carlos raised both hands in surrender and then walked away. "Sorry, lady. Can't help you."

"Please!" she yelled after him. "I'm begging you. If you can give me her phone number. An address. Anything!" Tears welled up in her eyes, but he just kept going. How could anyone be so cold and indifferent to someone else's suffering? She leaned against a long counter opposite the checkout lines, a place where customers bagged their groceries after paying. Random carts were parked in front of that counter, and all of the half dozen shoppers who'd been diligently organizing their purchases stopped to stare. A girl who looked young enough to be a high school student walked over and offered her a tissue, which she gratefully accepted. "Thank you," she said, dabbing at her eyes and blowing her nose. The girl nodded and returned to the counter to load up her cart with boxes and assorted plastic bags.

Grandma Nan knew defeat when she saw it. Mentally she went to plan B. She'd try calling Grinch again. Maybe now that she had Satira's name, he could use it to track Robert to wherever he and Logan were now. This wasn't the end. It couldn't be.

She slid the photo back into the envelope in her purse and looped it over her shoulder, trying to walk out of the store in a dignified manner. No slouch of defeat for her. She'd hold her head high.

She was almost to the car when she heard the patter of shoes coming up behind her and a woman's voice calling out, "Ma'am! Ma'am!" She turned to see the cashier, Marjorie, waving a bouquet of assorted flowers wrapped in clear cellophane. "You forgot your flowers!"

Grandma Nan turned to face her. "Those aren't mine. I didn't buy anything."

Marjorie got in closer, pushed the flowers into her hands, and said in a whisper, "Satira and I were good friends. I don't have her new address, but I know she got a job working at the Aldi on Pulaski Road in Chicago. She usually works the day shift."

Grandma Nan wanted to give her a hug and thank her, but she didn't have time. Once the message was delivered, Marjorie took off, jogging back to the store.

Grandma Nan held the flowers up in the air and yelled, "Thank you!"

In reply, Marjorie half turned and gave her a wave.

The Aldi on Pulaski Road in Chicago. She didn't even need to write it down. In a minute, it would be programmed into her GPS, and she'd be heading that way. In two hours, she'd be there.

CHAPTER SEVENTEEN

Joanne came home from lunch with a plan. A definite plan. First, she'd have to let Samson out, and once he was through, she'd put her plan into action.

The idea came to her after she met her neighbor Laura at the A&W for burgers and root beer. Laura had called that morning asking if she'd want to meet up for something to eat. The offer came out of the blue, but she didn't have anything else going on, and a person had to eat, didn't they? She brought tomatoes, cucumbers, and peppers as a gift, and Laura seemed genuinely delighted to receive them. "Are you sure you want to give all this away?" she asked, peering into the box.

"It's funny how gardens work," Joanne said. "You wait and wait and wait, and it seems like you'll never get any vegetables, and then all of a sudden, it all comes at once, and there's enough for a dozen families. I do some canning, and I donate a lot of it to my church's food pantry. I like to share."

Laura grinned. "And I like it when you share. Thank you!"

Joanne guessed Laura to be in her late thirties, maybe early forties. It was hard to tell nowadays. People used to wear different types of clothing at different stages of their life, but not anymore. Laura was trim and dressed almost like the teenagers at the next table: T-shirt, shorts, and flip-flops. Her purse was a small backpack with a drawstring closure, and her hair was pulled up into a messy bun. She was pretty, but her most appealing feature was her smile. Goodwill poured out of her. When Joanne walked into the place, Laura greeted her with an enthusiastic hug.

Joanne couldn't remember the last time she'd been hugged. It was kind of nice.

Once they started eating, Laura began telling her about the child she'd spotted in the woods next to her house. "As soon as I saw him, I went out to try to catch up to him." She took a slurp of diet soda. "Just flew out the back door, but I couldn't find him. He was either too fast, or he somehow looped back around and went past me." She shook her head. "I don't know. It was like chasing a ghost. I felt like I was right behind him, but when I got to the top of the incline, he was gone."

"You think it was the same child?"

"It had to be, don't you think?" Laura asked. "What are the chances it would be a different kid?"

Joanne thought about that for a second. Unlikely, it seemed. "He came back last night." She dipped a french fry into ketchup and bit off the end. "Returned my towel and knocked on the back door. When I answered, there it was, folded up nice and neat on my stoop. He was nowhere in sight. He must have knocked and then ran off."

Laura appeared fascinated. "Did you ever call the police?"

She shrugged. "No. He'd returned the towel, so I didn't see the point in getting him in trouble. I'm thinking he came home with a strange towel, and his parents made him return it."

They both were silent for a moment, working on their burgers. Outside, two boys, young teens, skateboarded in the parking lot. When they got up to the door, they tucked the skateboards under their arms and walked in and got in line. "That makes sense," Laura said. "But I wonder why he came back today, then?"

"I don't know."

"I checked, and there are no missing boys in the area. I even did a search and extended the range like one hundred miles and came up with nothing, so this kid has to live around here. It's just so odd."

"Kids around here have more freedom than in urban areas," Joanne said. "My son used to go camping with his friends when he was a teenager, and they'd be gone two or three days, on their own. Of course, that was thirty years ago." Glenn and his friends had camped out in the back acreage of a friend's property, just rolled up their sleeping bags and pup tents, packed up some food, and off they went. She'd worried then, even though Glenn and her husband, John, told her it wasn't necessary. Joanne knew it wasn't strictly necessary; she did it anyway because she just couldn't help it. Did they think she *enjoyed* worrying—the endless ruminating over what could go wrong, the fear that someone would get hurt or die, the knot of anxiety over the thought of bad things happening that she might have been able to prevent? No, she did not want to worry, but telling her not to worry was not a solution.

Many years later, Glenn told her he and his friends had smoked cigarettes and drunk beer and set off bottle rockets. One time, a few of them had dug a pit and covered it with branches, waiting for an unsuspecting friend to fall in. Boys. He laughed like it was funny, when all she could think was they that were lucky the kid didn't break his leg.

Glenn did have some other exciting stories, telling her about friends falling out of trees, burning their hands, and starting fires that almost went out of control. All the situations were funny after the fact, but the truth of it was that someone could have been seriously injured or killed. Knowing that she'd been right validated her worrying. Plus, she had been the one who insisted they take the fire extinguisher, which was how they were able to put out the runaway fire! Glenn hadn't told her at the time, but she'd always suspected as much when he returned the extinguisher with the pin removed. Score one for mother's intuition.

That was long ago, and now Laura was talking about a different, much younger boy. "I'm going to keep an eye out for him," Laura said.

"All I can think is what if this boy is a runaway or from an abusive home? He was by himself, which is odd. Don't kids usually travel in packs? What about the buddy system? Most kids hang out with friends or at least *one* friend. Something about this whole thing strikes me as being wrong."

It was too bad Laura didn't have any kids, because she definitely had the worrying part down pat.

"I'll watch out too," Joanne promised. "And I'll call you if I spot him again."

She thought about the conversation on the drive home and decided she wasn't going to wait to see if she happened to spot him again. Laura had said she'd gotten to the top of the incline and the boy had disappeared, seemingly into thin air. But people didn't disappear into thin air. A kid could hide better than adults could find, and she knew a thing or two from her years of being a parent.

Joanne whistled at the back door, and Samson came bounding in with his usual enthusiasm. She rubbed his head, talking at the same time. "Mom's just going out for a little bit, but you'll be staying here, okay?" Oh, Glenn would tease her mercilessly about referring to herself as the dog's mom if she ever slipped and said it in front of him. She was careful not to do that kind of thing when he was around. He already made comments about how Samson was treated better than most people's children.

Sadly, it was true. She'd fallen in love with her dog. She wasn't sure how it had happened. One day she was a normal woman with a dog; the next she was a crazy dog woman. The house was less lonely when she talked to Samson, and although he didn't talk back, he always had time to listen. She put her nose up to his. "I won't be gone for long. I promise." She got her keys. "You be good."

Maybe Laura left her house unlocked, but Joanne wasn't that brave. Laura had Paul, which made it different. When you lived alone, you allowed for every potential emergency. Having Samson gave her a measure of security, but she'd heard of intruders doing evil things to dogs before they robbed a house or attacked the homeowners. She tried to be prepared—even had Glenn's old wooden baseball bat wedged between her nightstand and her bed, just in case she was assaulted while she slept. She'd seen so many movies where the woman had some rapist break into the house and pin the poor thing down in her own bed. Imagine how surprised the criminal would be if his victim slammed him over the head with a baseball bat. She'd love to see that happen sometime in the movies.

After double-checking the knob from the outside to make sure it was secure, she was off to the tree house. It was the only place a person could disappear to at the top of the hill. Trust a kid to find it and an adult not to spot it. If the child was hanging around her property, that would be the place to look.

The tree house was old: Glenn's age minus ten years. He and his dad had built it together when he was just a kid. John was the kind of man who never did anything halfway, so it was a big tree house—solid, and high up. Too high up, in her opinion. "How about a playhouse on the ground?" she'd suggested when John and Glenn had first talked about it.

"A playhouse?" Glenn sounded downright offended. Even as a kid, he had set opinions. "That's for babies."

After that, she'd stayed out of it, just admiring the sketches and asking how much the supplies cost—the lumber, shingles, actual windows, and a hinged door. When it was finished, it was impressive. Three generations had found a use for the house. Glenn's daughters used it for pretending and for tea parties. Glenn and his friends used it as a sort of clubhouse. They had a whole secret-knock thing going and rigged up a rope for when they needed a faster getaway.

The third generation to use it was Joanne herself. After John died, she experienced all the stages of grief, sometimes all at once. Her grief was so deep that she felt lonely to the core, every fiber of her being bereft, even when surrounded by lots of love. She was unable to think past the moment. Everything was right now or not at all. Mourning wore her out, and she dragged through the days, sometimes climbing back into bed before the day was done. And she was angry too. Angry that John had died of a heart attack at sixty-three, right after he retired, when they had so much planned and were just starting to have so much fun. How was that even fair? She'd see couples at church, and it would infuriate her. Some of those women didn't even *like* their husbands, and yet, there the men were, escorting them in, and afterward, going out to pull the car up so their wives wouldn't have to venture out in the cold.

A year after John died, she woke up one spring morning expecting to feel better, but she didn't. She was still alone and sad and getting older by the minute. She went for a walk that day and wound up by the tree house. Impulsively, she climbed the ladder and went inside, sitting cross-legged on the floor, her back against a wall. She looked at the house's sturdy construction and thought of John teaching Glenn about framing and joists and what have you. How to safely use a nail gun. All the things men teach their sons.

And then Joanne thought about how much she wanted him back. She said it out loud. "I want you back." Hearing herself say the words made it even sadder, and she started to cry—a big, ugly gulping-for-air kind of cry. She sobbed and wailed. It was endless, and there was no one there to distract her or promise that time would heal all wounds. She wanted to feel normal again, to not be chained to this endless despair. Everyone said it would get better, but when? After she was all cried out, she used her sleeve to wipe her nose, even though it was disgusting, then she climbed down the ladder and went home and took a shower.

It took her six years to get over the loss of her husband. Six years until she was able to wake up and not be jolted by the thought that he wasn't lying next to her. Six years until she could see couples her age and not immediately think, *Must be nice.* When she talked to other widows, some of them confided that they'd had the same lengthy grief time line, so why did everyone act like you were an emotional wreck if you were still mourning past the one-year mark? It wasn't like she cried in public. She just still missed him.

The distance from her home to the tree house was farther than she recalled. She shuffled through leaves and stepped over roots and fallen branches. She'd forgotten how calming it was in the woods. The smell of pine and green freshness all around. No sound except her footsteps and the chirping of the birds. The air seemed purer, more oxygenated.

When she got to the base of the tree, she looked up, shielding her eyes with the flat of her hand. That ladder was steeper and more rickety than in her memory, and the tree house itself was higher than she remembered. She imagined getting to the top and having difficulty climbing down. There was no way she was dragging her old bones up there. Her muscles and joints weren't nearly as cooperative as they used to be. She was afraid she'd get up and be unable to climb back down. Anything she did was going to have to be while her feet were planted on solid ground.

"Hello," she called up. "Is anyone there?" Squinting, she thought the curtain might have fluttered, but it was hard to say for sure. "I'm Joanne Dembiec, the lady who yelled at you about the towel."

No response except the soft rustle of the breeze through the trees. She waited for a moment or two and then continued. "I'm sorry I yelled. I was just surprised. It was very nice of you to bring the towel back, and I want to thank you for that. You can tell your mother she raised you right. I can tell you're a nice boy."

The words came out without thought, and now that she'd started, she couldn't seem to stop. "You probably don't know this, but this is private property. It belongs to me, and I don't want you playing here." Looking up, Joanne estimated the distance from the tree house to the ground. Twenty or thirty feet? Just her luck the kid would fall and get seriously injured, and then she'd get sued by his parents. "There are lots of places for you to play, but this isn't one of them. You might get hurt." Even thinking he might be up there now gave her pause. The tree house belonged to her family. It had been designed by John and made by him and Glenn, and it was as much a part of her family as her own house. This was not a public park for random kids to use as they wished.

She kept looking up until her neck got a crick in it; then she reached back and kneaded it with her fingertips before trying one more time. "I'm going to go now, and you need to leave too, okay? When I check back later, I don't want to find you here. Be safe and go home."

CHAPTER EIGHTEEN

Grandma Nan checked in at the Sheraton, a hotel room that cost way more money than she'd been planning to spend, but the city of Chicago was apparently not a bargain destination. This was the cheapest room in the area, and she needed a place to sleep. The room was nice. Two queen-size beds, a bigger TV than she had at home, and some large framed artwork of some ferns. A generic space, but she was glad to be there. She was tired. So, so tired, and ready to settle down for the night.

Only earlier that day she'd been at Logan's elementary school talking to Ms. Tracey, but that conversation felt more like it had occurred the previous day, or maybe even the one before. It had been a long, emotionally trying day, but she was getting closer to Logan, so she felt that she'd achieved some degree of success. In the past twenty-four hours, she'd accrued some important information. She had talked to two women who had seen Logan just four months ago and assured her that he was fine. Or at least fine enough. Fed and clothed, if not speaking yet. She now knew Robert and Logan were living with a mother and daughter, and she knew their names. And she knew where that mother was employed.

She'd been to three Aldis in total that day. The first one, which was entirely wrong; the second, where Marjorie had given her flowers and hope; and the third, the one on Pulaski Road in Chicago. She'd pulled into the parking lot of that last one, sure she would walk in and see Satira at the register. She'd gone in and bypassed the manager, instead stopping a young guy with inked arms wheeling a pallet of paper towels through the store.

"Is Satira working today?" She tried to make her tone friendly.

He said, "She already left for the day. She'll be back in the morning at nine."

"Do you know where she lives, by any chance?"

He shook his head. "She's pretty new. I've hardly talked to her at all. You can ask the manager if you want."

There was no point in talking to the manager. She knew how that would go. Instead, she thanked the young man, bought some chips and bottled water, and got back into her car to search for a hotel. She made the reservation for the Sheraton over the phone, eating at McDonald's along the way. Stress, fast food, chips, and sitting in the car for hours. This was not a healthy way to live.

So the stop at that particular Aldi turned out to be a combination of good news and bad news. She'd come one step closer to finding Logan but couldn't do any more on that front until the next day. She tried to decide on a strategy. Would she talk to Satira, woman to woman, imploring her to let her see Logan? As a mother, Satira would know how much Nan was suffering. How heartless would a woman have to be to keep a grandmother from seeing her grandson? But there was Robert to consider. If Satira was living with Robert, she was either his girlfriend or else she relied on him for a place to live. Neither situation boded well for Grandma Nan's purposes. The woman's loyalty would clearly be to Robert. A pathetic thought but somewhat understandable. Satira had a daughter to think about too. Her motherly instinct would be to protect their lifestyle. This was not a new story. Since the dawn of time, women had made concessions to provide for their children.

That left one possibility. She could wait until Satira's shift was over and then secretly follow her home. Satira didn't know who she was, so she'd have no reason to suspect anything. Grandma Nan had gotten a new car last year, so there was no possibility of Robert recognizing it either. Trailing Satira would be easy to do too, as long as she went straight home after work.

To her way of thinking, this was her best chance of finding them. Robert would be caught off guard, and he'd have no one to blame for her sudden appearance. If she came bearing gifts, say, a fifth of Scotch or a case of beer, he might even be glad to see her. She hated to encourage his bad habit, but all was fair in love and war. If she needed to give Robert alcohol to see Logan, it was a small price to pay. It's not like she was tempting him as he walked out of an AA meeting. He was going to do it anyway.

Grandma Nan didn't want to get her hopes up, thinking she'd finally see Logan, but it was nearly impossible not to keep imagining how tomorrow might go. She thought of how exciting it would be to knock on the door and see Logan standing on the other side. If he thought she was dead, he'd be shocked to see her alive and well, but she also knew he'd be happy. She closed her eyes and tried to imagine how tall he would be and what his hug might feel like. Two and a half years was a long time in a nine-year-old's life, but he'd drawn the picture of her at school just a few months ago and labeled it "Grandma Nan." In his picture, he'd depicted her in her light-blue sweater wearing her black flats, the ones resembling ballet slippers. He hadn't forgotten her.

If his father wasn't home when she got there, she was tempted to just take him. Pack up his clothes, put him in the car, and drive back to Nebraska. Legally, it would be wrong. Morally, she was sure right was on her side.

She wasn't entirely sure Robert would pursue Logan if she did take him. He'd actually offered to let her take him the first month or so after Amber had died, but then reneged when he realized the Social Security check would go to her. The money was a nonissue as far as she was concerned; she would have paid to have Logan full-time. She had tried to offset his worries about the check. "Even if they send it to me, I'll cash it and send the money back to you," she'd suggested. "So you can set it aside for his college fund or whatever. And he can visit back and forth." She'd watched his expression and saw the gears turning. While he'd weighed all the variables, she desperately made her case. "You could see him whenever you want. I'm home all day, so I have more time to spend with Logan on homework and things like that." She'd been offering Robert a way out, but the frantic tone in her voice betrayed how badly she wanted Logan, and that made Robert suspicious.

Heartbreakingly, Robert had decided to keep Logan, and that was that. She had no legal grounds to take him away from his father.

Perhaps now things would be different.

CHAPTER NINETEEN

Logan mulled over what the woman, Joanne Dembiec, had said. She knew he was here. How did she figure it out? He'd been so careful not to be seen. He glanced around, wondering if there were cameras hidden in the trees, but who would bother to do that? It wouldn't make sense.

Joanne had said she was going to check back later, and he should be gone by then. Would she really come back? He considered the question. Probably. You can't just have a random kid hanging around your property even if no one was looking for him.

He didn't know what to do.

It was too soon for the police to discover him. Two days wasn't enough. He wanted it to be long enough that his father would be embarrassed to claim him after so much time. The idea of going home to his father drove terror up his spine. Starving in the woods would be better than being grabbed by his father and pinned against the wall, then shaken so hard his teeth rattled, his father's face so close he could see the blood vessels in his eyes. When he got like that, there was no telling what he would do. His father seemed to feed off Logan's fear, getting angrier and angrier when he didn't react, but if Logan *did* react by crying or shaking, his father grew disgusted by his son's weakness. Being dead would be better than facing him when he was like that. And there's no other way he could be, not after Logan took off and made him look bad.

He had only faint memories of his father from before the car accident. The accident that ruined their lives and ultimately killed his mother. The accident was his fault. He was in the back seat, complaining that he was hungry, and his mother reached back to give him a plastic bowl full of Teddy Grahams. This distracted his father, who drove through a red light, putting them right in the path of an oncoming truck.

He was five and sitting in the back seat at the time, so his memory of the accident was sketchy. What he did remember was the sound of squealing brakes, the car spinning around as metal hit metal, and the Teddy Grahams flying out of his mother's hands and into the air. He was strapped into a booster seat and escaped the worst of it. His parents sustained injuries that the doctor said were not life threatening, but they turned out to be life changing. His mother hit her head so hard against the side window that she had a concussion. His father broke his left arm and several ribs. Both of them had horrible bruises, particularly where the seat belts had crossed their bodies.

An ambulance arrived and took them all to the hospital. Grandma Nan came and picked him up, and he stayed with her for a few days.

His father missed four weeks of work and began drinking. Every time he told the story of the accident, and he told it a lot, he referred to Logan as "that damn kid" and talked about how he'd whined for the Teddy Grahams. The people he told the story to always gave Logan a look like they couldn't believe a kid could do such a terrible thing to his parents. Logan's mother had terrible headaches after that and had to take pain medication that made her sleep a lot. They had once been a normal family, but now they were angry and in pain. And it was all his fault.

Before the accident, his father had been different. Not as warm and cuddly as his mom, but different. Better. More like a regular dad. He'd explain to Logan how things worked when he fixed the faucet and take him out with him when he went to the hardware store. If they bumped into someone he knew, he'd rest his hand on Logan's head and tell the other person, "This is my boy, Logan. Kid's gonna be just like his old man." Proud like. After the accident, his dad didn't want anything to do with him. And no wonder. Logan had ruined everything. He could have waited for those Teddy Grahams, but he hadn't, and because of him, everything had changed.

Could he trust that woman Laura who said she was worried about him? Maybe. He could write her a note and give her a different story about where he'd come from. Then maybe when she called the police, they would put him in foster care with a nice family, and he wouldn't have to face his father.

But in his heart of hearts, he knew it wouldn't be that easy. Nothing ever was.

CHAPTER TWENTY

Grandma Nan held her breath as she knocked on the door. Following Satira home had been the easy part, but it was the end of a long process. She'd gone to the grocery store midmorning and purchased some canned goods and toilet paper, making a point to go through Satira's checkout line. When it came time to pay, she made small talk.

"Beautiful day outside," she said, handing over the cash.

"Yes," Satira said with a smile. Grandma Nan had not been sure how she'd react to meeting this woman, the one who'd replaced Amber in Robert and Logan's life. Satira and her daughter had been at a homeless shelter, according to Ms. Tracey. but there was nothing about this woman that indicated hard times. She was pretty, with dark glossy hair twisted and clipped up in back, and she had flawless skin and nice teeth. She had the build of a belly dancer—not stick thin, but what used to be called "pleasingly plump." Grandma Nan could almost imagine her as a mother figure to Logan: packing his lunch, reminding him to brush his teeth, washing his clothes.

Grandma Nan said, "It would be a shame to miss the sunshine. Are you getting off work soon?"

Satira sadly shook her head. "Not until two." She handed over Grandma Nan's change, counting it back to her. "Have a good day."

After that, there was nothing left to do besides wait for two o'clock. In the meantime, she filled her gas tank, found a liquor store, and bought the Scotch she knew Robert liked, tucking the bottle into her purse so that just the neck and cap stuck out, then returned to Aldi for her stakeout. She quickly figured out that the employees parked in the back. She waited and watched until two o'clock came around, and when she saw Satira come out carrying two grocery bags, she started up the engine. Satira climbed into a green Ford, and Grandma Nan followed her out of the parking lot. The first few minutes went well, but when a large truck did a kamikaze lane change, forcing itself between the two cars, Grandma Nan lost sight of the Ford for a frantic fifteen seconds. When Satira turned at the next corner, she was back in sight, and the world righted itself again.

Satira kept going, to the farthermost edge of Chicago, straight to a plain brick building. She pulled into a narrow driveway next to the building. Grandma Nan presumed there was parking in back, but she didn't follow. Instead, she maneuvered into a space across the street. After getting out of the vehicle, she dashed between traffic, then scurried around the side of the building, her back flat against the bricks, like a spy in a movie. Her stealthy method worked. When she reached the back of the building, she saw Satira sitting in her parked car, cell phone up to her ear. As Grandma Nan watched, she finished her call and got out of the car, a handbag looped across her body and a plastic grocery bag in each hand. When Satira got to the back door of the building, she shifted the bags to one hand and fumbled in her handbag for the key.

After she'd gone through, Grandma Nan darted out from her hiding spot and grabbed the door just before it closed. She watched as Satira climbed up the stairs and waited until she was at the top before trailing her. The door to the apartment clicked shut as Grandma Nan reached the top. Too late to see it happen, but she could tell which door from the direction of the sound.

Grandma Nan stood in the hallway, just outside the door for a minute or so, listening. She heard a woman's voice, presumably Satira's, and a man's voice responding. Even without hearing the words, she knew it was Robert. He had a deep voice and a gruff way of speaking, the words clipped and hard.

The carpeting in the hallway was a generic dark burgundy, stained in spots. The woodwork around the door was dirty, with what looked like oil or grease, and the white walls were yellowed, like someone had smoked cigarettes out here. Everything smelled musty and stale. A person would have to take the roof off the building to get the odor out.

She heard the back and forth between Robert and Satira, but nothing that indicated Logan was there. Of course, Ms. Tracey said he wasn't talking yet, so it was likely he was there, just not speaking. Grandma Nan took a deep breath and then rapped on the door. Once and then twice more.

She heard the sound of a chair scraping against a tile floor and then the heavy shuffling of feet. When the door jerked open, the look of surprise on Robert's face made the drive from Nebraska worth every mile.

"Nancy." He frowned.

"Robert. It's good to see you." In all the ways she'd mentally prepared for this moment, one thing stayed the same, and that was her decision not to be antagonistic. She knew from past experience that if she pretended nothing was wrong, there was a good chance he would go along with it. Her plan was to exchange pleasantries before she asked to see Logan, never mentioning the years that had passed or the fact that he'd cut her off and moved without notice, effectively ripping her heart in two. She peered through the opening but couldn't see much beyond Robert's beefy torso. "I'm sorry for not calling first. I was hoping to see Logan?"

"This isn't a good time, Nancy. Logan's not here."

She was close enough to smell the beer on his breath. "When's a better time? I'll come back."

"Give me your number, and I'll call you if he wants to see you."

"I brought you a gift." She pulled the Scotch out of her purse and held it up, just out of his reach. "Did I get it right? Is this your favorite?" Grandma Nan watched indecision flick across his face. Such a conundrum. He wanted the Scotch, but he also wanted her to leave. Before he could debate much longer, she said, "How about I come in for a quick shot with my favorite son-in-law? For old times' sake?"

He wavered, letting the door open another inch. She saw the hunger in his eyes, the wanting of the liquor, and for a split second, she felt guilty for using his weakness against him. This was a cruel trick. If he wasn't such a cruel man, this strategy would be despicable.

She continued. "I'll just come in for a minute. I'll leave a note for Logan, and then you can call me when he's available. I'd love to take him out for ice cream while I'm in town."

Robert opened the door wider and ushered her wordlessly into what she now saw was their kitchen. Satira was at the sink, her hands in soapy water. She turned slightly and smiled nervously, showing no signs of recognizing Nan from the store. Robert didn't bother to introduce her. He just went to the cabinet and got two juice glasses, then set them on the table next to a large knife with a jagged edge and took the bottle from her outstretched arm.

"Just one drink," he said sternly, showing her he was in charge. He pushed the knife aside and took a seat at the table, and she joined him, not waiting for an invitation. He poured two fingers in each glass and handed one to her.

Grandma Nan held up the glass. "To your health and happiness, Robert."

He shrugged. "Works for me." He downed the shot in one swift movement. Up close, she saw that he was even bigger than when she'd last seen him; his blue T-shirt was strained at the neck and shoulders by his muscular build.

Grandma Nan sipped from her glass, and Robert poured himself another. She needed to keep the conversation going. She looked casually around the room, at the tattered curtains flapping at the window and Satira's back as the woman slowly and methodically rinsed off glasses and put them in the plastic drying rack. All of them pretending there was nothing unusual about her showing up out of the blue after so much time. She kept her tone casual. "What time did you tell Logan to be home? I'd be happy to come back."

The mood in the room changed like a storm front had moved in. Robert cleared his throat, and out of the corner of her eye, she noticed Satira's shoulders hunch. He said, "You need to go home, Nancy. Logan's at summer camp and won't be back for a long time."

"Summer camp." She repeated the words, disbelieving.

"Yes, summer camp."

"Which summer camp? What's the name?"

"The name?"

He gave her the stare, the one that always stopped Amber from taking anything further, but Nan wasn't giving him that power. She said, "Yes, the name of the camp. I want to check it out."

"You don't need to know." He rolled the juice glass between his thumb and forefinger.

"I want to know. If it's close by, maybe I'll stop in and see him."

"Not a good idea."

"All I want to know is where he is, Robert."

Robert grabbed Grandma Nan's glass and threw it across the room. It ricocheted off the wall and landed on the floor. "Lady, you are out of line. We're done here."

He stood and loomed over her, then grabbed her elbow and pulled her to her feet. "Why won't you tell me where he is?" she cried out as he steered her to the door. "All I want to do is see my grandson!"

He shoved her roughly out the door and closed it, leaving her out in the dark, stinky hallway. She pounded on the door. "Robert! You need to tell me where Logan is. I'll call the police. I'll tell them he's missing." Her voice took on a shrill tone, and a door across the hallway opened. She saw two eyes peer out before it shut again. Grandma Nan rapped sharply on the door. "Robert, do you hear me? I'm not leaving until you tell me where Logan is. Answer me, dammit!"

The door opened roughly, and as quick as the lash of a whip, Robert's arm shot through the opening, pushing her so hard she lost her balance and teetered backward, almost falling. "Don't you threaten me," he said, emphasizing each word through gritted teeth. "Go now, or you'll be sorry."

Shaking, she turned and headed to the stairs. Robert wasn't going to tell her any more, but this was not over.

A vortex of thoughts whirled through her mind, none of them good. Summer camp? She didn't believe it for a minute. Robert would never spend that kind of money on Logan, and he'd never take charity either. No, something terrible had happened. Robert had somehow lost Logan. He'd given him up for adoption or sold him to someone for child labor. Maybe he had him chained up in the closet, or maybe, and she hated to even think it, maybe Robert had killed him. But no, she shook her head. Robert's mood got dark when he drank, but he wasn't a murderer.

She remembered how pleased and happy he'd been when Logan was born. The way Robert held him in the hospital, saying, "My son," like he couldn't believe his good luck. He'd loved Logan then, hadn't he? Or did he just love the idea of a son? It was hard to believe a man wouldn't love his own child, but to her it seemed like Robert didn't have the capacity to love anyone.

After leaving the apartment building, she returned to the front, trying to decide on her next move. She'd have to write down the address so she'd have it for the police report, but then what? She didn't want to go home without having seen her grandson. On the front steps of the building sat two little girls, heads together, looking at some kind of device. Grandma Nan gave a start as she recognized one of the girls from the class photo.

Satira Zafiris. Grade three.

Tia.

She went over to where they sat and crouched down in front of them. They both looked up, startled.

Grandma Nan said, "Hi, is your name Tia?"

"Yes." The girl's eyes went wide, probably wondering how she knew her name.

"You were in Mrs. Park's class last year, right? I was at your old school today."

After hearing the school connection, Tia's face lit up. "I was Mrs. Park's favorite. And Mr. Baird, he was the principal. He said I'm a real piece of work."

Grandma Nan gave her a smile. "I'm hoping you girls can help me. I'm trying to track down Logan Weber. Do you know where he is?"

Tia held her hand up in the air, as if wanting to get called upon. "I do! I do! He got in big trouble 'cause he wasn't supposed to leave his room, and then Robert got mad . . ." All the details spilled out then, the vomiting and how Logan ran out of the apartment with Robert going after him screaming his name. The little girl went on and on as if describing a scene in an exciting movie. All Grandma Nan could think about was how Logan must have experienced it. The poor child had to be terrified. "And then Logan never came back," Tia said, thus concluding the story. "He runned away for good, and now I'm the only child!"

Grandma Nan took a breath. "Wow, that's quite a story. When did all this happen?"

"The day before yesterday."

~

After pushing Grandma Nan out the door, Robert returned to the table and poured himself another shot.

Satira stood, her back to the sink, watching him brood. "This will be a problem for us," she said quietly. Handling Robert when he was in this kind of mood took great delicacy. She'd found that a soft voice worked best to calm and soothe him. A woman had to proceed with caution. Not like Amber, who Robert said sometimes argued with him, sticking up for the boy. Satira knew the art of letting things go when necessary, and she also knew how to make Robert think things were his idea.

"What do you want me to do about it? Damn kid just disappeared. Couldn't find him anywhere."

"You could look again," she suggested.

"He's probably staying with some friends. Just to piss me off."

"Tia says he doesn't have friends." She paused for a beat, then kept going. "He is just a little boy. He could not have gone far without money."

Robert poured another drink and said nothing.

"I think it would be good to ask around and show people his picture. Someone had to see where he went."

Robert ran his finger around the rim of the glass and grunted. "I can tell you one thing. The kid is going to be sorry he was born once I get through with him." He lifted the glass to his mouth, and when he was done, he wiped his lips with the back of his hand and got up from the table.

CHAPTER
TWENTY-ONE

Logan's third-grade teacher used to say everything happened for a reason, but if that were true, there was a reason his mother died and a reason he and his father kept moving and a reason his grandmother died, which were all terrible, awful, horrible things. And what kind of reason would there be for him not being able to talk and the other kids making fun of him?

If every one of these things happened for a reason, they had to be stupid reasons.

Being able to talk would solve so many problems. He could answer questions in school, tell Tia to stop taking his stuff, and answer his dad when he was at his angriest, when he insisted Logan was keeping quiet just to make him look bad. Sometimes his father called him *dummy*, and the word plunged a steak knife into his heart. Because he wasn't a dummy. He was one of the smarter kids at school. He knew this because he heard the other kids groan about how hard tests were—tests that he found easy. And when his teacher passed back papers and tests, he usually got everything correct.

He knew lots of things—not that it helped, because the things that made him stupid at home weren't things anyone could learn. They were rules that changed all the time. Suddenly he'd be expected to do something that had never been mentioned before. Like one time he got up from the dinner table carrying his dishes to the sink, and his father came after him and smacked the back of his head, saying, "Where do you think you're going? Get back there and push your chair in." Logan went back then and pushed the chair so it fit snugly against the table. It wasn't hard to do, but it was confusing. When had pushing the chair in been a requirement? Never, that he remembered. And then his father said to Alicia, a woman who lived with them at the time, "If I don't keep after him, he tries to get away with things."

His home life was befuddling. Even when he was careful, one thing led to another, and when he realized later that he shouldn't have whined for Teddy Grahams or believed Tia or eaten the marshmallows, it didn't matter. Knowing afterward didn't help. And knowing beforehand was impossible.

It had gotten worse after his mother died. One time his father shook his head and said, "Stop looking at me with her eyes." Logan knew his eyes were exactly like his mom's. Grandma Nan had said so many times. But he didn't have her actual eyes, so his dad saying that was totally confusing.

He thought maybe it had something to do with his mother's death. All three of them had been home that evening, all linked forever in the awful accident that wasn't an accident at all. His dad had been drunk, not as bad as usual, but still drunk, and his parents had been arguing. He was downstairs at the time and heard them shouting on the landing above. Their fight was mostly his fault because his mother had been defending Logan, telling his father he should cut him a break, that he was just a little boy. That he was still learning and that constantly berating him wasn't helping. His father hated anyone telling him what to do, so this made him even madder, and it got worse from there.

If it weren't for Logan, she would still be alive.

He pushed the memory away, trying to think about better times. There were a few. Sometimes for a day or two, his dad was fine. Once in a while, he even laughed or smiled, something that made Logan happy. Tia's mom had a knack for calming him down as long as his anger wasn't too far gone. About once a week, she'd suggest they watch a movie on TV together. Then she'd make microwave popcorn, and he and Tia would each get their own can of soda while the grown-ups drank beer. It was nice.

The problem was that he could never let his guard down because his father could fly into a rage about anything—or even nothing, for that matter. If only Logan had a way of knowing what was coming and when, it would have been better. The uncertainty left him twisted in knots, knowing that at any moment, there might be an explosion coming his way.

Being hit with his dad's belt was the worst physical pain he'd ever experienced, and like everything else, it seemed to be random. He never knew when an infraction might be severe enough to incite him to take off his belt and whip him across the back. One time, he was standing at the sink brushing his teeth, and his dad came tearing in, screaming about the mess he'd left in his room. The belt was already in his father's hand, and it cut across his back with such force that it pushed him forward, making him gag on the toothbrush. The sting of the leather made him lose his breath. Inside, he screamed, but still his vocal cords were frozen, and no audible sound left his mouth.

The mess his father had referred to had been a project for school, a collage for his social studies class. Logan had left only the cut-out parts spread out on the floor of his room for a moment, and then just to go to the bathroom. He'd intended to come back and glue them onto the poster board, but when the whipping was over and he was vanquished to his room, he saw that all the pieces had been ripped to shreds.

That night, his back bled through his T-shirt. He hid the shirt in his room and later threw it out when the grown-ups weren't home. If his dad had seen it, he'd have been in trouble for wrecking a perfectly good shirt.

When he considered going home, he thought about these things. The yelling, the name-calling, the hitting. Even the idea of going home filled him with an awful sense of dread. There was no way his father would be overjoyed to have him return. His temper ruled over all of them, but Logan the most.

Of course, being on his own had brought a mess of new troubles. Anything could happen to him out here in the middle of Wisconsin. Up until now, he'd been too focused on figuring things out, but now that things had settled down, loneliness gripped him. He was homesick for a different life, one that didn't exist anymore. He missed snuggling up against his mother when they read together. He missed making cookies with his grandma and going for hikes with her out in the woods. He missed Ms. Tracey. If he knew where she lived, he'd be heading there now, even if it took a month and he had to walk the whole way.

CHAPTER
TWENTY-TWO

Grandma Nan sat in her car, still parked across the street from the apartment. It was a shock to see how much Robert had changed since she'd last seen him. Physically he'd aged, with lines around his eyes, his face bloated and puffy. He'd lost the aura of charisma he'd had when he first met Amber. Then he could have charmed anyone with his good looks and confident patter. People even forgave him when he was being difficult or testy because he'd come around later and apologize in the most engaging way, making excuses and begging forgiveness. This new version of Robert wasn't even trying to keep up appearances.

He'd pushed her hard, and she had no doubt he would have hit her if she'd refused to leave. Without the Scotch, she wouldn't have made it past the door in the first place. He'd become a middle-aged drunk, ready to beat down anyone who stood in his way. His own son had run away in terror, and he wasn't doing a damn thing about it. Logan could be anywhere. Someone could have abducted him. He could have been hit by a car and be in the hospital right now, with no one even looking for him. Her eyes flooded with emotion at the thought.

She'd made a point to ask Tia if the adults had called the police to report that Logan was missing. With wide eyes, the little girl shook her head and answered, "Not the police!" as if the police were the enemy. Tia had reported what Robert had said about Logan: "When he's hungry, he'll be back."

Now, with trembling fingers, Grandma Nan dialed the number for the private investigator, relieved when he answered on the first ring. "This is Nancy Shaw," she began, and told him everything she'd just discovered about Logan. "How do I go about issuing an AMBER Alert?" As the words left her mouth, she ruefully realized that the alert had the same name as Logan's mother. A coincidence, of course—it was named for a child who'd been abducted—but the reminder of her daughter pained her.

"First of all," Grinch said, in a way she didn't like, "a private citizen can't issue an AMBER Alert. That's a judgment call made by the authorities, usually the local police."

"So if I tell the police, they'll do it?"

He sighed. "In theory, that would be how it would go. But they'll want to investigate themselves. They won't just do it on your say-so."

Flabbergasted, she said, "What's to investigate? Logan is missing."

"You know that, but they don't." She could picture Grinch in his cluttered office, one hand flat against the desk. "What they'll see is a parent saying his kid is at camp, and a grandmother who has no legal authority over the child who is saying something else. The two of you have contradictory stories, and they'll want to check out the whole situation. Believe me, they don't just issue AMBER Alerts half-cocked. There's a process. Now if a witness sees a kid abducted, say, grabbed off the street and thrown into a car, they'll move on it pretty quickly, but in your case—"

He kept talking, but it was just background noise to Grandma Nan because her eye was drawn across the street to the front door of the brick building, where Robert came out clutching a small white square of paper. He'd changed clothes and now wore a white T-shirt and narrow, dark sunglasses, like he was undercover, but she'd have known him anywhere. Tia and her friend were no longer sitting on the steps. They must have gone inside while she was on the phone.

Robert stepped onto the sidewalk, looking up and down the street. What was he doing? As she watched, he called out to a jogger, a young woman in athletic leggings and tank top, earbuds attached to an iPod strapped to her upper arm. The woman slowed to a stop, gazed down at the paper in his hand, gave him a sad smile, and shook her head. Grandma Nan found herself able to read her lips. *Sorry, no.* At that second, realization hit hard, and she knew exactly what he was doing.

On the phone, Grinch was still speaking. "They'd most likely interview the neighbors to try to determine when Logan was last seen by—"

She interrupted him. "I'm across the street from Robert's apartment building now, and I can see him showing people Logan's photo like he's asking if they've seen him."

"Sounds like you shook a tree, and down came some fruit."

"I guess." Whatever that meant.

Grinch said, "If that's what he's doing, it's something you can tell the police that will definitively back up your story. Does your phone take pictures?"

"Yes."

"Do you know how to use your phone's camera?"

"Of course." It came out more snappish than she intended.

"Don't sound so irritated. Not everyone in our age group knows how," he said.

It occurred to her then that he was probably referring to himself. "So what should I do with the camera?"

"Your son-in-law sounds potentially dangerous, so don't leave the car. From where you are, take pictures of him and whomever he's talking to. The fact that he's asking other people about Logan's whereabouts will back up your story. If he sees you, just drive away. You do not want a confrontation."

"Got it," she said.

"Then drive to the closest police station and tell them what you told me. Show them the photos, and give them all the information you have regarding Logan. His birth date, his dad's current address, that type of thing. They'll want that recent photo. Keep calm and stay neutral. You don't want to sound hysterical or make them think you're holding a grudge against Robert. Keep it all about Logan."

"Okay."

"If you need anything else, call back. I'm here for you."

They exchanged goodbyes, which made the phone available for photo taking. She was glad she let the young man at Best Buy talk her into a phone that took such excellent photos from a distance, although at the time she didn't think it would ever be so advantageous. "Eight times larger," he'd enthused, showing her how it worked by taking pictures of a display on the other side of the store. Who knew she'd be using it for something like this?

Her side window was down, but the engine wasn't running. It was an inferno outside and even hotter in the car, but she didn't dare start up the engine and turn the air-conditioning on. She didn't want to attract attention. Robert wasn't looking in her direction, but that could change.

Grandma Nan slouched down so that only the top of her head was visible. She watched Robert through the phone's screen. He paced back and forth in front of his building, like an anxious caged tiger. He showed the photo to a woman pushing a stroller and a minute later to a guy going out to his car. Both shook their heads, the guy saying, "Sorry, man." Grandma Nan got multiple shots of both encounters.

Snap. Snap. Snap. Snap.

The images were so sharp that the people were readily identifiable. She hoped the photos would be helpful.

Robert pushed the sunglasses to the top of his head and wiped his sweaty brow with the palm of his hand. Nan knew how he felt. Too hot to be out here. He was probably wishing he was inside drinking a cold one. And she was wishing for cool air coming out of her dashboard vents, but as long as he could stand the heat, she could too.

He sat down on the front steps, the same place where Tia had been sitting with the other little girl her age. A spot that provided partial shade. Why he didn't walk down the street was puzzling because that's what she'd be doing if she were in his place. That's what anyone would do if they had a missing kid. Robert had always been lazy and conniving. He spent more time trying to get others to do his work than it would have taken to do it himself. Amber had admired it when they were first married, thinking he was good at delegating, but Nan hadn't been so sure. At the time, she'd hoped she was wrong, but she hadn't been. Robert was a waste of a human being.

She was almost to the point of giving up and driving to the closest police station when two young men rounded the corner, heading right toward Robert. It was like watching a movie, knowing what would come next. Just as she could have predicted, Robert stood up when they came near, called out to them, and then thrust the photo in front of their faces. She waited for the shake of the head, the apology, accompanied by the walk away, but that didn't happen. Instead, the two guys exchanged an uneasy look before one of them said something to Robert. Something that made his face crease with anger.

She sat up, not even caring anymore if anyone saw her. She had to remind herself to keep taking pictures. Robert jabbed an accusatory finger at one of the guys, and in return, the young man held up both hands in the surrender position. All three men spoke rapid-fire. She couldn't make out the words. It seemed to her that the two younger men were trying to defuse the situation. *Good luck with that,* she thought.

Robert finally took a step back and pulled out his phone. She thought he was going to call someone, but instead, he entered something, tapping his phone as one of the guys seemed to be dictating. Was he texting? She wished she knew some genius tech guru, the kind in the movies who could hack into Robert's phone and tell her what was going on. The movies always made it look so easy. The only way she'd ever see what was on his phone was if she grabbed it out of his hand. Even then, she probably wouldn't be able to figure out how to access his texts.

Robert put his phone back in his pocket and said something else to the two guys, saluting them with two fingers before spinning around and sprinting into the apartment building, like a man on a mission.

"He knows something," Grandma Nan murmured to herself. Without giving it much thought, she was out of the car and darting through traffic as she crossed the street. The two young men had continued walking and were talking between themselves, one of them tapping a pack of cigarettes against his hand. The sun's rays were full-on radiating off the pavement. "Excuse me!" she yelled as she got closer. At this range, she noticed they looked like tough customers, with their bulky arms and military-length haircuts. One had a tattooed neck, and the other had a long chain at his waist, starting at his belt and leading to the back pocket of his jeans. They were so similar in appearance they had to be brothers.

They regarded her expectantly. The taller one said, "Lady, you better watch where you're going. You almost got hit by that car."

Did she? She hadn't noticed. Unzipping her purse, she said, "I think you boys can help me. I'm a grandmother to a little boy named Logan." She fumbled through the contents of her purse, pushing aside her bulging wallet, pack of gum, clear plastic bag of cosmetics, and comb until she found the envelope with the photos she'd gotten at the elementary school. "He's lost," she said, sticking the photo out for them to see. "And I think you know something about where he is."

Grandma Nan saw a look pass between them but wasn't sure how to read it, so she added another branch to the fire. "I'm not looking to blame anyone here. No judging, I promise. I just need to find him. He's the other half of my heart." And wouldn't you know it, despite her best efforts to stay cool and collected, her eyes welled up with tears. Worse yet, her tissues were still in the car. With tears streaking down her face, she said, "Can you please tell me what you know?"

They barely registered what she said. The shorter one put a cigarette to his mouth, cupped his hand around it, and lit it with a Zippo lighter. His friend said, "Sorry, lady, we can't help you."

"I just saw you talking to Logan's father," Grandma Nan said, reaching back into her purse. "I know you told him something. Tell me what you told him." She pulled out a wad of cash—two twenties, a five, and a bunch of singles—and thrust it toward them. "Look, I'll give you money." She pushed the cash into the taller one's hand, and he accepted it. "This is everything I have. That, and . . ." Rummaging through her wallet, she pulled out an Amazon gift card. "And this!" She held it up in the air. "It's for fifty dollars, and I haven't used any of it yet. Just tell me where Logan is. I need to get to him before his father does."

Her words were having an effect. She could tell. The taller one asked, "His dad—does he whale on him?"

"Whale on him?"

"Beat him. Does his dad beat him?"

Grandma Nan sucked in a breath. She'd never seen Robert hit Logan, but there were plenty of times he'd been short with him, yelled, or pushed him when he'd thought Logan was moving too slowly. Other times he'd threatened the boy in such a mean way it made her wince. Amber had always managed to placate Robert, but that glimpse of rage just below the surface was still scary. The tip of the iceberg, most likely. So she couldn't answer definitively, but she sensed this question was important. "Yes."

"That sucks. Poor kid." The brothers both looked sympathetic now.

"So you can see why I need to find him. He's been through so much."

"Okay, Grandma. We'll tell you what we know," the guy with the cigarette said, inhaling so the tip glowed red. "The kid hitched a ride in our moving van the day before yesterday. We didn't know he was back there. Only found him when we opened up the truck at a gas station off I-39 north, first exit past Banfield."

"We pulled up the door, and he was just there," his brother said. "Kid didn't say a word. Just jumped out the back and took off."

"He wouldn't have said anything," Grandma Nan said. "Logan doesn't talk."

"At all?"

"No, not at all."

"He's deaf?"

"No," she said, shaking her head. "It's complicated." None of this was helping. She needed to get them back on track. "So he ran out of the truck. Did you notice which way he headed after that?"

"He took off down this country road, away from the interstate." He flicked the ashes off the end of his cigarette. "We yelled after him and tried to catch him, but he's a quick little guy."

"Did he have anything with him?"

"Only a can of soda. He boosted it from our cooler." He grinned.

"What was he wearing?"

They looked at each other and shrugged. The taller one said, "Jeans, a T-shirt, shoes? Just regular kid clothes."

Grandma Nan said, "When was this?"

"Sometime in the afternoon."

"Thank you, thank you, thank you. Can I ask one more question?"

"Go ahead."

"Is this what you told Robert just a few minutes ago?"

"Pretty much, but when we talked to him, we said it happened to some friends of ours, 'cause that guy looked mean," the one with the tattoo said. He shrugged. "We made it sound like something some dude told us about."

"Okay." She nodded. "Got it. Thanks."

CHAPTER
TWENTY-THREE

Logan found that he had more hours in a day in the woods of Wisconsin than he'd ever had in any day anywhere else, and every minute belonged to him. He used the paper towels from the mini-mart to clean the tree house as best he could, getting some of them wet and wiping off the table and cushions, then drying them off with the remainder. He propped the cushions against the walls to let them air out. The sandwich and cookie had been consumed, but he arranged the toy dishes on the table along with the soda can and banana. When he stood back to take a look, he was pleased with what he saw.

He played in the creek for a bit, splashing around in his bare feet, his jeans rolled up to his knees. He had fun seeing the water swirl, feeling the soft mud between his toes and watching as the clear water clouded up with his every movement. When Logan tired of it, he got out and lay down on the shore on his belly, holding a stick out and watching it bob on the current. Without the constant noise of apartment neighbors or the TV set, it was easier to hear his thoughts. It was so peaceful outdoors. He rolled onto his back and looked at the sky, puffy white clouds against the blue, hovering high above the tree branches. Logan imagined Grandma Nan up beyond the clouds, watching over him. He imagined she would be proud of the way he'd returned the stolen towel. She'd also be glad he was safe. Would she disapprove of him being away from home by himself? He'd made his father angry, but Grandma Nan had never gotten mad at him. The worst he'd ever gotten from her was quiet disapproval when he hadn't listened once. The look on her face that day almost killed him, he felt so bad.

When his feet had dried, he put his socks and shoes back on and decided to go exploring. About twenty feet away from the tree house, near a forked tree, he found a huge hole that looked deep enough for him to stand in. He crouched next to it and peered down, spotting what looked like the skeleton of a small animal, partially covered with leaves. *Yuck.* Who knew what other gross things were down there?

He wandered off, and when he got to the edge of the woods, he watched as the old lady gathered up vegetables in baskets and took them inside the house. Later, he saw her car back out of the driveway and head down the road. Earlier, he'd noticed an SUV back down her neighbor Laura's driveway, so he knew both houses were empty.

Feeling bold, he ventured through the woods to the patio of the house closer to the street, the one where Laura lived. He'd watched earlier as the couple had erected a pole with a hook in their backyard, then hung something that resembled the spine of an umbrella to it, and attached different pieces of metal off the ends of those pieces. The lower pieces were able to pivot so that they spun around in the breeze, making the whole thing revolve. A hanging sculpture, like the mobiles that hang above baby cribs, only huge. Logan stepped out from the trees, wanting to get closer, to see more. From the back of the house, the big windows revealed so much of the interior he felt certain no one was home.

The moving sculpture was a marvel, maybe ten feet wide, with large polished pieces of silver. Some of them had pieces of clear cut glass that shone rainbow beams onto the grass as it moved. He reached out and let a piece graze the tip of his finger as it swung by. So shiny and beautiful. It was the kind of thing his mother would have loved. She had a piece of glass like this that hung on a window with a suction cup, and when the sun shone into the window just the right way, the rainbow colors were magical. He didn't have it anymore. The rainbow glass had been left behind one time when they had moved. He hated to think that the landlord had thrown it out. Maybe the new people were able to enjoy it.

Walking around the mobile, he saw now that it was cockeyed, leaning slightly to one side. The fact that it was off balance bothered him, and he put his fist over his mouth, trying to figure out what was wrong. Each lower piece had a counterpart to provide balance, so it should have been in perfect alignment. He puzzled over this for a moment, until it hit him. The decorative weights on the end of each bar determined the spacing between them. Logan had an idea. He unclipped one of the rods and moved it over by several inches. He stepped back and watched as it moved. Only slightly better. He puzzled over it some more, studying the angles and lengths of the crosspieces until finally a solution came to him. When it came around again, he stopped it from rotating, removed two different rods, and exchanged their positions on the mobile. It was a risky move, monkeying around with someone else's artwork. He glanced back at the house, the gleam of the windows bright in the sunlight, but there was no one inside that he could see. The mobile rotated slowly in the breeze, and he smiled as he realized that now it was perfect.

He'd figured it out, proving to himself he was no dummy, no matter what anyone said.

The silver sculpture was mesmerizing, almost dizzying in its beauty, and he sat on the grass, viewing it from another angle. He sat there for a long time, just watching as it circled and swayed. When he heard a plane fly overhead, he reluctantly left the yard and headed back into the woods. It was doubtful anyone was looking for him, much less searching by plane, but it was best not to take any chances.

Logan was almost to the tree house when he heard Samson yowl. Not the aimless barking of a dog that had spotted a squirrel or was bored and wanted some attention. A raw, tortured kind of bark, the howling of a dog in trouble. He stood still, listening, waiting to see if the problem would resolve itself, but the dog's yelling and crying went on until he couldn't stand it anymore, and he took off running to see what had happened.

When he burst out of the woods into the old lady's backyard, he saw Samson, his leash caught on the wrought iron metal supports that held up the patio overhang. Logan got closer, trying to figure out what had gone wrong. One end of Samson's leash had been hooked to an eye hook next to the back door. From there he'd crossed the patio and circled a corner post on the far edge of the patio numerous times, and Logan guessed, in an effort to get loose, he had jumped up and gotten the part of the leash closest to his neck hooked onto the decorative S-curve of the wrought iron support beam. When Samson stood on his hind legs, it alleviated the tightness of his collar, but he couldn't keep it up for long, so he was alternately jumping and crying.

When Logan unhooked the leash from the curve of the support beam, the dog yelped in relief. Gently pulling on Samson's collar, Logan guided the dog around and around the post until he was completely free.

Logan had never seen a dog look so happy. Samson's tail wagged furiously, smacking the patio. He nudged him with his nose and made soft, whimpering sounds that sounded like a dog's version of "Thank you." Logan rubbed his head, behind his ears, and under his chin. Even without a voice, they'd made a connection. Samson rolled onto one side, and Logan knew he wanted his belly rubbed.

Sitting cross-legged, Logan kept up a steady petting motion, as much a comfort to him as to the dog. A living thing that welcomed his touch. A few minutes later, Samson got up and crossed the patio, coming back with a red rubber ball in his mouth, which he dropped in front of Logan. A person didn't need words to know what that meant.

He debated what to do next. Helping the dog get unstuck was one thing, but releasing him from the leash to play fetch was another. What if Samson ran away? What, then? Logan shook his head, but Samson gave a soft whine and put his muzzle on the boy's knee in a way that was too endearing to ignore. Finally, Logan unhitched Samson's collar from the leash, grabbed the ball, and stood up. Samson bounded around the yard like a crazy, happy thing, anticipating the game of fetch to come. Logan threw the ball over and over again, his heart filling with joy at the sight of the dog leaping as gracefully as a ballet dancer and catching the ball with uncanny precision.

If only life were this good all the time.

When the dog stopped the game to slurp up some water from his bowl, Logan was pretty well spent too, so he took the opportunity to hook the leash back to Samson's collar. The dog lapped some more before curling up in the shade. Logan gave him one last rub behind the ears before going back into the woods.

CHAPTER
TWENTY-FOUR

Joanne had driven home from her errands with Samson on her mind. He'd been left under the covered patio and had water and food, but still she didn't like to leave him alone for more than an hour or two if she could help it, and she really couldn't help it this time. Between picking up her prescriptions and running into one of Glenn's childhood friends in the produce section at the grocery store, it took longer than anticipated. Glenn's friend knew who she was right away, but she had to really think to match this gray-haired, middle-aged man to the face of the boy he'd been. Halfway through the conversation, she realized his name was Barry. Barry was under the impression she was moving to Seattle, of all things. "Glenn is pretty excited about having you live with them," Barry had said, holding an avocado in one hand. "You're going to love it there." Correcting him took a good chunk of time. He'd seemed certain she was moving.

She left her car keys and purse on the kitchen table, along with the one bag from the grocery store containing frozen items—orange juice cans, frozen vegetables, chicken breasts—which she emptied immediately into the freezer. The rest of the groceries were still in the car, where they'd stay until she let the dog in and got herself a glass of water. The heat today had gotten to her, which struck her as ridiculous. She'd gone from an air-conditioned car to an air-conditioned store and actually became chilled in the freezer aisle. Barely outdoors at all. Really, she had nothing to complain about compared to so many people in the world. So why did she feel so light-headed and fatigued? Probably just dehydrated.

When she opened the back door, Samson lifted his head and yawned, which was another odd thing. Normally he'd be ahead of her, bounding onto the stoop before she barely turned the knob. So many times she had to open the door slowly for fear of hitting him. Today he just lay there. Was he sick? He looked okay, probably just waking from a nap. "Come on, boy," she called out, and when he didn't move, she tugged gently on his leash. He rose slowly, shaking out his haunches before coming to greet her. He moved more slowly than usual but looked happy enough. "That's it. Come on in." When he was inside, she leaned over to unhook him and noticed that the leash was clipped onto the collar instead of the metal loop. "How did this happen?" Joanne wondered aloud, and for the millionth time wished John were still alive, for so many reasons, but this time so she'd have someone to bear witness. Had she really done this? Made such a big mistake? She frowned, looking again at the clip, which was not fastened in the right place. She'd never done it that way before, not even in her ditzier moments. When she thought back, she actually couldn't remember any specifics about letting Samson out before she left, besides making sure his water bowl was full and accessible. At the time, she'd been mentally tallying what errands she'd be running and what she'd need to bring along. So much of her daily routine was done on autopilot. "Woman loses her mind, film at eleven," she said, and laughed.

Hearing the words and her laughter echo in the kitchen confirmed it: she was really losing it. Too many years of living alone was the source of the problem. In a way, getting mentally off track was not entirely unexpected for someone of a certain age. She might even concede it was an inevitable phase of the human condition. If anything, it was amazing that people could hold so much stuff in their minds for as long as they did. Dates and memories and all manner of information. When to file income taxes and how to cook a turkey. How often to replace furnace filters and what to do if the smoke detectors went off. So much to keep in your head! History and holiday traditions and anniversaries and birth dates of family members. The human brain constantly sifted through data and memories, retaining what would be useful in the future and deciding what could be discarded, and it did this day after day, year after year, for decades on end. Astounding how much stuff rattled around in a person's noggin. No wonder some of it leaked out on occasion.

If she was getting a touch forgetful, she could live with it as long as it didn't progress any further. She didn't relish the idea of living in a memory care unit in some facility somewhere. Of course, no one wanted that.

CHAPTER
TWENTY-FIVE

Grandma Nan went back to her car with a new sense of purpose. "Hang in there, Logan. Help is on the way," she whispered. She turned the key, and the engine came to life, hot air blowing out of the vents. Hopefully that would change in a few minutes.

She was still parked across the street from Robert's apartment building when one of the young men appeared at her open window, handing her the clutch of bills she'd given him. "Here, Grandma," he said. "I can't take your money."

She looked up and saw his scarred face and his neck, covered in dark-blue inked letters. It had made her wary originally, but now she saw him with new eyes, and in an instant, his tough-guy persona melted away. He was someone's grandson too. "Thank you." She took the cash. "I appreciate it more than I can say."

"I'm keeping the Amazon gift card, though." He flashed a smile. "I've got a bunch of stuff in my cart, and it'll cover most of it."

"That's fine. I hope you enjoy it."

He tapped the roof of her car. "You drive safe now. I hope you find the little guy." He ran back across the street to join up with his brother.

They continued walking down the sidewalk, and she watched them round the corner until they were out of sight.

Grandma Nan had brought a small notebook with her on this trip, all the better to keep track of anything she discovered along the way. She'd written down the address of Robert's apartment, the names of Tia and her mother, and the name and address of Logan's elementary school, along with the names of the school assistant, Jenny Barnes, and the speech therapist, Ms. Tracey. Now she took out her phone and took photos of Logan's school picture and classroom photo. Grinch had said to document everything, and she thought it was a good idea. Once she had it all down, her next destination was the closest police station.

She looked at her phone, trying to figure out the exact location of the gas station off I-39 north, the one at the first exit past Banfield. Grandma Nan input every combination of searches she could think of and finally came up with a gas station called Mallick's Gas and Go. Once again, her smartphone was smarter than she was. Grandma Nan was more than a little proud she'd figured out the location all on her own. The younger generation grew up online and navigated the Internet like it was their hometown, but to her, it was a foreign country.

She had just programmed the address into the GPS when a car came roaring up out of the apartment building's side drive. It was the green Ford, the one Satira had driven home from Aldi, but now Robert was at the wheel, the only passenger in the car. Even from this distance, there was no mistaking the determined look on his face, the cold concentration of a hunter. There was only one reason he'd have that kind of look. He was, she realized with a sickening feeling, on Logan's trail, ready to drive up to Wisconsin and drag that kid home. Once that happened, there was no telling what would happen next, but she knew it would be something terrible. Robert hated being inconvenienced, and he also hated it when someone made him look bad, and Logan had done both.

Change of plans. There was no time to go to the authorities. Logan was three hours away, give or take. By the time she explained the situation to the police, and they checked her story out, Robert would be there already. She needed to beat him there.

She waited until he was halfway down the street before pulling away from the curb. At the stop sign, she was right behind him. She waited for him to glance back and realize it was her, but when nothing happened, she exhaled in relief, glad for her oversize sunglasses and new car. Robert wasn't known for noticing much beyond himself. Maybe, just maybe, she could get away with driving the same route without him spotting her.

She followed him down city streets, unaware of where she was, but certain he had a handle on directions since her GPS backed it up. He was a smart enough man when motivated. They drove on, and she lagged behind, not wanting to be too obvious. He paused at another stop sign, and she spotted a sign ahead for the interstate going north, the exact route that would take them to Wisconsin. He crossed the street, and instead of heading for the interstate, he pulled into a gas station. Grandma Nan continued past.

When she'd successfully merged onto the expressway, she breathed a sigh of relief. Robert was behind her, which meant she'd get there first.

CHAPTER
TWENTY-SIX

Logan ran out of things to do, so once again he found himself walking to the mini-mart. He was out of money, so there would be no shopping at the food station, but at least he could wash up in the bathroom and take some paper towels. There was always a chance too that he could scavenge something from the garbage for tomorrow. People were so wasteful. A half-eaten discarded candy bar would be trash to someone else but heaven in a wrapper to him. As long as it wasn't buried under garbage and he could eat around the part someone else's mouth had touched, it would be okay. He had enough food for now, but he had to think ahead.

The day was warm, but the sky had turned gray and cloudy, making the heat feel less piercing. Knowing he could douse his head with water in an air-conditioned bathroom lifted his spirits. He was on his own and doing fine. Logan kicked at a stone in the road, and when he got to it, kicked it again and continued that way for a good stretch until the stone disappeared into a ditch. If he had shoes that fit him correctly, this walk would be nothing, but each step hurt, so he took wide strides, which helped, but only a little. When he got back, he would take his shoes off and sink his toes into the creek. That would feel good.

When he got to the gas station, he waited until a couple was entering the mini-mart and walked in behind them. The place was fairly busy, so busy that he was sure no one would notice a boy heading into the restroom. It felt good to use an actual toilet and then wash up at the sink. He splashed water on his face and neck, then squished the liquid soap between his fingers and used it to scrub his face, hands, and arms. When he was done, he considered his reflection in the mirror. He'd picked up some sun since he'd left home. Without his baseball cap, his face had developed the pink tinge of sunburn, and his arms were darker than they'd been before. He could see an actual tan line where his T-shirt sleeve ended. His hair, which was getting long, now seemed shaggy and stringy. It made him look dirty. He frowned, and then without thinking about it, he stuck his head under the faucet, feeling the water wash over his eyes, drip into his nostrils, and splash over the back of his neck. He didn't lift up his head until his hair was completely wet. While trying to keep his head over the sink, he got a handful of liquid soap and scrubbed his hair. It didn't lather up like shampoo, and it didn't smell as nice either, but at least his hair would be clean. He stuck his head back under the faucet, waiting until the water ran clear, then ran his hands over his head to wring out as much as he could. He finished with the brown paper towels, rubbing until his hair was only slightly damp.

When he was done, he used more towels to wipe up the sink and floor, and he raked through his hair with his fingers until it lay flat. He smiled, and the boy in the mirror smiled back. Not as good as taking a shower, but pretty close.

Someone knocked on the door, and out of habit, he opened his mouth to say, "Just a minute," but his throat closed up before even one word could escape. He hated that. Luckily, he was done. He walked out, and the guy, an older man in a Packers jersey, pushed past him in a hurry.

The mini-mart was starting to have a familiar feel, and he made his way to the exit down a side aisle. At the picnic table near the front door, a mother sat with three boys, all of them younger than he was. Each one had a can of soda. Full-size bags of snacks were in the middle of the table—chips, pretzels, and popcorn—and the mother pulled them open one by one and passed them around. Logan lingered nearby, his mouth watering as the boys mindlessly popped chips and pretzels into their mouths. As much as he wanted to stay anonymous, he wouldn't have minded if the mother had noticed him standing there and offered him some, but she was too busy keeping her sons in check. They were a squirmy bunch. One began throwing the popcorn in the air toward his brother's open mouth, even as their mother told them to knock it off. Logan watched as the boys swatted at each other, poking and whining and laughing, and getting more and more riled up until the smallest one fell off the bench seat and crashed to the pavement, then began crying—a dramatic, fake-sounding cry. Their mom, not the least bit sympathetic to the boy's wailing, gritted her teeth and said, "I've had it with you boys. We're leaving."

She grabbed the fallen child by the hand and pulled him to his feet, then snatched up two of the bags, motioning for the other kids to follow her to a minivan parked a few feet away. The nearly full bag of popcorn stayed behind on the table. Was she really going to leave it there? Logan stood by, guarding the bag, and waited to see if she'd return. Getting all the boys strapped into the minivan turned out to be a major production, with a lot of yelling on the part of the mother. When they finally pulled away, Logan swooped in and grabbed the bag, claiming it as his own.

He wandered to the back of the building, finding the dumpsters enclosed by walls, the top exposed. Undoing the latch to the entry door, he was able to get inside to look, but the dumpster was stinky, and all the garbage was enclosed in black plastic bags. He wasn't desperate enough to open them up. For now, he had food.

As he walked back down the country road eating his popcorn, he still couldn't believe his good luck. An almost entirely full bag of popcorn! And they'd left two pretzels on the table as well, which he'd eaten right away. What a score. It definitely made the long walk worthwhile.

Logan was in such a good mood that the return back to the tree house seemed to take no time at all. When a truck approached, he automatically moved off to the side, hiding behind some bushes while still popping kernels into his mouth.

When Logan got back to what he thought of as his woods, he veered off the road and headed toward the tree house. The popcorn wasn't overly salty, but he was ready for a sip of water, and then maybe after that, he'd go take a look and see if Samson was out. If the dog was out and he was sure the woman was not at home, he might be bold enough to go and pet him again.

He was deep in thought when he felt himself pelted by something that came from above his head. A hard object hit his shoulder and slid down his back, bouncing off the ground. His heart jumped, and he stopped in his tracks, sure someone had thrown something at him. It felt that way, anyway, but the woods were silent, except for the rustling of the leaves in the wind and the far-off cry of a bird. At his feet, he saw the object now. It was an apple, and above his head, branches with more apples. A grin crossed his face when he realized he'd discovered an apple tree. Wisconsin was full of surprises. He picked up the one on the ground and wiped it on the front of his shirt before taking a bite. Despite its small size and imperfect shape, it tasted even better than one from the grocery store. He plucked a few more off low-hanging branches, cradling them in the stretchy fabric of the front of his shirt. He'd wash them off in the stream and have them for dessert.

This was turning out to be a pretty good day.

CHAPTER
TWENTY-SEVEN

By the time Paul and Laura returned from dinner at the local café, the sky had gotten overcast, and the wind had picked up. Clearly a storm was brewing. "We should leave the car out and put the mobile in the garage," Laura said as Paul pulled into the driveway.

"I was just thinking the same thing." He pulled up and pressed the remote to raise the door. "If any of those pieces come flying off, they'll turn into projectiles." He made a throat-slashing gesture that made her laugh.

He parked the car, and they went around the side of the house, both of them wanting to be done with the chore before the storm hit. Laura hadn't looked at the mobile since they'd put it together, hadn't even allowed herself to view it through the window. Knowing it wasn't hanging right weighed on her, made her feel like the project was a failure, even as Paul assured her they'd work it out together. But when? The date to deliver and install the project was less than two weeks away. Her one big artistic triumph, and her biggest fear was that she'd messed it up.

Maybe once it was in the garage she could figure out what was wrong. If not then, maybe the maintenance crew at the hospital who were scheduled to suspend it might have some insights. It should have worked. The virtual model did, and her calculations were correct, so why it hung lopsided was anyone's guess.

A gust of wind lifted her hair off her shoulders. "Where did this come from?" Laura asked. It had been sunny earlier in the day, a perfect August morning.

Paul said, "I saw the forecast earlier, but I didn't think anything of it."

When they rounded the back corner of their house, they could still hear the wind, but the trees on one side and the house on the other gave the yard a sheltered feeling. Her mobile still hung off the pole, the whole thing intact, to her relief. It swung around, the prisms casting rainbow lights on the grass. Each piece was perfectly balanced, all of them working in sync, exactly as she had envisioned it and just the way it had appeared in her virtual plan. "Oh," she said, stopping to look. "It's fixed." Looking at Paul, she asked, "Did you do that?" Without even waiting for a response, she gratefully threw her arms around him and gave him a hug. "Best husband ever." When she smiled up at him, he was shaking his head, a confused look on his face.

He said, "I'd love to take credit, but I haven't touched it since we were out here before. Maybe it just corrected itself?"

"Maybe." She didn't think that was possible, though. If something was lopsided, didn't it stay lopsided? Things didn't just fix themselves.

"Anyway." He kissed her forehead. "Let's get it inside before it rains."

They kept the mobile intact, swinging the pieces to one side so it could be easily carried. Once it had been safely moved into the garage, Paul stepped back to admire it. "Even in our garage it looks like a masterpiece."

"I'd love to know how it got fixed." Laura frowned. She circled around the thing, trying to determine what had changed, if anything, but it looked the same to her.

"Sometimes it's best not to overthink things when they're going well."

"I guess you're right, but you can be sure I'm going to label the parts and include the numbers in the diagram."

Once they were inside, Laura switched on some lamps, and they settled down on the couch to watch the rain. Storms came hard and fast out in the country, or at least it seemed that way in this house made of glass. Wind knocked on the sides of the house, and rain pelted the windows like it was a person made of water, trying to break in. When lightning struck, it seemed close. The thunder that followed shook the house, the noise so resounding it went all the way to Laura's spine. Knowing they were safely inside made it amazing and thrilling, but if she were on the other side of the window, she'd find it terrifying.

"I knew we were getting a storm, but I didn't know it would come up so fast," Paul said. "I'm glad we decided not to go to the movie."

Laura, who was nestled in the crook of his arm, lifted her head and said, "Is there a tornado warning?"

"Not that I heard." He consulted his phone. "High winds and plenty of precipitation, but nothing about a tornado."

"That's good."

They watched the trees outside bend and shimmy in the wind, the rain on the windows blurring their view so the scene resembled a painting by Monet. Real-life impressionism.

"I hope that boy I saw isn't outside," Laura said.

Paul shook his head. "Trust me. No one would be outside in this. I'm sure he's home by now."

CHAPTER
TWENTY-EIGHT

Logan's day took a turn for the worse when the skies darkened and it began to rain. He was safely nestled in the tree house by then and feeling pretty good now that he'd cleaned himself up and consumed enough food and water that his stomach was full. The popcorn and apples were a good combination, the salty crunch contrasting with the sweet, juicy fruit. He'd savored every bite. After he'd eaten, he'd spied on Samson's house, hoping to catch a glimpse of the dog, but all he saw was the old lady through the kitchen window. From her movements, he guessed she was doing the dishes. He watched for a bit, thinking she might let Samson out, but when it didn't happen for what seemed like a long time, he left, disappointed.

He killed some time playing in the creek. Scooping up water with his hands and splashing it on his face and neck felt good, and the muck on the creek bottom eased the parts of his feet that had been pinched by his shoes. He'd discovered on the way home that undoing the laces gave his feet some breathing room, which caused less pain and rubbing as he walked. Not having his shoes tied slowed him down some, though. That was the bad part.

When the wind picked up and the sun disappeared behind some steel-gray clouds, Logan gathered up his belongings and climbed up the ladder to his new home. He placed the popcorn bag and the remaining apples on the table, amusing himself by putting two of the apples in the plastic teacups. Then he took the cushions off the chairs to create his makeshift bed. It was too early to sleep, but there was nothing else to do, so he took off his shoes and settled back, listening to the wind cry and watching the branches outside his windows twitch and thrash.

It wasn't until the wind started howling that a worrying thought crossed his mind. Would this tree house withstand a big storm? It looked sturdy, but then again, it was attached to a tree. He'd seen tree branches that had broken off in windstorms. Tornadoes were another thought. One time, Grandma Nan had told him about a tornado that had hit her hometown in Nebraska when she was a little girl. The tornado had sliced off the front of a house so that you could see the inside as plain as day. "It was like looking at a dollhouse," she'd told him. "You could see the dresser in the bedroom and the mirror on the wall, all untouched." It was hard to imagine a wind so strong it could cut a house in half, but Grandma Nan would never lie to him, so it had to be true.

When the rain started, it didn't come in a mist and build from there. No, it was as if the sky had a huge bucket it emptied right over Logan's tree house. He frantically closed the windows once the rain began to pound against the roof. The tiny holes that had made the ceiling look like planetarium stars that morning started to leak, the water dripping in steadily and pooling on the floor. Alarmed, Logan stood up, holding his finger over the closest hole. Upon realizing it worked, he looked around to see if there was anything that could block the holes.

He went over to the table and pulled a few kernels of popcorn out of the bag and tried to cram one into an opening, but it wouldn't stay, and all he got for his trouble was a stream of water running from his wrist to his elbow. Finally, he gave up and moved the cushions underneath the table, where he sat hunched over, his arms around his knees. The rain pounding on the roof was an assault, a sign that he wasn't safe. Logan closed his eyes and rocked, repeating the mental mantra he'd used when his father used to hit him. *Please stop. Please stop. Please stop.*

The words were just as ineffective now as when his father's belt came relentlessly slamming down on his back.

Lightning flashed, and shortly thereafter a clap of thunder shook the thin walls of the tree house. Most of the floor was wet now, and Logan was damp too. If it stopped soon, he could mop it up with his clothing and wring it out. If it was sunny the next day, he'd dry his clothes in the sun.

It was a fine plan, but the storm kept on, and soon the floor of the tree house was slick with water, which meant it was all around him. With the windows closed, it was stiflingly hot and hard to breathe. Without warning, he got that weird closed-in feeling, the precursor to the heart-attack-like spells he got all too often. As the wind whipped harder, he felt his heart pound so hard he thought he was dying. No doubt about it, he had to get out of there. He grabbed his shoes and stuck them on his bare feet, then bolted out of the tree house, leaving the apples and popcorn and his wet socks behind.

Down the ladder he went. By the third rung, he was soaking wet, his hair hanging in wet clumps, rivulets of water streaming down his face. His first thought was to go to the gas station. Maybe he could sit inside without being noticed or hide in the bathroom until the storm played out. He hopped off the bottom of the ladder onto spongy ground and started to walk in the direction of the road. A bolt of lightning lit up everything around him for one freak second, and then it was dark again. After his eyes had adjusted a little, he kept on, going slowly because his shoes were unlaced and it was hard to see. He almost stepped into the huge hole, the one with the animal bones in it, but at the last minute, he realized it was there and went around it. He tried to concentrate on his breathing in order to slow it down. Sometimes that helped.

Logan wiped the water away from his eyes, pushing his hair back off his forehead. He was being so careful that when he tripped over a tree root and fell to his knees, the unexpectedness of it made it feel like someone had come up from behind and smacked him down. His outstretched hands started to break his fall, but then he skidded forward on the wet ground and landed, *thwack*, full body down, his head hitting something hard. The impact took the wind out of him and sent one of his shoes flying.

The storm wailed like it was mocking him, and he found himself unable to hold back the tears springing to his eyes. He could hear his father's voice in his head. *Such a baby. You disgust me.*

Slowly he got up, wiping his muddy hands on his jeans. He looked for his lost shoe and couldn't find it, something so puzzling it troubled him. How could it not be nearby? He stepped cautiously, feeling the poke of something sharp on the sole of his bare foot and crying some more, which was the stupidest thing ever, because if it was hard to see in the first place, it was even harder to see through tears.

There was no going to the gas station now, not soaking wet and muddy and with a missing shoe. But he had to go somewhere. Almost by instinct, he headed to the closest place he knew he could take cover. Walking with most of his weight on the foot with the shoe, he nearly hopped in the direction of Samson's house. It was slow going, but when he reached the edge of the woods, he was relieved to see that although there were lights on in the house, the light next to the back porch was off, making the space under the overhang dark.

Logan hobbled over to the patio, grateful to get out of the rain and more grateful still to see one of the striped towels folded up on the bench next to the stoop. Even though it wasn't his, he used it to wipe his face. Using a towel was not the same as taking a towel. The old lady might be angry to find her towel dirty and wet, but there was no helping it. This was an emergency.

Once he'd toweled off the best he could, Logan lay down close to the house, where the rain couldn't reach him. Covering himself with the towel, he curled up, making himself as small as possible. He was wet and tired, but his heart had relaxed, and he no longer felt as if he was about to die. There was no telling what he would do tomorrow, but that was tomorrow's problem. For now, he would wait out the storm.

CHAPTER
TWENTY-NINE

Most of the time, Joanne didn't mind living alone. She had Samson, busy days, and a comfortable routine. There was no one there to mind if she wanted to channel flip or decided to eat cereal for dinner. No one to account to and no one to object. She could do whatever she wanted, whenever she wanted. Most of the time it was freeing, but tonight, the sudden onset of the storm troubled her. She wasn't sure what the problem was—she was safe enough in the house, and the forecast didn't mention tornadoes, so at least she could rule that out. She just didn't like the way the thunder made the house shake and the way the rain made so much noise that she had to turn the TV up louder than she liked.

Samson was a little nervous too, so instead of sitting in her recliner as she usually did, Joanne parked herself on the end of the sofa and patted the space next to her, which gave him permission to come up, something that wasn't usually allowed. He climbed up clumsily, but she could tell he was grateful, and when she patted her lap, the dog plunked his muzzle right on her thigh. She stroked his head as she watched her shows.

The woods in back shielded the house somewhat, but the front window, close to the sofa, was getting slammed with rain. She'd closed the drapes earlier so the flashes of lightning wouldn't trouble the dog, but even so, both of them were aware of what was going on outside. "It's okay, boy," she murmured, rubbing behind his ears. "It's okay. We're safe."

The *Lifetime* movie she'd settled on took place in a beach town. A young woman with a secret past had come to live there and was befriended by a good-looking young widower with an adorable little daughter. It seemed to Joanne she'd seen this one before, or was this just a common plot? Regardless, it was fun to watch TV people, all of them young and beautiful, with problems much more dramatic than usually found in real life. It was nice to have someone to root for. During commercials, she flipped to another channel, to a movie she'd seen so often she should be sick of it, but it starred Sandra Bullock, who was one of her favorites. So often, actresses were beautiful *or* funny. It was a rare treat to watch one who was both.

She went back to the first movie, knowing how it would go, but still along for the ride. Despite reaching the exciting part of the movie, where the woman's abusive ex-boyfriend finally caught up to her, and also in spite of the fact that the storm still raged on, Joanne found herself with her head back, resting her eyes. It had not been an especially tiring day, but sometimes sitting for too long made her sluggish. If she didn't get up now, she'd fall asleep in the chair and wake up with a backache. She shook herself awake, shut off the movie, and made her way down the hall.

After being in the heat all day, a shower would hit the spot, but that wasn't the smartest idea during a thunderstorm. A bath, she decided, would have to do. She went into the bathroom and ran the water, checking periodically to make sure the temperature was right. Samson had followed her initially, then lost interest and wandered out of the room. When the tub was two-thirds full, she heard him barking in the kitchen.

"Okay, okay, just a minute." Joanne shut off the water and got to her feet. Samson sounded frantic, which was odd because she'd let him out not that long ago.

By the time she got to the kitchen, Samson was whining by the back door and pawing at the floor like he was digging for something. What a goofy dog. She opened the door to let him out and heard the machine-gun pounding of the rain on the overhang. She hoped he would be quick about it because she wasn't in the mood for a drenched dog.

She waited for him to bound outside, but Samson stood still, alternately looking out the door, then back at her. His whole body quivered with anticipation. "Go ahead," she urged, but the dog just whined and looked up at her. Turning on the back porch light, she told him, "You're on your own. I'm not going to pee for you."

But when he didn't go, she realized there must be more to it than that.

There was something out there. Joanne peered into the darkness, wondering what wild animal lingered nearby. A coyote, maybe? Not a wolf. They'd be farther north. She'd heard locals sometimes say they'd spotted bobcats, but she'd never seen one herself, and she'd never heard of one confronting a dog.

She sighed, then took hold of Samson's collar. "Come on."

He allowed her to walk him out. When they were on the stoop and she'd let go, he didn't head out to the yard to urinate but went around the bench, nosing at a towel bunched up on the concrete next to it.

Joanne followed the dog. "What are you . . . ?" She stopped, taking in the sight of a small child, curled up on his side, Samson's striped towel covering most of him. She reached down to pull off the towel, and the boy flinched as if expecting to get hit.

CHAPTER THIRTY

Logan heard the back door open and would have run away if he'd had enough time or the strength or a place to go. He'd once heard Grandma Nan say she was all out of energy, not a drop left, and that was how he felt. Not too long ago he'd had an endless supply of it, but he'd been battered by this storm and drained by the wind, and now he was all tapped out. All he could do was lie still, hoping the old lady would let Samson out and then back in again without noticing him.

He closed his eyes, feeling that if *he* couldn't see anything, he wouldn't be seen either, but that didn't work. The back porch light went on, and the lady came out with Samson. The dog wasn't out one minute before he began nosing at Logan, giving him away. When the lady pulled the towel back, he opened his eyes and looked at her, sure she was going to yell at him for trespassing or using her towel or getting mud on the patio, but instead, a startled, soft expression came over her face. Their eyes met, and she didn't say anything for a minute, just had a look like she was trying to figure out a crossword puzzle. When she finally spoke, her voice was kind. "That doesn't look too comfortable. I think you should come inside." She extended her hand, and he took it, letting her pull him to his feet.

Samson wagged his tail and darted around both of them. If Logan had to guess, he'd say the dog was happy to have found him.

The lady guided him with one hand on his shoulder. "Come along," she said. "It's cooler in the house." Opening the screen door, he found himself ushered into the kitchen, the same room he'd seen peering through the window earlier. Inside it was nice: braided oval rug inside the door, a bowl of fruit on the counter, nice cabinetry, and a small wooden table.

He didn't move off the rug, not wanting to track in dirt, and the old lady must have had the same thought because she pulled a kitchen chair away from the table so it was closer to the door and put a dish towel on the seat. She said, "Go ahead and sit down."

Numbly, he followed orders, waiting for her to interrogate him or call the police or tie him to the chair, but instead she got a handful of dish towels from one of the drawers and knelt down in front of him, taking off his one remaining shoe. "This one has seen better days," she said, almost to herself. She examined the patch job done with duct tape before setting the shoe on the rug. She wiped Logan's feet, dabbing at them gently, and frowned when she noticed the raw spots. Samson plunked himself right next to the chair, his head bumping against Logan's leg.

"Okay, then," she said, pulling herself up on the edge of the table. "Now we talk."

She sat down in a chair opposite him. "My name is Joanne Dembiec. You can call me Joanne or Mrs. Dembiec. Either one works. What is your name?"

This was the part Logan always hated. When he didn't answer, people always thought he was being rude. He pointed to his throat, then mimed writing on some paper.

"You can't talk?"

He shook his head.

"But you can hear me, obviously. Just a minute." She went to one of the kitchen drawers and came back with paper and pen, which she set down in front of him.

He wrote out his name in block letters: LOGAN WEBER. Staring at what he'd just written, he realized with horror that he'd forgotten to give a fake name. Too late now.

"How old are you?" she asked. "Seven, eight?"

He held up the right number of fingers.

"Nine, then."

He waited for her to make a comment about him looking younger or being small for his age, but she didn't say anything about that.

"Where do you live, and why were you out on my patio? Your parents must be worried."

He shook his head.

"You don't want to answer my questions, or you don't know?"

Logan pressed hard with the pen, writing: DON'T KNOW.

"You lost your memory?"

He blinked a few times and then shook his head.

"Surely someone is looking for you?"

With a shake of his head, he indicated a negative. No one was looking for him, he was sure of that. Something about acknowledging he wasn't missed by anyone at all made the tears start, something he hated. *Such a baby. You disgust me.* He sniffed, trying to rein in his crying, and lowered his gaze to the floor. When he finally glanced up, the lady had her head tilted to one side, her lips pursed.

"Did you run away?"

He blinked. How to convey that he *accidentally* ran away? Finally, he shrugged his shoulders.

She said, "Are you hungry? I can make you a grilled cheese sandwich if you'd like."

The idea of a grilled cheese sandwich momentarily distracted him from his misery, and he managed a small smile and a nod. Joanne Dembiec was turning out to be nicer than he would have expected.

While she bustled around the kitchen, taking butter and cheese out of the refrigerator and getting out a pan, Logan looked around the room, his eyes settling on the refrigerator that was covered with various photos held up by kitchen magnets. Most of the pictures were of two girls older than he was, but there were a few of the dog and one of the parents with the same two girls. Joanne caught him staring and said, "Those are pictures of my granddaughters. And Samson, my dog." She gestured toward the dog. "You already know him. If you want to get up and look, Logan, go ahead. Just don't sit anywhere but on that towel."

He got up and went over to examine the photos more closely. The two girls were clearly sisters, and they obviously got along. In the photos, one always had her arm around the other. There were Halloween costumes and water fights and one picture of them pretending to sword fight. There was a lot of laughing in that family, based on these photos.

"My son, Glenn, his wife, Belinda, and their two girls," she said. "They live in Seattle. They want me to come live with them. What do you think? Should I move in with them?"

Logan looked at the pictures again, the happy faces of people who clearly loved one another. Who wouldn't want to live in that house? He turned to Joanne and gave her a thumbs-up, and she grinned. He sat back down and watched as she expertly flipped the grilled cheese in the pan.

A minute later, she presented him with a plate containing the sandwich, a pickle, and some potato chips. "Just like at a restaurant," she said. "Eat what you want and leave the rest."

He gave her another thumbs-up when asked if he wanted lemonade and had half the sandwich finished before she even had the glass poured. She sat at the table, watching him eat. He tried not to wolf it down, but he was hungrier than he'd realized, and it was a real meal, something someone had prepared just for him. The thought filled him with gratitude. This lady reminded him of his grandmother. Maybe all grandmothers were the same—old and kind and good at making food.

When he was done, she took the plate away and rinsed it off in the sink, leaving him behind to sip on his last bit of lemonade. He glanced nervously at the door, wondering if he should take the opportunity to grab his shoe and make his escape. But there really was no place to escape *to*. That was the problem. The tree house wasn't much better than being out in the storm. Besides, this kitchen was so pleasant. His wet clothes clung to him in an uncomfortable way, but at least the air-conditioning allowed him to breathe deeply, and the dog at his feet gave him an odd sense of security.

On the other side of the door, it was raining as hard as before, maybe even worse. Through the window, he saw it coming down in sheets. Lightning flashed, followed by thunder, rumbling like a mountain avalanche. It was, as Grandma Nan would say, a good day to be a duck.

Joanne took a place across from him at the table. "So what am I to do with you, Logan Weber?" she asked, tapping her fingertips together.

Everything had been going so well, and now, just as he'd feared, the situation had taken a turn for the worse. He shook his head, an all-purpose answer he hoped would convey the idea that she should do nothing.

As if she read his mind, Joanne said, "I can't just do nothing, honey. Someone, somewhere, has to be frantically looking for you. Your mom? Your dad? I know I would be sick with worry if you were my boy and I didn't know where you were."

Again, he felt tears well up in his eyes, and all he could do was shake his head. He opened his mouth to beg her to just let it be, but all that came out was a garbled sound, a noise from the back of his throat that sounded like he was about to be sick. It wasn't a word, but the fact that anything came out of him was a shock.

Joanne didn't know that a noise coming out of his mouth was a momentous event, so she kept on, sliding the pad of paper over to him. "If you write down your home phone number, I'll make the call for you."

Seeing his hesitation, she added, "It doesn't have to be your home phone. If you know the cell phone number of any family member, that would work."

He picked up the pen and put it to the paper, writing: *No. Please. No.*

Joanne sighed. "Then you leave me no choice, Logan. I'm so sorry, but I have to notify the authorities that you're here." She stood to pick up the receiver of the phone that was fastened to the wall above the kitchen counter. It was attached with a curly cord, the kind Logan had seen only in old movies. Holding the receiver out, she had one finger ready to push a button when she turned and said, "Last chance, Logan. Can you give me your parents' names or number? Maybe you have a legal guardian, or an aunt or uncle I can call? Otherwise, I'm sorry, but I have to do this."

He shook his head firmly and wrote "NO" in big letters on the pad, then held it up for her to see.

Before she could react, lightning struck nearby, and the room lit up for a split second, followed by a deafening boom. A moment later, it was pitch-black. Samson rose up and howled, and from her spot across the room, Joanne shushed him.

Logan heard her hang up the phone, followed by the sounds of fumbling in one of the drawers. The next thing he saw was the strike of a match and a candle being lit. "We seem to have lost our power," Joanne said, her face aglow behind the flame. "And the phone's out too."

CHAPTER
THIRTY-ONE

Grandma Nan saw the Wisconsin-shaped sign by the side of the road welcoming her to the state and found it reassuring. Knowing she was headed in the right direction made her even more determined to get there before Robert. The look on his face as his car had barreled out of the apartment driveway had been chilling, the countenance of an unhinged maniac. She wouldn't want to be on the receiving end of that much rage, and it would be so much worse for a helpless child.

She didn't want to imagine how terrified Logan had to have been, trapped in the back of a truck for hours. There was a possibility, of course, that the boy wasn't Logan at all. It could have been another child. Or maybe there was no child at all, and this was just a story someone made up. If that were the case, this trip would be for nothing.

One thing she knew—if there was a boy trapped in the back of a moving van who hadn't called out to be released, Logan and his lack of voice fit the scenario. If it was him, what happened to him after he took off down the country road? She patted her purse, glad to have a recent photo to show the police. Someone, somewhere, must have noticed a kid all by himself. She was counting on it.

She'd been in Wisconsin only an hour when she had to turn on the windshield wipers. The formerly sunny sky had darkened, and a mist began to fall. As she went along, the rainfall increased, dropping in large splatters against the glass. Now she switched the wipers on all the way, watching them furiously whip back and forth. Driving in her hometown, she listened to music in the car, but her nerves couldn't handle the combination of uncharted territory, weather, worrying about Logan, and watching the road all at once, so she gripped the steering wheel, stared ahead, and drove in silence.

Along the way, she kept an eye out for Robert in the green Ford. Not seeing him, she assumed she was still ahead of him. Robert had a tendency to speed, which wasn't her style, but the urgency of the situation required her to floor the gas pedal far beyond her comfort zone. A few times she considered pulling off the road and making a phone call, either to 911 or to Grinch, but knowing Robert might be right behind her made her dismiss the idea each time. She didn't have time to make a convincing phone call. Not only that, but the whole story was so involved, and frankly, even to her, it sounded concocted. The police would think she was loony. Talking to them in person was the only way to present a believable case. The information in her notebook and the photos would help as well. Something tangible to go with an old lady's assertion her grandson was missing.

She drove on.

When Grandma Nan saw the sign for Banfield up ahead, she ignored the speed limit and stepped on the accelerator. No random number on a sign could hold her back. The rain hadn't let up—not one bit. It pelted angrily against her windshield, the wiper blades pushing it aside as fast as it fell. She passed the Banfield exit and eased up on the gas pedal, knowing her exit was coming up soon.

She found herself leaning forward over the steering wheel and was relieved when she was finally on the ramp and could see the gas station off to one side. It wasn't right off the interstate, but on a frontage road, the tall sign easy for travelers to spot.

Grandma Nan kept on going, feeling more like the car was being pulled than she was doing the driving. A slightly anxious feeling came over her, the worry that this long drive would lead to nothing, and she'd be right back where she'd started. "Nothing to it but to do it," she whispered to herself, pulling into the gas station parking lot. She drove past the pumps and took a space close to the door, the nose of her car facing the front window. A neon sign declared the business open. Underneath the neon were posters advertising soft drinks and cigarettes. A picnic table was on the pavement to one side of the door. It seemed an unlikely place for anyone to eat, so close to the pumps.

Grabbing her purse, she dashed out of the car and went through the door as quickly as possible. The top of her head had gotten wet, but the rest of her was spared. Grandma Nan ran her fingers through her hair. The place was empty, except for one man buying beer up at the front counter. She got in line behind him, getting out Logan's photo while she waited.

"Your card is not going through," the man behind the counter said in a hushed tone. "Do you have another one?"

There was a time that having a card declined would be embarrassing, Grandma Nan thought, but that day was long gone. "I got another," the man said, fishing around in his wallet.

The transaction with the new card probably took all of a minute, but it was as if time had slowed for her. She had the urge to push him aside, tell him his beer could wait, or maybe—this was a thought—he didn't need beer at all. Honestly, it took everything she had to wait to get up to the counter, but when it was her turn, she suddenly realized she didn't know what to say. The young guys in Chicago had said the boy ran *away* from the gas station. It was unlikely anyone working here would have seen him. She straightened up, remembering this was just a starting point. Besides, the man behind the counter looked nice, and the photos posted on the wall behind him showed he was a loving family man.

"Yes?" he said as she stood there mutely.

"I'm not sure if you can help me," she said, sliding the photo across the counter. "I'm looking for my grandson. He's missing. His name is Logan Weber, and he's nine years old. The last reported sighting of him was in your parking lot two days ago. Can you tell me where I can find the local police station to follow up on this?"

He gestured to the photo. "May I look?"

"Of course."

The man glanced at it for only a moment before sliding it back. He tapped on the counter with his pointer finger. "I have seen this boy."

"The day before yesterday?"

"No, today. And yesterday too. I remember him. Not a very big kid. One of his shoes was wrapped up with duct tape."

Grandma Nan felt something warm rise in her chest. Hope. "You're sure it was him?"

"Oh, yes, it was him." He nodded. "He bought bananas yesterday. Today he didn't buy anything. Just used the restroom."

"He was by himself?"

"Yes, I believe so."

"You didn't think that was odd? A little boy all by himself?" She looked out the window. "I mean, there's nothing around. You're way out in the boonies. You should have stopped him and asked . . ."

"I am sorry," he said, looking very sorry indeed. "The first day I thought he walked in with some other people, and today he was in and out the door so fast I barely had time to notice him. There were people lined up paying, and I was here by myself." When she didn't respond, he added, "Besides, there is a community only a few miles away, and some houses even closer than that. Some of the local kids ride their bikes or even walk here to buy candy or soda. And I did not hear of a missing child, so it did not strike me as all that unusual."

"I'm going from here to the police station to notify them that Logan's missing. Would you be willing to tell the police you saw him so they don't think I'm crazy?"

"Of course, but I don't understand. If he's been gone for days, why wasn't he already reported missing?"

She sighed. "It's a long story. I lost touch with the family and just discovered he's gone. His father didn't report him missing. I don't know why."

"I'll tell you what," he said, picking up a cell phone from underneath the counter. "A sheriff's deputy usually stops in here around this time every evening. I'll see if they can come now and talk to you."

"Oh, thank you!"

After dialing, he rested one palm against the counter, speaking quickly. "This is Devan Mallick from Mallick's Gas and Go off I-39. Do you know if Scott is going to be coming by soon? I have a lady here who's looking for her grandson. She needs some help." He turned to give her a quick smile. "Uh-huh. Okay, then. Sounds good. Thanks." He nodded. "She's going to put out a call to have him come right away."

Relief flooded over her. Having a witness who'd seen Logan recently would be a huge boon in talking to the police. She was thanking him again, saying words of gratitude that Mr. Mallick brushed off, saying it was no problem at all, when the door swung open, punctuated by an electronic chiming.

Both of them turned to look, and Grandma Nan let out a gasp as Robert came through the door in a rain-splattered T-shirt, his movement more lurching than walking. Even from ten feet away, it was clear he was angry and drunk.

"Can I help you?" Mr. Mallick asked.

Grandma Nan backed away from the counter, trying to ease herself out of sight. Robert went right by without even giving her a look, staggered to the counter, and pulled his cell phone out of his pocket. He fumbled with it for a moment before thrusting it right into the other man's face. "This kid. You seen him?" Nan noticed a knife holstered to his belt; she recognized the handle from seeing it at Robert's kitchen table. She swallowed and quietly eased herself even farther away, trying to stay hidden behind a display.

Mr. Mallick leaned over, eyebrows furrowed to look at the picture and then glanced over to where Grandma Nan stood. "Ma'am, this looks like the same boy you're looking for. Logan, right?"

She sucked in a breath, not saying a word, but Robert turned and noticed her standing there, his bloodshot eyes narrowing in anger. "You!" Like a bear, he lunged at her, his finger pointing accusingly. The smell of Scotch hit her in the face like a furnace blast. "What are you doin' here? Stickin' your nose where it doesn't belong!"

"I have every right to be here, Robert."

"You never could mind your own business." He sneered and grabbed her arm, dragging her toward the door before she even had time to react, while the owner yelled, "Stop it! Stop it right now!"

The two grappled, with Grandma Nan crying out from the pain of having her arm in his vise grip. She reached for a shelf holding a display of candy, and it came loose, the candy spilling on the floor. Her feet skidded as she tried to resist. She hit at Robert with her free arm, but it wasn't much of a deterrent. When they got to the door, she swung out a leg to keep from being pulled through the opening, something that infuriated Robert, who yanked even harder.

He roared into her ear. "This has nothin' to do with you. He's my son. My. Son."

"He's my grandson," she said, still struggling to come loose.

Mr. Mallick was at their side now, pushing at Robert with both hands. "Let go of her. You must leave at once!"

Robert shook off Mr. Mallick, who went reeling backward, falling to the floor, and for the first time, Grandma Nan was afraid. She kicked both legs, but still Robert managed to yank her out of the store and into the storm. His voice was a scream above the howl of the wind. "Why don't you just die, old woman?" He shoved her hard, pushing her into the parking lot. She fell over and landed hard on the pavement, her outstretched hands stopping her just before her face hit the asphalt.

"Stop that. Leave now!" It was Mr. Mallick, calling out to Robert from the doorway. Grandma Nan heard a metallic thud and lifted her head to see Robert kicking her car. He knelt down next to the back door and made a punching gesture to her tire. Through the pouring rain, she caught the glimpse of a blade as he pulled his hand back, and she realized he'd slashed her tire.

The shock of the assault and getting her breath knocked out of her made moving difficult. If Mr. Mallick hadn't come out to help her to her feet, she might have had to crawl to the door. "Are you okay?" He fussed over her, grasping her gently under her arms and lifting her up. When she was on her feet, she saw Robert's car tear out of the parking lot and head down the adjacent country road.

"I'm okay. I'm okay," she said as he helped her walk back inside the building. The words came out automatically, but the truth was she really wasn't okay at all.

CHAPTER
THIRTY-TWO

Laura and Paul went to bed early that night. Once the power went out, their plans to watch Netflix fell by the wayside, and when Laura got up to do the dishes, he silently took her by the hand and led her on a detour upstairs. Rounding the corner at the top landing, she bumped into a wall and laughed. Being in the dark turned their house into something else entirely. They navigated by touch and the occasional flashes of lightning. An unexpected adventure.

Afterward, they lay intertwined in bed and talked. "How long before the power comes back on, do you think?" she asked.

It was cute the way she assumed he knew these kinds of things. "Depends on what we're looking at and how widespread the damage is out there," he answered. "There might be a lot of downed lines, and if that's the case, it might be a while."

Laura speculated on how long the house would stay cool without air-conditioning, and after discussing it, they decided it was better to leave the windows closed regardless because the humidity was pretty fierce. She said, "When this happens, I always think about people who don't have air-conditioning at all. Or people in other countries who don't have power or clean water ever. They live like that all the time."

"Yeah, we have it lucky." Truthfully, he never really gave it much thought, but he wasn't surprised that she did. Laura had a giving spirit. Sometimes she wrung herself out emotionally worrying about other people. She sucked up the emotions of those around her in a way that was both endearing and alarming.

She nestled against him, her head on his shoulder, and when she said, "Can I ask you something?" he knew what was coming next.

"Have you thought about it? Applying to be foster parents? I can't do it without you, you know."

Even though they were touching, as close as two people could be, the silence hung between them. "I know."

"I understand your concerns," she said. "I do. I really do. And they're valid, but this is not the kind of thing that you decide by checking off boxes and making lists of pros and cons."

"You're right."

"Of course I'm right," Laura said. "So what's holding you back?"

A hundred things were holding him back, and all of them had one name: fear. Fear of having his marriage usurped by a child, fear of getting attached to said child, only to have that child taken away from them, fear of losing their freedom—the ability to pack up and go for the weekend, or even go see a movie on a moment's notice. And then there was the fear that they'd have a problem child, one who would destroy furniture or set fires. He could go on and on with reasons, but he knew Laura was aware of all these possibilities and wasn't afraid at all. "It's just a big decision," he said, knowing how lame this sounded.

His mother's words played out in his mind: *You can't have half a child. You're either in or you're out. Laura's always been there for you. Don't you want her to be happy?* He did, in fact, want Laura to be happy.

"Of course it's a big decision," she said. "But it's not a hard decision. Look . . ." Now she was above him, propped up on one elbow. "I'm going to lay it out for you. I had dreams when I was young, and I've been lucky enough that most of them have come true. I'm an artist, have a great husband, beautiful house. But I always imagined I'd be a mother. It was heartbreaking to find out I'd never get pregnant, but I learned to accept it. Then, you ruled out surrogacy, and I understood your reasoning. Private adoption for infants can take years, and the woman I talked to on the phone said most birth parents pick couples in their twenties and thirties." She sighed. "And we've spent a lot of money building this house, which was your dream." He started to talk, and she put a finger to his lips. "Not yet. Let me finish. Yes, I know I was excited about building the house too, and I'm happy I can stay home and work on my art. I wanted it to be enough, but when it comes right down to it, I need more. I tried, really I did, but I'm forty-four, getting older by the minute, and I can't imagine my life going from beginning to end and never having a child to guide and love. I've been thinking about this for a long time and reading everything I can find on foster care and foster kids. Sometimes I even dream of children, and then when I wake up, I feel like something's been taken away from me."

She paused, and he said, "I'm sorry."

"But, see, that's the thing. I'm not asking for your sympathy. I'm telling you that this feels like the logical next step. I really believe this is my calling in life. There are kids out there who need parents and a loving home, and we have so much to give. I have a lot of love in my heart, Paul." Laura's voice was trembling with passion. "I need to do this, but like I said before, I can't do it without you."

His mother had told him to wait for a sign, saying it wasn't always an actual physical sign, but that sometimes it was a still, small voice that would point him in the right direction. He'd been waiting for a sign, and it hadn't happened, not yet, but apparently Laura had gotten her own sign, and that was good enough for him.

"Okay, we'll do it," he said.

"Really?" She kissed his cheek, delighted. "You mean it?"

"Absolutely. You've never steered me wrong before. Count me in."

"Thank you, Paul. I'm so happy." She kissed him again, her lips lingering over his cheek. "You're the best."

"Just one thing—this might mean not going to Spain next summer."

"That's fine. I don't care about Spain. It was just something to do."

CHAPTER
THIRTY-THREE

Joanne had a feeling letting Logan stay the night wasn't the best decision, but without phone service, there was no way for her to contact
the authorities, and besides, the kid was sopping wet and dirty, and
something had to be done about that. And putting him in the car and
driving to the police station was not an option. Her night vision was
terrible, and in the rain, it would be even worse. She wasn't risking both
their lives over something that could wait until the morning. Besides,
Logan seemed resistant to the idea, and she couldn't physically force
him into the car. Even a scrawny nine-year-old could overpower her.

When the lights went out, Joanne had gotten some candles and
found her flashlights, including one that worked like a lantern. In the
kitchen, the flicker of the flames gave off a cozy glow. She'd experienced
outages in this house many times over the years, and they'd lasted anywhere from ten minutes to twelve hours. This one could go in either
direction. There really was no way of knowing. "I'll tell you what," she
said to Logan. "Why don't we get you cleaned up and into some dry
clothes? If the power is still out after that, you can spend the night in
my guest bedroom, and we can talk tomorrow morning about what we
want to do next. Would that be okay with you?"

A sense of relief washed over his face, and he nodded enthusiastically. She ushered him into the bathroom. "You're in luck," she said. "There's already clean water in the tub, just for you." It didn't seem necessary to tell him she'd intended the bath for herself. What difference would it make now?

While he stood waiting in his filthy, damp clothing, she set the flashlight lantern on the counter next to the sink and put out a large bath towel for him to use. She told him to feel free to use the shampoo and soap on the edge of the tub and found an extra toothbrush, still in the package, which she set out on the counter next to the toothpaste. "I'm going to find you some dry clothes to wear while you clean up. I'll check back with you in a little bit, okay?"

He nodded yes, and she left him to it, knowing that a nine-year-old wouldn't need any additional assistance. In fact, sticking around would be considered creepy. Again, she wondered at her decision to have him stay, but it was just for a few more hours, and there was nothing else she could have done. Except. She put her hand to her forehead as it occurred to her that she could have walked the boy down to Paul and Laura's place. Their cell phones might have worked, and if not, one of them could have driven Logan to the police station.

But she didn't want to just drop him off somewhere. Even in the short time he'd been in her house, she felt a responsibility toward him. Such an odd kid, the way he flinched as if sure she was about to hit him. The look on his face when eating the grilled cheese sandwich too was really something. Like he was eating the best meal in the best restaurant in the world. He all but smacked his fingertips to his mouth. How often did you see a kid have so much appreciation for such a basic thing? And was it her imagination, or did he seem excited to be able to take a bath? His face had certainly lit up when she'd pointed out the toothpaste, soap, and shampoo. Her motherly instinct kicked in, wondering what this kid had been through. She had the urge to hug him and tell him everything would be okay, but he wasn't hers to hug, and she wasn't quite sure everything would work out for him. At least for one night, he'd be safe and well fed and dry. She prayed that she wasn't delaying his return to loving parents who were worried sick about him. Somehow, though, she doubted that was the case.

After rummaging around in her room, she found a pair of running shorts one of her granddaughters had accidentally left behind on their last visit. They'd be big on him but should be fine for sleeping. She had a T-shirt too, one that she'd won at a church raffle. It was your basic man's white T-shirt, size medium, with a panda head imprinted on the front. She tried it on once she'd gotten home from the church carnival, and quickly decided she had neither the body type nor the inclination to wear a man's panda T-shirt. Besides, it was made of a flimsy, cheap fabric. Why she never donated it to Goodwill was a mystery, but it turned out to be a good thing because now she had something for him to wear. It was brand-new and would be big on him, but that didn't matter.

Using her flashlight to guide her, she navigated back to the bathroom with the clothing clutched in her free hand. She knocked once before turning the knob. Finding it unlocked, she swung it open, intending to just set the clothes on the counter. "Logan, I—"

He wasn't in the tub, as she'd assumed. Her flashlight caught him standing outside of the tub, towel wrapped around his waist, one arm reaching into the tub to pull the plug. At the sound of her voice, he turned, but not before she saw his back, a narrow expanse of flesh scarred with red crisscrossed ridges like he'd been whipped. His shoulder blades stuck out pitifully, like sharp-looking knobs. "I'll just leave this here," she said quickly, dropping the clothes on the floor. Closing the door, she added, "Bring me your wet things and I'll hang them in the laundry room to dry."

She stood outside the door in disbelief. Could something besides abuse have made those kinds of marks? She wanted to believe that there was another explanation, but deep inside, she knew the truth. Someone had beaten the hell out of that sweet little boy. No wonder he didn't want to go home. With her fingertips, she wiped away her tears. She didn't want him to see her crying. Making him feel bad wasn't going to help.

By the time he came shyly into the living room, holding out his wet clothing, Joanne had managed to compose herself. He followed her when she went to hang his clothes on the indoor clothesline next to the washer and was right on her heels when she went to make sure the guest bedroom had everything he might need. The dog, not wanting to be left out, took up the caboose end of their train. In the guest room, Joanne fluttered around, adjusting the blinds and plumping up the pillow. "We'll keep the flashlight right here, so if you need it, you can just reach over," she said, tapping the nightstand. "And I'll have Samson sleep right next to you on the floor. He'll keep you safe." What she didn't mention was that Samson would rouse her if Logan tried to leave the house in the middle of the night. Both doors were locked, and the front door also had a chain fastener, but a smart boy could have it all undone and slip out in a minute.

Logan, who was sitting on the edge of the bed, his legs dangling down, nodded.

"It might be a little early to go to sleep, but we don't have any power, and I think both of us had a big day. Do you mind going to bed right now?" she asked.

In response, Logan climbed under the covers. Instinctively, she tucked him in, covering him with a sheet and light blanket. "Sweet dreams, Logan. If we have our electricity back tomorrow morning, I'll make pancakes. Would you like that?" He gave her a thumbs-up and a smile as an answer. She switched off her flashlight and left the room, leaving the door wide open.

When she checked on him half an hour later, he was sound asleep, one arm trailing over the side of the bed, his fingers resting on Samson's back.

CHAPTER
THIRTY-FOUR

In the mini-mart bathroom, Grandma Nan switched out her muddied blouse with a T-shirt she selected from a revolving rack in the store, then cleaned her bloody elbow, applied a gauze pad, and taped it in place. Mallick's Gas and Go, she reflected, really was equipped for most emergencies. Mr. Mallick hadn't wanted to take her money, but after she'd insisted, he'd reluctantly rung her up, but not before throwing some candy bars and a bottle of water in the bag and saying, "We're having a special today. Buy a T-shirt. Get some candy."

She heard an enormous boom of thunder while still patching up her arm, and then the light went off. Before she even had a chance to open the door, the light was back on, accompanied by the humming of an engine, somewhere toward the back of the store. When she walked out, Mr. Mallick said, "So now we know the emergency generator still works."

"Do you always get bad storms like this?" she asked.

"Not often, but it happens," he said. "The worst is when trees go down. They can do a lot of damage."

"To power lines?"

"And property too. At my house, we had a tree come completely uprooted and fall on the garage last year and crush the roof. Our very first insurance claim." He smiled, showing a line of straight, white teeth.

"Hopefully your last."

"Maybe. But it's good to have insurance. Life is so uncertain."

It was odd to make small talk when she'd just been assaulted and had her tire slashed by a man who'd once promised to love, honor, and cherish her daughter. But wasn't that what people did—make small talk when they were too shocked to talk about anything else?

When the deputy sheriff arrived, he greeted Mr. Mallick like they were old friends, and it turned out they were, having known each other since they were young.

"Scott played defense on our high school football team," Mr. Mallick said, clapping Scott on the shoulder. Grandma Nan didn't know much about football, but judging from Scott's massive size, she assumed he did his fair share of keeping the ball going in the right direction.

She answered all his questions, and he took copious notes. Three different times she turned down his suggestion to go to the hospital. "You might have more serious injuries than you realize," Scott said. "You should get checked out."

"I'm fine," she answered.

Mr. Mallick backed up her account of being assaulted at the gas station and took the two of them back to his office to watch the footage from the outdoor video camera. It was in black and white, and a bit grainy, but it supported what she'd said. When Scott peered over Mr. Mallick's shoulder at the tape, he said, "Too bad you can't make out his license plate number."

"I remember it," Mr. Mallick said, rattling it off as easily as if it were his own. "They were Illinois plates," he added. Even Scott looked impressed. In explanation, he turned to Grandma Nan and said, "When you own a gas station, you become aware of things like license plate numbers."

Scott took photos of the picture she had of Logan and copied down all the other pertinent information. "I'm sending this in, and we'll need to coordinate with the Chicago PD regarding the missing child," he said.

"How long will that take?" she asked.

"Longer than I'd like," Scott said, giving her a sympathetic smile. "Everything by the book. But if it helps, they do give cases with missing children top priority."

The two men talked to each other quietly, with Mr. Mallick telling Scott everything he remembered about seeing Logan in his store. "The first day, he bought a sandwich, I believe." He cleared his throat. "This morning he bought bananas, three of them. A very polite boy, waiting very patiently in line for his turn." This was directed at Grandma Nan. "And then later today, he came back but didn't buy anything. He just used our restroom. When he came out, his hair was damp, like he had washed it in the sink. But perhaps it was wet when he came in? I can't say for sure."

"If it was raining, that could explain it," she said.

"This was before the rain."

Scott didn't look up from his notepad. He just kept writing. "And he was always by himself?"

"Yes."

"Could someone have been waiting outside for him?"

"Anything is possible, but I don't think so," Mr. Mallick said. "He seemed very much alone."

The words "very much alone" hit Grandma Nan like a wrecking ball. Outside, the rain pummeled the roof over the pumps, pouring off the sides in torrents. How could a little boy be out there in this weather? Worse yet, what if someone, some person, had gotten ahold of him? If it was the wrong sort of someone, Logan could at this very moment be in some basement being held prisoner or even tortured, and here the three of them were just standing, doing nothing. The idea made her want to scream. She had to stop thinking about all the worst possibilities, or it would surely drive her mad.

She took a deep breath, weighing the positives and mentally ticking them off. Logan had been seen recently. Mr. Mallick had said he'd bought three bananas today, so he wasn't starving, and he looked to be on his own. She knew him to be a smart kid, a resourceful kid. They would find him, and he would be fine, and that was that.

Scott pulled up a chair now, and the two men reviewed footage from the three days that Logan had been present at the Gas and Go. They watched both versions, the indoor camera that covered the counter and the outdoor camera aimed at the pumps. On TV, this process went quickly, but in real life, it was arduous, scrolling through the recordings looking for one little, quiet boy minding his own business. When they first spotted him, buying a sandwich and a small bag of chips, Grandma Nan's heart swelled with happiness, and it only grew when they found him buying bananas that morning and coming past the counter to leave the store that afternoon. His hair was damp, just as Mr. Mallick had said, but the swirly cowlick on the top of his head was evident. She'd traced it with her fingers a hundred times, and God willing, she'd do it again, once he was found.

Now that they had the time stamps for his comings and goings, the deputy sheriff and owner were able to watch Logan's arrival and departure from outside the store. "There he is," Mr. Mallick said, at one point, a finger to the screen. "And it doesn't look like he's with anyone."

"Could there be someone in a car, outside the view of the camera?" Grandma Nan wondered aloud. A criminal would certainly know to avoid security cameras.

"Doesn't look like it," Scott said. "See how he's kind of meandering?" His finger followed Logan's walk across the screen. "He's not looking around for someone else, and he doesn't seem to be in a hurry. Anything is possible, but my guess is he's on his own."

They played the footage again, noting that Logan wore the same clothing all three days. "See right there," Mr. Mallick said, pointing, "how he has duct tape wrapped around one shoe? That's why he walks a little oddly. The duct tape caught my attention right away."

You noticed a child all alone and dressed like a vagrant, and yet you did nothing, Grandma Nan thought. A second later, she guiltily wiped her bitterness away. This man had no idea Logan was a lost child. And he was helping her now. She had to believe that if he'd known the situation, he would have stopped Logan and gotten him some help. It wasn't his fault. There was no way for him to know.

It did make her feel better to see the recording of Logan taken earlier that day. Proof he was alive and fine. And if he was alone, on foot, he couldn't have gone too far, so he had to be close by. She imagined walking down the road, calling his name. If he were hiding and heard her voice, she knew he would come out.

"We'll need that footage," Scott said, after they'd gone over every second of the tape when Logan was in view multiple times.

"Of course," Mr. Mallick said.

As Scott had said before, all of this was a process. He called in to the sheriff's office and talked to someone named Amanda, giving her all the information from his notes and explained about the security camera. "I'll send you the digital files," he said. "Put out an ATL on the boy's father. He assaulted the boy's maternal grandmother at the Gas and Go and slashed one of her tires. We have a witness and video footage of the crime. He is armed with what appears to be a hunting knife and is reportedly inebriated." He rattled off the make and model of the car along with the license plate number. After that, he listened for a minute and said, "Yeah, that's what I thought too. I'm going to do a quick drive around, and then I'll be coming in to help coordinate all this. No, I know. Part of the job."

When he clicked off, Grandma Nan asked, "What's an ATL?"

"Attempt to locate," he explained, then put a fist to his mouth to stifle a yawn.

"Is it almost the end of your shift?"

"My shifts don't have definite beginning and end times," he said. "Depending on what's going on, sometimes I wind up putting in more hours." Seeing her face, he said, "Don't worry about it. I don't mind working a little bit longer. We need to find your grandson."

"That's what I want too."

"I don't think you're going to be able to get your car towed tonight," he said. "The closest hotel is about nine miles up the road. I'd be glad to drop you off there."

"But I want to stay, in case Logan shows up again." She glanced at the door, as if doing so would make him appear, but of course that was just wishful thinking.

Scott said, "In all three cases, he came here during the day." He gestured to the window. "In this weather, I would guess he's not going to venture too far from wherever he is. You should get some sleep and let us do our job. I promise I'll call you if I hear anything."

Mr. Mallick joined in, saying, "I will be closing at eleven anyway, so you'd need to go then. You might as well take Scott up on his offer."

She shook her head. "But then how would I get back here tomorrow? I'm guessing you don't have taxis around here. I don't have one of those car transport apps on my phone, and I wouldn't even know how to use one if I did . . ."

"You will call me," Mr. Mallick said firmly, "and I or someone in my family will come and get you in the morning and bring you back here."

"Oh, no, you've been so kind already. I really couldn't—" Nan stopped, realizing she was out of options. "Thank you. I accept both of your offers."

CHAPTER
THIRTY-FIVE

Deputy Sheriff Scott hadn't even gotten the key in the ignition when Grandma Nan said, "If you don't mind, I don't want to go to the hotel just yet." He gave her a curious eye, probably wondering, *What now?* He'd already waited while Mr. Mallick called the hotel to reserve a room for her. She'd noticed his impatience then, the way he jiggled one leg, like that would speed things up. Not wanting to cause any more delay, she made a point to be quick about getting her suitcase out of the trunk of her car and her travel umbrella out of her glove compartment. She hated inconveniencing him and wouldn't be asking for yet another favor now, if not for Logan.

"Where else do you want to go?" he asked, starting the engine and then turning the windshield wipers on high, making them a blur of movement across the glass.

"I almost hate to ask this of you, because you've been so kind already, giving me a ride and looking for Logan. I can tell you're a caring person, and I appreciate this more than I can say, but—"

"Ask already," he interrupted. "Just say it." He turned in his seat and watched for a moment as she fumbled with the seat belt before reaching over, taking the buckle out of her hand, and making the two ends connect. Click. Locked and loaded.

"I was just about to get that," she protested.

"Just helping out. Now what is it you want to ask me?"

"Before you offered to drive me to the hotel, I heard you on the phone saying you were going to do a quick drive around, before you went back to your headquarters, or whatever it is you call it. Am I right in assuming you were going to drive around the area looking for Logan?"

"That's part of it, yes."

"I want to go with you, then. Two sets of eyes are better than one. I can help you find him."

"Mrs. Shaw."

"Please, call me Nan."

"Okay, Nan." He sighed. "I understand where you're coming from, I do, but taking citizens along for the ride is not generally done. I'm not just looking for Logan. I'll be on patrol, and I have to be available if someone calls something in. Someone else might report a crime or something suspicious while I'm out, and if so, I'll be heading that way. I'll also be on the lookout for your son-in-law, who is armed and potentially dangerous. I don't want to put you at risk, and like I said, as soon as I hear something, I will call your cell number. I promise."

It was a long way of saying no. "So if you don't usually drive citizens places, why did you offer to take me to the hotel?" she wondered aloud.

"I have a grandmother. I'd like to think someone would help her out in a pinch."

Rain splattered against the windshield like someone had poured it out of a bucket. Off in the distance, a zipper of lightning lit up the sky. Would this storm ever end?

She pressed his arm, needing to get his full attention. "I am begging you, as a grandmother, to please let me ride along when you look for Logan. I know if I yell out the window and he hears my voice, he'll come. I know my grandson, and I'm pretty sure that he'll hide from a police car. Logan hates getting into trouble."

"It's not that I don't want to help you or that I even mind having you along. It's a safety issue, you understand. For your own protection."

"I will take full responsibility for my own safety," she said. "You will not be liable. I promise you."

"Those words mean nothing if you're injured or killed. Then it's my fault. Besides me getting in trouble, I would feel terrible that something happened to you."

"Then I promise not to get injured or killed."

He tapped the steering wheel in a way that made her think he was deliberating. "You're not going to let this go, are you?"

"No. Not until Logan is found."

"You understand the risks? Your son-in-law sounds very unstable. He has a grudge against you, and he already attacked you once this evening."

"I'm with an enormous guy with a gun. How much more protected can I get?"

That made him laugh, and when that happened, she knew she had him. He was going to let her drive along. He got on the radio to tell his dispatcher the change in plans, letting her know his current mileage. After he signed off, he turned to Grandma Nan. "This is only for fifteen minutes, and you have to do exactly as I tell you," he said. "If I say to stay in the car, that's it. No arguments."

"Of course," she said primly, clutching her purse to her front. "I'm just a grandmother. What else would I do?"

"Hmm." He swung the car out of the parking space and headed for the side road. "I think we can drop the sweet old grandma act. You're clearly more of a force than you let on."

They drove in silence down a country road, a wall of darkness on each side. "I have a confession to make." She'd been feeling guilty ever since encountering Robert at the mini-mart.

"Yeah? What's that?"

"My son-in-law—Robert? He's drunk because I gave him a bottle of Scotch back in Chicago. I knew he had a drinking problem, but I gave it to him anyway, because I knew it would increase my chances of finding out where Logan was. I could smell it on him when he assaulted me, and his eyes were bloodshot. He was slurring his words. I hope he doesn't get in a car accident and kill someone. I couldn't live with myself."

"So you gave him the bottle of Scotch?"

"Yes."

"Did you know he would drink and drive?"

"No. We were at his apartment at the time."

"Did you hold a gun to his head and make him drink?" Scott asked.

"Well, of course not, but I know he's an alcoholic or close to one, anyway. I feel like I gave him something dangerous, knowing full well he couldn't handle it."

Scott tapped on the steering wheel. "If it makes you feel any better, I absolve you of this particular sin. Giving a drunk a bottle of Scotch was not a great idea, but ultimately you're not responsible for what other people do. I believe we each have enough to do working on ourselves. Other adults are in charge of themselves. Don't beat yourself up over this."

"Thanks, that helps," she said, the wave of regret receding.

"Just don't do it again." He got to a stop sign, paused, and kept going.

"It seems like there's nothing out here," she said, eyes focused on the window.

"Mostly woods, some farm fields. A few miles down the road, we'll get to some houses, but if their power is still out, we won't be able to see much."

"I guess I'm just used to streetlights." Her face was so close to the glass her breath created a foggy circle. She cleared a space with her fingers. "And you're going so fast."

"I'm not even doing the speed limit."

Grandma Nan saw now that what she envisioned doing, stopping periodically to get out of the cruiser and yell Logan's name, wasn't going to be feasible. Logan could be anywhere, and what chance was there that he'd hear her over the storm? And even if she did yell, how long would she wait for a response? Besides, Deputy Sheriff Scott was clearly humoring her by letting her ride along. He wasn't going to let her leave the vehicle or even open the window in the rain. She'd have been better off going on foot on her own. Of course, she didn't know the area, and it was dark. Crestfallen, she asked, "What exactly are you looking for?"

"A green Ford with Illinois license plates. Barring that, anything out of the ordinary."

They rode along, both concentrating on what they could see in the beams illuminating the road ahead. The road was a snake, randomly bending and twisting. At one point, they drove over a wooden bridge, the car's tires thumping, the rush of water below even noisier than the rain coming down from above. There were houses now, just a few, dotted here and there. She no sooner registered seeing one than they were past. Most of them small and squat, one with a large boat parked in the driveway. "Couldn't Logan be hiding in that boat?" she wondered, her head whipping back to look. "The one in the driveway?"

"Maybe. You want to look?"

"Yes, please."

Scott swung the car around and pulled into the driveway, aiming his headlights at the boat and turning on the overhead flashing light.

"Is that really necessary?" she asked.

"It is. People around here might shoot first, ask questions later, if you're on their property after dark. You stay here."

He left the car running, slamming his door as he darted out in the rain. The boat was smaller than she'd originally thought—not a yacht, but a large fishing boat covered by a waterproof cover. As Scott peered under the cover, the front door to the house opened, and a man stood in the dark of the doorframe, a flashlight in hand.

She rolled down her window an inch and heard the man yell, "Scott, that you?"

In the headlight beam, she saw Scott clear as day, perfect posture as he stood in the rain. "Yeah, I'm looking for a missing boy. A nine-year-old. You seen him?"

The man hadn't seen him but came running out to help Scott lift the cover. When they tacked it back down, she realized this whole stop had been for nothing.

The man pointed to his house. "Do you know when we're getting our power back?"

"Not a clue."

Both men jogged back to their respective safe spots, the man to his house, Scott to the car. When he slid into the seat, he brought some of the rain with him. Glancing at the rearview mirror, he ran his fingers through his wet hair. "Talk about looking like a drowned rat."

"I'm sorry."

"Why are you sorry? You're not in charge of the rain."

"I know, but it was my idea to check the boat."

"It was a good thought. It would have been a great hiding place for a kid. I should have thought of it myself." He turned off the flashers and backed down the driveway. She had a feeling he'd be dropping her off at the hotel soon. Knowing Logan was still lost, there was no way she'd be able to sleep tonight.

CHAPTER
THIRTY-SIX

Logan wasn't sure how long he'd been lying in bed in Joanne's guest room when he heard a metallic thump coming from somewhere outside. It wasn't loud enough to fully rouse him, and he would have settled back to sleep, except for the dog's reaction. The noise apparently bothered Samson, who gave a small yip before rising from his place on the floor and trotting out of the room. Curious, Logan threw back the covers, grabbed the flashlight, and followed.

When he got to the end of the hall and rounded the corner into the living room, he found the dog at the window, his head stuck through the gap in the curtains. For the first time since leaving the bedroom, Samson barked, three short gruff yaps. Logan shut off the flashlight and pulled open the curtains, then pressed his forehead to the glass to see what was upsetting the dog. There was light down by the road, the headlights of a car. Once his eyes focused and he could see past the light, he saw that a car had hit Joanne's mailbox and was now sideways in the ditch.

The wheels of the car were spinning but not getting anywhere. Still, the driver revved the engine as if more horsepower would overcome the simple truth: he was stuck.

When the driver's side door flew open and a man emerged, nearly toppling over before regaining his balance, a shock wave of terror came over Logan. It was his father. How had he found him? His father hung onto the door, looking straight at the house when a bolt of lightning lit up the sky and everything else too. For a split second, he saw his father in perfect clarity—sunglasses perched atop his head, a look of drunken disgust on his face—and in that second, his father saw him too, framed in the front window of the living room.

His father's roar could be heard over the storm and through the glass. "Logan!" There was only one person who could say his name with so much anger that it sounded like a curse word. Logan watched in horror as his father staggered up the driveway. Reflexively, he stepped back into the room, off to the side, away from the window.

As if echoing the pounding of Logan's heart, Samson barked over and over again, so many barks in a row that it was a continuous stream of objections and warnings, but if his father heard the dog, it didn't deter him. He lurched up the driveway, not in a straight line, but with a determined perseverance. With each step closer, Logan wanted to run, but he was paralyzed with uncertainty. Besides, where would he go?

"Logan! Get out here!"

How did his father know it was him for sure?

"Logan!" His voice charged through the window and above Samson's barking, the sound of it more than angry. He was enraged, and Logan knew this was it, the end of everything. All of it was over. Just when it seemed like things were getting better in his life, it would all be snatched away.

"Boy!" Lightning flashed again, making his father look like some kind of creature, something the angry storm had created.

A hand squeezed his shoulder from behind, and he jumped before he realized it was Joanne. She wore a blue bathrobe, the sash tied around her middle, but she hadn't bothered to do anything with her hair, which hung wildly around her face. "Samson, shush," she said, quieting the dog. "What's going on?" She peered out the window.

"Logan, get out here, boy! Don't make me come after you!" He was only ten feet away now, and his voice boomed loud as thunder.

She crouched down and held Logan's face in her hands. "Do you know this man?"

Logan nodded, trembling.

"Is he your dad?"

He didn't answer, couldn't answer, didn't want to answer. A dribble of pee came out on its own and traveled down his leg. Logan clamped his hand against the shorts but couldn't stop it from dripping all the way to his ankle.

With a creak, the screen door flew open. The pounding on the main door meant his father was on the other side. "Who's there?" Joanne shouted, her hands on both of Logan's shoulders. "What do you want?"

"I want Logan!"

"You're on private property. Leave before I call the police."

Bam. Bam. Bam. "I'm not leaving without the boy."

Joanne spoke quietly in Logan's ear. "Take it easy, Logan. I won't let him in." She reached up and yanked the curtains along the rod until they met in the middle, then braced herself against the door, making sure the eye-level chain was securely fastened. "There's no one named Logan here. Get off my property *this instant*." Her raised voice sounded like it came from a different person, someone far removed from the kind old lady he'd come to know in the last few hours. Just from that voice you'd think she was a formidable woman, ready to fight if necessary. Logan had heard this same tone from his mother and his father's other girlfriend, Alicia. They had also thought they could stand up to him, but it never ended well.

"I've already called 911. The police are on their way!" she cried out.

The door heaved in its frame. Logan knew he was close to breaking in. They needed to hide. He thought about what he knew about the layout of the house. Maybe they could take the dog and lock themselves in the bathroom? He pulled at Joanne's bathrobe, but she was concentrating on his father.

"I'll have you arrested!" she shouted.

His voice came through, gruff and mad. "Logan! Get out here now!"

The door broke free of the frame and popped inward, providing a gap only secured by the chain. Samson opened his mouth to protest—not the growl of guard dog, but the yowling of a worried dog.

Joanne pressed against the door, trying to hold back the inevitable. "I have a gun," she said, but her voice had lost some of its strength.

"Open the door!"

In a moment, Logan knew, his father would barrel through it and be in the living room. A place that had felt welcoming and safe earlier would become a battleground. His father would not let anything stand in his way, and when he realized Joanne had lied about Logan not being there, something really bad was going to happen.

Both Samson and Joanne were in danger because of him. If he hadn't been there, they'd be sleeping right now. With this thought came another one. It was Logan his father wanted. He didn't care about the lady and her dog. Only Logan.

"I have a gun!" she repeated.

"Lady, I will stick that gun—"

Logan didn't wait to hear the rest. Muscles pulsing with adrenaline, Logan ran to the back of the house, through the kitchen, and out the back door. He was momentarily blinded by the dark and rain, but he knew the way to go, rounding the corner of the house until he was in the front yard. The door had been smashed in, and when he reached the front stoop, he saw his father inside, holding Joanne by the shoulders and shaking her so hard that her head bobbed violently back and forth. Joanne was screaming, hysterical words that blended all together while Samson growled and jumped up on the intruder. "Where's my boy?"

his father yelled over and over again, his voice thick with whatever he'd been drinking.

Logan rapped frantically on the door to get his father's attention but couldn't be heard above the commotion, so he ran into the room to make it stop, but he was too late. Logan watched horrified as his father threw Joanne down in disgust. The nice old lady flew backward, hitting her head against the wall and sliding down to the floor, her limbs limp, her body still as death. Samson rushed to Joanne's side, barking anxiously, circling around her.

For a split second, Logan couldn't move, couldn't even breathe. Thundering over the pounding of his heart came the memory of his father saying, *Not a word*, on a different and yet not-so-different occasion, and he realized with a sinking heart it was happening all over again, and once again, it was his fault.

What Logan heard next was a loud, throaty "No!" He was shocked when he realized it had come from his own mouth, that he'd thought a word and then said it. His father heard it too, pointed at him accusingly, and said, "You!" That one word said everything; it said that Logan was the one who'd made him go to all the trouble of having to hunt him down, that anything that his father had done was his fault. That Joanne wasn't moving because of him.

His father was across the room in a flash, grabbing hold of the back of his T-shirt and dragging him to the door, all while Logan struggled to get away. When they got to the step of the front stoop, his father stumbled, losing his balance and momentarily losing his grip on Logan's shirt.

Logan ran.

CHAPTER THIRTY-SEVEN

It hadn't been that long ago that Grandma Nan had slept in her own bed, rising in the morning and following a varied but somewhat usual routine. She generally had eggs for breakfast, although sometimes in winter there was nothing like a bowl of oatmeal with raisins and brown sugar. When she got home from running errands, her keys went right to the hook by the door. She went to bed at eleven and arose at six thirty. Most of the time she slept well, but she kept a book on her bedside table, prepared for unexpected insomnia. She shopped at the same grocery store without exception and knew the cashiers by name. She attended church weekly and found it a comfort, a way to explain life in all its shining glory and all its dreadful, ugly atrocities.

Those days seemed a world away. It felt like she'd been plunked down into another person's life. Now she was the type of woman who hired a private investigator, followed an Aldi cashier home, and went on patrol with a deputy sheriff. More excitement than usual, but it wasn't a good excitement. None of this was anything she wanted. Once they found Logan, she'd petition for guardianship and bring him home to Nebraska. Under the circumstances, a judge would have to see that she was more fit to raise Logan than his father.

Scott had driven for about fifteen minutes, only stopping when Grandma Nan thought she spotted movement in a ditch. It turned out to be a piece of loose plastic sheeting, the kind they used to wrap shipments on pallets in warehouses. It was really just garbage flapping in the wind. The crazy thing was that for a moment she actually thought she saw her grandson lurking underneath the plastic. Amazing the way the mind plays tricks when you're desperate.

The rain was still constant but not pounding quite so much. Finally, it seemed possible that the sky might run out of water. Scott drove assuredly down country roads, all of them blending together for her, a mass of fields and modest houses all encased in unrelenting dark. If he dropped her off now, leaving her by the side of the road, she wouldn't even be able to point toward Mallick's Gas and Go. Country landmarks all looked the same to her, but maybe that was how country people would feel about the suburbs or the big city. It was all what you were used to.

When Scott turned to her and said, "That's about it," her heart sank.

"But we just barely got started," she said.

"We've covered a lot of ground," he said, and went on from there, explaining how unlikely it would be to find Logan under these circumstances. That a better bet would be media coverage, where they could get the word out in a big way. One photo, he explained, could reach thousands of people in a short period of time, and then it was like having eyes and ears everywhere. One car driving around was like looking for a needle in a haystack. He said all this as if it might be news to her. She understood, and knew driving around was not the most logical approach, but her grandmother's instinct made her want to be part of the search. That same instinct told her Logan was nearby and that he was afraid. Scott ended his one-sided discussion by saying, "And if your son-in-law is smart, he's long gone by now."

"He's not my son-in-law anymore, and he's not all that smart," she said. Robert was the least of her worries. In all honesty, she'd almost forgotten him, but now that Scott had said his name, she was aware of a pain in her shoulder, probably from when he'd pulled on her arm. "How about just a little bit longer? I just have a feeling Logan's not too far away. You did say looking in the boat was a good idea." She gave him her most plaintive look and put her hands together in a pleading gesture, but the car was dark, and he wasn't looking her way.

"Sorry," he said, his tone unyielding. "I've already stretched this out longer than I should have. I need to get you to the hotel, and then I'm back to work."

He drove ahead and swung the car around, doing a complete hairpin turn in the middle of an empty intersection. Grandma Nan said nothing as they drove farther and farther away from Logan. She imagined leaving him behind while she crawled into bed at the hotel, snug and safe. What kind of grandmother would do that? But then again, what else could she do?

When she spotted the lit-up Gas and Go sign ahead on the frontage road, she finally got her bearings. They drove past, and she turned her head to catch a glimpse of her car, abandoned in front of the building. Soon they would be on the interstate going faster and faster, farther away from where she wanted to be, but like a kid strapped in a car seat, she didn't have a say in the matter.

CHAPTER
THIRTY-EIGHT

Logan was familiar with this plot of land, but not at night in the rain. As he ran across Joanne's yard and dove into the woods, all his senses kicked in. He was aware of the smell of wet wood filling his nostrils, the spiky ground poking at his bare feet, and branches reaching out like fingers as he made his way through. The rain was a heavy mist now, dripping off the trees and onto his head. The dark made it difficult to see but not impossible. He just had to be careful.

When he got into the thick of it, he slowed to keep from running into anything. Behind him, his father lumbered, crashing into branches.

"Logan!"

The hoarse, angry way he shouted his name twisted Logan's belly. At home, he could wait out his father's anger, hide until the drinking wore off, and then later pretend whatever bad things happened had never happened at all. But this went beyond that. His father had attacked Joanne, a complete stranger. And Logan had done something unforgivable. He'd openly defied his father.

No, there was no turning back.

He slipped on the mud and grabbed onto a branch, then winced as he stepped on something sharp. A nail, a thorn? Whatever it was cut right through the skin, and he stepped on the foot carefully but kept going. Behind him, he heard his father getting closer, crashing his way through without caution, more like a bulldozer than a man.

Logan had gone another thirty feet or so when he realized his father was gaining on him and he needed a new strategy, so he stepped behind a tree, trying to make himself invisible. Pressing his body against the trunk, he kept quiet, a soldier's trick.

His father lurched nearby, mumbling to himself, and was almost past Logan's hiding spot when his head whipped around. Backtracking quickly, he was on Logan, his bulky form hovering over him and blocking out everything else, one large meaty hand grabbing hold of his shirt. "Gotcha!"

Logan glanced down and saw the trouble—his white T-shirt had given him away. The clouds must have moved away from the moon because his father's face was close now, and he could clearly see his big dark eyes rimmed in red. His father shook Logan so hard his teeth rattled, and then he smiled.

"You like that?" he asked, his voice low and growly. "Is this fun for you?"

Another test. If Logan nodded yes, he'd do it again, this time even harder. If he shook his head no, his father would say, "Too bad," and do it again anyway. There was no right answer. That was the way it had always worked. Up until now.

It occurred to him that this was the second time he'd ever gone against his father. The first time he'd wound up in a moving van crossing state lines. He'd lived on his own and found food and a place to stay. And he'd bought food at the gas station, cleaned his clothes in the stream, and saved a dog from choking. Pretty good for a kid his father called dumb.

Such a baby. You disgust me. His father's words had been said so many times that Logan had begun to believe him, but he knew now they weren't true. Sometimes you had to leave to get a clear view of where you'd been.

Logan thought back to Joanne falling to the floor. The shocking sight reminded him of his mother's death. In an instant, the whole scene scrolled through his brain. It had happened when they'd lived in the rented house just a few blocks from Grandma Nan. He was downstairs at the time fearfully listening to his parents' angry shouting upstairs. They were arguing about him.

The yelling went back and forth between them, his father saying that Logan would wind up a mama's boy if she kept babying him. She defended him, saying, "He's just a little boy! You have to stop being so hard on him." Logan listened, his breath racing and stomach churning, hoping it would stop.

At the end, his mother yelled, "I'm not putting up with this anymore." He saw them struggling on the top landing, his mom trying to wrench free of his father's grip. As his mother batted at him with her free hand, Logan yelled, "Mom!"

His father gave her a rough shove, and Logan watched in horror as she lost her balance and tumbled down the stairs. The awful thumping sound of her body hitting against the hardwood steps didn't stop until she hit the bottom, her head smacking against the tile. His father lumbered down the stairs, stepping over her still body at the bottom. His bloodshot eyes narrowed. "Look what you've done." He smacked Logan so hard, it knocked him onto his butt.

Reeling from the impact, he looked up to see his father looming large over him. He pointed at Logan, and his booming angry voice filled the room. "Not a word about this, do you understand? Not a word. Tell anyone and you'll be sorry." Blood began to pool around his mother's head. She was still, so still, that Logan, even at that young age, knew she had to be dead. His father sent Logan to bed then, and he curled up under the covers, not knowing what else to do. Later, when the police arrived, he agreed with everything his father said. Logan had been asleep when it happened. His father had come home from the bar to find that she'd fallen down the stairs. His drinking friends at the bar vouched for him.

He'd wanted to speak out for so long, but whenever he'd tried, the words were packed tight in his mouth, and he couldn't spit them out. Something had shifted in his vocal cords, though, back at Joanne's house. He'd made an actual sound, a word. It had rushed out of him like a balloon losing air. It was something. The start of something, anyway.

He'd been so afraid for so long, waiting for someone to help him, but no one ever did. No one had come to save him. For the most part, it had just been him and his father, and his father was bigger, louder, and angrier. "What about this?" his father taunted now, pulling the knife out of his belt holster and holding it against Logan's stomach. "You like this?" He poked and waited for Logan's reaction.

The old Logan would have shrunk in terror, shook his head wildly, and pleaded with his eyes. But wishing for it to stop never stopped it. Nothing was ever going to change until he changed it.

Almost as if he had read his thoughts, his father said, his voice menacing, "Just you wait until we get home." The blade glinted in the moonlight as his father grinned.

Logan's mouth tightened. He tried to push the knife away, grabbing for the handle but slicing one of his fingers instead. Reacting to the pain, he swung his fist at his father, hitting his jaw and catching him by surprise.

"Ouch. Why you little—"

When his father let go of his shirt, Logan took off, heading in the direction he thought would lead to the road.

His father bellowed, "Get back here!" And he heard him follow, large footsteps right behind him. Too close. Too close. Too close.

When he reached the forked tree, he realized he was going in the wrong direction. He knew the deep hole with the animal skeleton was right in front of the tree and circled around it. His father, intent on catching up, didn't notice it. Behind him, Logan heard the sound of his father go heading toward the muddy hole. *Whump.* "Aw, hell!" came his father's voice loudly from behind him, signaling to Logan what had happened. He hadn't deliberately lured him into a trap but knew his father would never believe him.

Logan's heart jackhammered in his chest. He paused for only a second and then kept moving—darting around trees, pushing back branches, not looking back. When he stepped out of the woods into a clearing, he recognized the back of the house that was closest to the road, the one with all the windows. Laura's house.

He hobbled as quickly as he could over the lawn and to the back door and pressed the doorbell over and over again. When he realized it wasn't ringing, he pulled open the screen door and pounded on the interior door. He shot a glance back at the tree line, thinking that any second his father would come bursting through, and then it would all be over.

Hurry. Hurry. Hurry.

CHAPTER
THIRTY-NINE

Paul was the one who heard it first, but it didn't immediately awaken him because his mind incorporated the sound into a dream in which he was lost in a cave. It was a bad dream he'd had on and off since he was a child. Usually he was being chased by some unnamed, unseen horror. This time, his brain turned the pounding on the door of his house into a miner tapping at the walls of the cave, searching for gold. When he woke up enough to realize the noise was happening in real life and that someone must be at the back door, he nudged his wife. "Someone's knocking on the door. Who in the hell could be here at this hour?" He glanced at the clock, which was dark. Still no power. "Laura?"

"What?" She sat up from a sound sleep, a talent he'd always admired but didn't have himself. It made her seem ready for any emergency.

"Someone's banging on the back door."

Without saying another word, she got out of bed and groped around in the semidark, finding her way into her bathrobe, then getting her phone to use as a flashlight.

They went down the stairs together, Paul half fearing they were about to be robbed or maybe that there was a gas leak in the area or something else so life threatening they'd have to evacuate their home.

When they got to the kitchen, his fingers groped for the switch out of habit, but of course, there was no electricity yet.

The banging was relentless, giving credence to his fears, but when he opened the door, there was no one there but a small boy with a bleeding hand, ripped shirt, and mud-covered legs standing in between them and the open screen door.

"Help," he said in a croak. "I need help." The kid leaned against the doorjamb, looking as if he was about to collapse.

Paul did a double take, and for a split second wondered if he were still dreaming, if the foster child Laura had wanted to take in had somehow materialized in front of him, but the rush of humid air and the mist of the rain against his face brought him back to reality. "What happened?"

The boy looked as if he were in shock. His wet hair was plastered to his head, rivulets of water dripping off the ends.

"Let him in, Paul." Laura gently pushed her way in next to him, beckoning for the child to come inside. She put her arm around his shoulder and helped him to a chair. "You're bleeding, honey. What happened?"

The boy shook his head. "Call the police." He gulped between each word. "It's okay. I can tell now."

Paul picked up her phone off the table and gestured to Laura. "I'm going to call 911."

Laura nodded and crouched down next to the chair. "I'm sorry, but I don't understand what you're saying. Why don't we start at the beginning? What's your name?"

"My name is Logan Weber." He enunciated each word carefully, like speaking a foreign language.

"Are you the little boy I saw in the woods the other day, Logan?"

He nodded. "Thank you for the sandwich and the cookie."

"Do you live around here?"

"No." He shook his head.

"Where are you from?"

He hesitated before saying, "Chicago."

"Did you run away?" She thought it was a simple question, but he didn't answer. From the stricken look on his face, she could see it was a sore subject. She brushed past that question and tried another one. "What happened, Logan?"

Logan closed his eyes and took two deep breaths and then said, "He killed my mother. I think . . . I think maybe he killed Joanne too."

"Who did this?"

"Can you tell me his name?"

Logan raised his eyes to Laura's face. "My father. He pushed her down the stairs."

"He pushed Joanne down the stairs?" Laura shot a look at Paul, who was talking to the 911 operator, filling her in on the injured boy who had showed up at their back door, saying he thought someone had killed their neighbor, Joanne Dembiec.

"No, my mother. Joanne he pushed down on the floor."

After Paul was done talking to the 911 operator, she told him to stay on the line, that she was sending help, so he stood there with the phone to his ear, listening as Logan filled in the details. It came in bits and pieces, but slowly Laura was able to draw the story out of him. Paul found it incredible that this kid had lost his mother and grandmother along with his ability to speak, then was trapped in a moving van, finding himself hours away from home in another state, and yet he somehow managed on his own for several days. Some of the story was fuzzy, which made him wonder if this was all true. Like, how did his father track him down? And what were this tree house and the huge hole in the woods? Those were small details, though, and presumably they'd find out later.

Laura brought out a bowl of soapy water and some paper towels and cleaned up Logan's hand. The cut on his hand had only started to clot, so she put some toweling over it and applied pressure. "I think you might need stitches," she said. "Have you ever had stitches before?"

"No."

"They'll numb it first, so it shouldn't be too bad. I'll stay with you if they take you to the hospital. Don't worry. It's going to be fine."

"Okay."

Laura rested her hand on his shoulder. "You're a very brave boy. Not too many people could have gotten through what you did."

"I'm not afraid anymore," Logan said, sounding amazed. "I'm not afraid at all."

"Nothing to be afraid of," she said. "You're safe here."

"Yes, I'm still here," Paul said to the 911 operator. "Logan has a pretty deep cut on his hand. My wife cleaned it, but he's going to need medical treatment. Uh-huh. Okay." Paul covered the phone and said to Laura, "Maybe I should go check on Joanne?"

Judging from the look on her face, she didn't like the idea of having her husband head outside with a killer on the loose. "She said to stay on the line, didn't she?"

"Well, yeah."

"You said they'd be here any minute, right?"

He nodded. "Yeah, one of the deputy sheriffs happened to be in the area and is on his way. They're sending an ambulance too, just in case."

"Logan said his father fell in the woods. Let's give it a minute." Just as she spoke, the lights came back on.

CHAPTER FORTY

They'd been on the expressway for only a minute when Scott's radio crackled and a voice came over the line. Grandma Nan had just been staring out the window praying for something to happen, anything that would stop the car from moving forward and, instead, take her back to where Logan might be, and still the noise nearly startled her out of her skin. Deputy Sheriff Scott answered. It was Amanda, the one he'd talked to earlier. "We have a 911 call coming from 630 County Road H," she said. "I have another car heading there, but they're going to need backup. How close are you?"

"I can be there in less than five," he said, turning through a gap in the median. "What's the situation?" The rain had slowed to mist, but still the wipers whipped from side to side.

Amanda's voice came through loud and crisp. "The homeowner, Paul Sutton, reported that a child, a nine-year-old boy, came to his back door claiming he witnessed his father attack a woman, Joanne Dembiec, at a neighboring house. The boy, who is a stranger to the Suttons, is currently safe inside their home. The father is still at large. I've been calling the Dembiec residence, but no one is answering the phone. It's a potentially dangerous situation. Proceed with caution. There's another officer on his way. I have a call out for an ambulance as well."

Grandma Nan sat bolt upright. "It's Logan, isn't it?" she whispered excitedly, but Scott wasn't paying attention to her. Instead, he had Amanda repeat the address. "I went to school with a Glenn Dembiec. He was a few years ahead of me. The Dembiecs have the house farther back from the road, right?"

"Yes, that's the one," Amanda said.

Grandma Nan was hitting him on the shoulder now. "Ask her if the boy is Logan!"

Scott said, "Is the boy's name Logan Weber?"

"I'm sorry. I don't know."

"It's okay. I'll find out in a minute." He clicked off and kept driving, the cruiser retracing its path past Mallick's Gas and Go and onto the country roads they'd just left. His calm demeanor was infuriating, although Grandma Nan guessed it was good that one of them was keeping it together.

"It has to be Logan," she said, ticking off the facts one finger at a time. "He's nine years old. The people don't know him. Which would fit because he's not from around here. Also, Robert would be the father who attacked the neighbor, which frankly, I wouldn't put past him."

"Whoa, whoa, whoa," Scott said, his eyes still on the road. "If there's one thing I can tell you from my years of working in this job, it's never to assume. Do you know why?"

"Because it makes an ass out of you and me?" Grandma Nan said, repeating the childhood refrain.

He grinned. "Kids say that in Nebraska too?"

"Kids say that everywhere. I think it's universal."

"No, it's because you shouldn't make assumptions until you have all the facts. We don't know for sure if it's Logan or Robert. You're right. It would be an incredible coincidence, but I've seen stranger things happen."

"It's Logan. I know it is." She opened her purse to take out her compact, then studied her face by the light of the mirror. So much time had passed. Would she look the same to him? She hadn't changed her hair or gained any weight. Regular old aging would account for the only difference, and she didn't think she'd fared too badly in that area. "Aren't you going to turn on the siren and the lights?"

"No need. I'm going as fast as I would, regardless. And if the father is still in the area, I'd rather not scare him off."

When they turned onto County Road H and were approaching the Sutton residence, they saw a car ahead in the ditch, its headlights aimed toward a house. When they got closer, Scott slowed long enough to ascertain the driver's door was open and the interior lights were on as well. The front grill of the car faced away from the road. The engine was still running, but no one was in sight. "That's Robert's car," she said excitedly, recognizing the green Ford. "It is Logan. I knew it. I knew it!"

"It appears that way," he said, pulling into the Suttons' driveway. On the neighbor's driveway, there was another police car, its lights on. Presumably it was the one Amanda had mentioned. "You wait here," Scott said. "If it's Logan, I'll be right back. I promise." He turned off the car, pocketing his keys before he left.

He was loony tunes if he thought she'd sit in that car and wait, but she didn't argue. That would just be a waste of time. The front porch light was on, and the inside lights too. There were so many windows the house was like a square aquarium. She could see the front room with its boxy couch, big-screen TV, and starburst wall hanging, but she didn't see anyone inside until after Scott bounded up the walkway and rapped on the front door. In a moment, a young woman came and ushered him inside, closing the door behind both of them.

Grandma Nan unbuckled her seat belt and got out, going straight to the front door. From the porch, she heard the wail of an ambulance coming down the road, but she was too close to having her grandson in her arms to wait for its arrival. Unlike Scott, she didn't knock but turned the knob and went in.

Holding her purse to her side, Grandma Nan walked through the entryway and past the living room, following the sound of the voices coming from the back of the house. If Scott had gone out the back for some reason, she had no way to prove she'd come with him. There was a possibility that the Suttons would think she was a trespasser or burglar, although, given her age, it was unlikely. One of the benefits of old age was that she appeared completely harmless to younger people, so she wasn't worried that she'd alarm anyone too unduly. She had Logan's picture in her purse and, of course, Logan knew who she was.

Ahead she saw an arched doorway leading to the kitchen. Scott's back was to her; he was talking into the radio strapped onto his front. Facing her was a large man, tall and broad-shouldered, wearing a bathrobe over what looked like pajama pants. And sitting on one of the kitchen chairs with his back to her was a small figure with brown hair, a cowlick swirl at the crown of his head.

She picked up her pace, and when she walked into the room, she ignored the puzzled looks of the man and his wife, the woman who'd let Scott into the house. She quietly surveyed her grandson. He was wet and dirty, dressed in a thin white T-shirt and some ill-fitting shorts. His feet were bare and muddy. One hand had been wrapped in gauze, and his hair was long and straggly, but even with all that, she'd have known him anywhere. Of course she would, he was her grandson. "Logan?" She pulled up a chair next to him and put her hand to his cheek.

Logan's eyes widened in astonishment. "Grandma? Grandma Nan!"

Grandma Nan took in a breath, shocked to hear his voice after so much time. He flung himself off the chair, threw his arms around her neck, and buried his face in her shoulder. He was so overjoyed to see her that it brought her to tears. She pulled him onto her lap to get him even closer. Normally she'd think he was too big for that, but this was way beyond normally. He hugged her so tightly, it was like he was afraid she'd disappear if he let go.

"I thought you died," he said, the words breaking her heart. "He said you died."

"Oh, no, honey, that must have been sad news, but as you can see, it's not true. I'm sorry you were told that. I've been looking for you, Logan," she said, stroking the back of his head. He was so big now. She'd been out of his life for way too long, but that was over now. "I missed you so much. I love you."

"I love you too, Grandma." She'd never heard sweeter words.

Scott finished his radio conversation and said to the couple in the room. "This is Logan's grandmother, Nancy Shaw."

"I figured as much," the woman said. "I'm Laura, and this is my husband, Paul." She jabbed a thumb at her husband. "You have a very nice grandson. I'm glad to meet you."

CHAPTER
FORTY-ONE

Later on, the Sutton kitchen was filled with people, but Grandma Nan was the only one who mattered to him. The minutes before he first saw her he was feeling pretty low. His hand was throbbing, and his foot hurt from the sharp thing he'd stepped on, and he felt left out, because the deputy sheriff and the Suttons were talking about all kinds of serious stuff and not paying much attention to him, which gave him time to think, and his thoughts weren't good ones. He felt bad for Joanne, who was probably dead and didn't deserve to be dead, just because she'd been trying to help him. He had a pang of guilt about his father too. Logan had wanted to get away from him, but he wasn't trying to kill him, and that's what must have happened, since his father never got out of the big hole to chase after him. If his father were alive, he'd have kept on coming. There was no stopping his father when he got that mad.

So he sat in the chair feeling like he was there and yet like he was not there at all. His emotions and memories were all jumbled together in a big mixed-up mess. He was tired and dirty. He wanted nothing more than to go home, but then he remembered he had no home. There was no place in all the world where he belonged. Realizing that made him so sad, he could barely stand it, and he wondered what the point of it all was. He was so tired. Why even live when bad things just kept happening? And then Grandma Nan was suddenly there and said, "Logan?" and he felt everything inside of him break loose until he was crying like a little kid. Grandma was crying too, though, so that was okay. Seeing her show up in that kitchen was like watching a miracle happen. All this time he'd thought she was dead, but she wasn't. She'd missed him and had been looking for him. She'd hugged him so hard, and he had hugged her back, and then everything was all right.

Soon after that, the kitchen filled up with all kinds of people, most of them in uniform. Some of them talked just to each other or into what looked like walkie-talkies, but a lot of them wanted to speak to him. A woman from the ambulance checked him out and spoke kindly to him and gave him a sticker. Nine-year-olds were too big for stickers, but he didn't want to hurt her feelings, so he took it and thanked her. The police officers asked him a million questions, sometimes the same ones over and over again. They seemed confused as to what had happened that night and what had happened before, when he was a younger kid. His grandmother finally had to interrupt and sort it out for them. "My daughter, Amber, who was Logan's mother, died three years ago from injuries after falling down a flight of stairs. Logan's father's story at the time was that he wasn't even home when it happened. What Logan is telling you now is that his father *was* home, that there was an argument, and he pushed her down the stairs." Her voice trembled as she spoke like she was holding in more tears.

Both police officers became silent. Finally, one said, "And this was never investigated?"

"I wasn't there," she said. "I was told the injuries that killed her were consistent with a fall. She was taking a lot of pain medication at the time."

After Grandma explained, it got easier because Logan could tell them about being trapped in the moving van and how he found the tree house and everything else that had happened the last few days. His throat got kind of sore from all the talking, and his voice wasn't coming out very good, but then Laura Sutton brought him a glass of water, which helped a lot.

When they were finished questioning him, two guys came in wheeling a skinny bed to take him off in the ambulance to get checked at the hospital. Both of the guys were big, like his father, but they had baby faces so Logan decided they couldn't have been grown-ups for very long. The two baby men were volunteers with the local fire department and were trained EMTs. He knew this because that's what they answered after Grandma Nan had asked, "Excuse me. Might I ask what your credentials are?"

The ambulance lady cleaned his foot and looked at the hurt part, then dabbed it with something wet that stung. She had warned him first, but it still took him by surprise. She also unwrapped the gauze Laura Sutton had put around his hand and inspected the cut before looking to his grandma. "He's definitely going to need stitches," she said. Then she patted Logan's arm and said, "They'll get you all patched up at the ER."

He didn't want to go to the hospital until his grandmother said she'd be going with him. She traced the swirl at the top of his head and said, "Are you kidding? I just found you. I'm not letting you out of my sight for a minute!" which made him feel much better. They helped him climb onto the skinny bed, covered him with a blanket, and belted him in. Grandma Nan gave Laura Sutton a hug, which was odd because they didn't even know each other, and then Laura leaned over him and said, "Good luck, Logan. I'll never forget you." Her husband stood right behind her, but he wasn't looking at Logan. Instead, his focus was on his wife, and he had a look of wonder like people have when they open a present to find out it's just exactly what they wanted.

～

While one of the EMTs, a cute young woman named Janine, was cleaning up Logan's foot with antiseptic, Scott took Grandma Nan aside. "Your son-in-law was found in the woods, down in a pit by the forked tree, right where Logan said he would be."

"Dead?" Grandma Nan asked, not sure if it were wishful thinking or not. She'd never wished for someone to die before, but it would be a fitting end in this case.

"No." Scott shook his head. "Very much alive. Drunk as a skunk, mad as hell, and it looks like his leg is broken, but from what I understand, he should make a full recovery." He leaned in. "I've got some good news, though. The lady he attacked—Joanne Dembiec? She's alive and in pretty good shape. Hit her head pretty hard when your son-in-law"—he paused to correct himself—"I mean, your *former* son-in-law knocked her down. She lost consciousness for a bit. They suspect concussion."

"And here poor Logan thought she was dead," Grandma Nan said, shooting a glance her grandson's way.

"Yeah, I thought it would be best if you gave him the update. Poor kid will probably be relieved to hear she's okay."

She nodded.

Scott continued. "Robert is going out in the first ambulance. Logan and Joanne will share the second one. Both vehicles will leave around the same time. It's department policy not to transport victims with their attackers. The hospital staff knows to keep them separate too."

"That's good." Especially since she couldn't trust herself around Robert at this point. She wasn't a violent woman, but she felt like throat punching him. "Are you going to arrest Robert?" She looked back at Logan, who was staying strong, answering all their questions in his hoarse little voice. "He won't be able to take Logan back, will he?"

Scott's mouth twitched into a slight smile. "You don't need to worry about that. He's under arrest for breaking and entering, assault, and trespassing. And that's just at the Dembiec place. We're also charging him with driving under the influence as well as for attacking you and slashing your tire, and that one is pretty open-and-shut since we have the security footage and Devan Mallick as a witness. And I have more news. When we checked, we found out Robert Weber has a whole slew of outstanding warrants in other states. The worst offense is that he beat the hell out of a woman named Alicia Mendez and set her car on fire in Indiana. There were witnesses, but he fled before he could be arrested."

"Who's Alicia Mendez?"

Scott shrugged. "Honestly, I don't know. A woman unlucky enough to get involved with the wrong man, would be my guess. My point is that in my opinion, it wouldn't take much for you to get guardianship of your grandson."

"What about what Logan said about his father pushing his mother down the stairs? Can they charge him with murder?"

"If it were up to me, I'd say yes, but it's not my call."

There was so much more she could have asked, but just then Logan called out, "Grandma!" and her grandson took precedence. She excused herself to rush to Logan's side, staying with him as they transferred him to the gurney. Grandma Nan, in a surge of gratitude, gave Laura a hug, and then the couple said goodbye to Logan.

As they wheeled him out to the ambulance, Grandma Nan walked alongside. If the EMTs were annoyed at her presence, they didn't show it. The only time she let go was when they lifted him into the vehicle, but she followed right behind and was inside, her hand in his, by the time they'd connected the gurney to the floor.

"I have some good news for you, Logan," Grandma Nan said. "Mrs. Dembiec is alive and well. The deputy sheriff told me she had a pretty good bump on her head, so the doctor will have to examine her, but they expect she'll get out of this just fine."

He nodded, a slip of a smile crossing his face. "She's a very nice lady. I like her dog. His name's Samson."

"I knew you'd be relieved to hear she was okay." Grandma Nan took a deep breath before continuing. "I also have other news. They found your dad in the woods right where you said he'd be. He was injured from the fall. A broken leg, they think, but nothing that can't heal. You didn't hurt anyone, Logan, and none of this was your fault."

"Grandma?" he asked, clutching her hand. "What's going to happen to me?"

Grandma Nan caught the eye of the paramedic riding in back with them, but the young man kept busy attaching a blood pressure cuff, allowing them to have a semiprivate conversation. "They'll check you over and take care of the cut on your hand and your hurt foot. I'll be with you the entire time, so you don't have to worry about a thing."

"No, I mean what's going to happen to me *after* that?"

"Oh." She paused, thinking of the best way to reassure him without lying to him. "Your father is in some legal trouble, actually a lot of legal trouble, which means he won't be going home for a very long time. How would you feel about coming to live with me?"

"Could I?" His eyes lit up.

"Of course. I wouldn't have it any other way." Grandma Nan silently prayed that it was just that easy. She couldn't imagine that any of Robert's relatives would fight for custody, and even if they did, all of them had questionable lifestyles: constantly changing jobs and moving, money issues, having cars repossessed, that kind of thing. She'd learned so many troubling details from being on Facebook. She knew she compared well. As grandmothers went, she was relatively young, owned her own home, and as a bonus, had every hour of every day wide open and available for Logan. If it came to it, she'd hire the best attorney no matter the cost and show the court system she was the best choice.

"But then my dad would get me back later?" he asked.

She wasn't sure what answer he wanted. Robert was a horrible father, but he was still Logan's father, and there had to be some good times mixed with the bad. "Probably not, honey. I don't know for sure yet, but if I get custody, and I'm hoping I do, then you're stuck with me until you're a grown-up. You can keep in touch with your dad if you like. Phone calls and letters and visits. But if you don't want to, that's fine too. It will be up to you." It wasn't her imagination; he was clearly relieved. He kept a tight hold of her hand but closed his eyes. She said, "Just rest, Logan. I'm not going anywhere. We'll work out all the details later."

When she'd said goodbye to the Suttons, Grandma Nan had thought she'd never see them again, so when the ambulance doors opened up to admit Joanne Dembiec, she was surprised to see her accompanied by Laura.

"Hello again!" Laura said. She stayed outside the ambulance as they lifted Joanne's gurney into the back. Joanne was similarly bundled into the gurney, most of her body covered with a blanket, the neckline revealing she was still in her nightgown. She had gray, bobbed hair, a lined face, and the same kind of turkey skin Grandma Nan was just starting to notice (and abhor) on her own neck. Joanne smiled wanly, and Grandma Nan smiled back.

"I didn't expect to see you again," Grandma Nan called out to Laura.

"Joanne doesn't have any family in the area, so I'm going to be her honorary daughter. Paul is going to stay here and take care of Samson."

"That's her dog," Logan said, straining his head to look at her.

"That's right," Laura said. "I'll ride up front with the driver. I'll see all of you when we get there." She tapped the door. "You okay, Joanne?"

"I've been better, but thank you." The woman's voice was weak.

"Take good care of her, Dean!" Laura called out.

"I will!" After they shut the doors, the paramedic, Dean, sounding pleased, said, "I didn't know she knew my name." To no one in particular, he continued, "My little brother is a student at the high school where Mr. Sutton is principal."

Grandma Nan looked at his dear, serious, young face and couldn't help but think that children were running the world now.

When the vehicle was on the road, Dean hovered over Joanne and said, "It's about half an hour to the hospital. We called ahead, and they're waiting for you. If the pain in your head gets worse, let me know right away."

Joanne lay with her eyes closed, her hand next to her head for most of the trip. When they got to the hospital and were driving up to the ambulance bay, it was as if she noticed Logan for the first time. Her arm stretched across the gap between the gurneys, and she stroked his arm with one finger. "Hi there," she said in a soft voice.

Logan turned his head to face her. "Hi."

"You can talk now." It was a statement, not a question. Joanne didn't seem shocked. Maybe, after last night, nothing surprised her anymore.

"Yes."

"I'm glad I got to see you again, Logan, because I wanted to thank you."

Logan gave her a puzzled look. "For what?"

"For coming back to help me. You were very brave. So thank you."

"You're welcome." He smiled—a shy, satisfied smile.

CHAPTER
FORTY-TWO

TWO MONTHS LATER

When Joanne said she'd be there at 6:30 a.m., she'd really meant it. The doorbell rang at that exact minute, and even though it was, as Paul had wryly commented only minutes earlier, "the butt crack of dawn," Laura was ready. She hadn't slept much the night before, her mind racing with all the details of the day. Dropping Joanne off at the airport on the way to the hospital to supervise the installation of the mobile made sense, since the timing aligned, but it also added another layer to her day. One good thing: the parts to the mobile had been shipped to the hospital ahead of time, and she had been assured that all of it had arrived in good shape.

That didn't guarantee there wouldn't be problems, though. All night her mind had whirred through all the things that could go wrong before they even arrived in Milwaukee—everything from a car accident while they were en route, to Joanne's flight being canceled, to her artwork looking like garbage once it was hung, resembling something a third grader made with wire hangers (and the resulting shame of the hospital demanding she take it down, leave, and darken their door no more).

She tried to drive these worries out of her brain by concentrating on happy thoughts and doing some deep breathing, but every time her body relaxed even a little bit, another crazy thought popped into her head. Finally, she decided the insomnia had won and got up at four to take a shower. Paul slept through all her anxiety, but he was awake now, sipping coffee at the kitchen table.

Laura opened the door, and there was Joanne, her face flushed with color, a large suitcase parked next to her and Samson on the other side, his tail wagging. She ushered them both in, helping Joanne lug the hard-sided suitcase into the front entryway and giving Samson some major head rubs. "Aren't you a sweetheart?" she cooed.

"As soon as I started packing, he knew something was up," Joanne said. "He's a smart one." She smiled down at the dog. "It's just for a week, baby. Just for a week."

"You know I was planning to pick you up, right?" Laura said.

Joanne waved her hand dismissively. "It was no trouble to walk down my driveway and up yours, although I will admit yours was easier. Besides, Samson and I need the exercise."

Paul was there now, leaning down to talk to Samson. "We're going to have fun, aren't we, boy?" The dog quivered with excitement, dancing and leaping from one person to the next, glorying in all the attention.

"I can't thank you enough for taking him for me," Joanne said, smiling. "Knowing he's in good hands makes leaving that much easier."

"We're happy to have him," Laura said.

"No problem," Paul said. "We've got this."

Laura gathered up her laptop and notebook. She'd packed an overnight bag as well, in case the install took a lot longer than expected and she needed to check into a hotel, but she hoped not to have to use it. Paul grabbed Joanne's things, and all together they went outside and loaded up the back of Laura's car. Paul shut the trunk with both hands. "Have a good trip, ladies," he said, giving his wife a kiss. "Call when you get there and keep me updated."

Laura found that having Joanne in the car lessened the stress of the drive. Summer was over, and it was warm for October. The expressway traffic was light for a Saturday. The GPS was set, so getting lost wasn't even an option. Joanne was easy to talk to, which made the time go faster.

Joanne mentioned she hadn't visited her son and his family in what seemed like ages. "We talk on the phone, but it's not the same. The girls are growing up. The older girl, Serena, is a junior in high school and already talking about looking at colleges."

"Are you going for a special occasion?" Laura asked. "Is it a birthday or anniversary?"

"No. Just time to go." She let out a long sigh. "That's not quite the truth. The reason I'm going now is because of Logan."

"Logan Weber?"

"Yes. Meeting that little boy changed my view of the world. Seeing him reunited with his grandmother and hearing how she'd searched for him was so touching. It made me realize I have a family of my own who wants me to spend time with them, and I kept doing this to them." She put up a hand in a stopping gesture. "I've gotten set in my ways, and I was content enough, but having Logan's father break into my house made me feel vulnerable. And it was nice of you to come with me to the hospital when I had the concussion, but really, that's the kind of thing family members do."

"I didn't mind," Laura said. "Honestly, I was happy to do it."

"You're a wonderful neighbor and friend. I'm so grateful that you were there for me in my time of need, but it was an eye-opener, that's for sure. It really brought home the fact that I didn't have any family members who live nearby. My son Glenn's new house has a mother-in-law suite, and he's been asking me to come live with them. He said I can bring Samson and I can keep my car. They'll even let me tear up their lawn and put in a garden."

"It sounds nice," Laura said, shooting a glance in her direction.

"Yes, it does. But every time he's mentioned it, I've told him no. I was so resistant. It felt like the beginning of the end, you know? Sell your house, move in with someone else, next step—the old folks' home. I'll end up shuffling down the hall with the rest of the old codgers."

"You don't seem like the shuffling type."

Joanne smiled. "I'm not yet, but there's still time. You know, I've always prided myself on being independent and not counting on anyone, but I'm starting to think that attitude doesn't serve me very well. So I'm going to visit and look at the mother-in-law suite and give this some serious consideration. It might be nice to be part of a family again. I mean, they're my family right now, but if I lived there, I'd be in the thick of things. You understand."

Laura did understand. "It's worth looking into, but just for the record, we would miss having you for a neighbor."

Joanne smiled. "Thank you for that. And I'm never going to forget that little Logan. I wish I could be sure he had a happy ending."

"I know I mentioned his grandma and I are Facebook friends. It sounds like he's adjusting well to living with her. When you get back from Seattle, I'll show you what she's posted. She has some photos of the two of them, and he looks like a different kid."

They arrived at the airport right on schedule. Laura parked in the structure and accompanied Joanne to the airline desk to get her boarding pass printed, and then helped her check her suitcase. From there, they went to the security line. After a hug and a quick "Bon voyage," they parted ways.

Later, as Laura was overseeing the installation of the mobile, Joanne's words in the car came back to her. *Meeting that little boy changed my view of the world.* She'd almost told Joanne that Logan had changed her life too, but it was really Paul's story to tell, not hers. When she'd returned from the hospital, Paul, her very practical, not-one-to-look-for-signs husband, had told her he had a confession to make.

"I'm listening," she'd said. The word *confession* had thrown her off. She'd usually thought of it in terms of affairs or embezzling, neither of which she could imagine would be true for Paul.

"This is going to sound ridiculous," he'd said. "It does, even to me." He'd gone on to tell her about the conversation he'd had with his mother, the one where she'd suggested he wait for a sign. Laura loved her mother-in-law, but she had been a little peeved to find out he'd been discussing their private business with her. A moment later, when she found out his mom was on her side, she softened slightly. He'd continued. "I thought all this looking for signs was pretty woo-woo, but you know, after Logan came to our door, it occurred to me that without his grandmother, he'd probably be in foster care. And he seemed like a really great kid who'd just been put in a terrible situation. Then I realized that I'd been thinking about this all wrong. These kids need loving homes, and we have a loving home. I saw how you were with Logan, and you were such a mom, the way you talked to him and cleaned his cut hand. You're a natural at this mother thing. And that was my sign. We need to be foster parents."

After that day, they'd filled out the paperwork and made a commitment to do the required training. The social worker had felt that they'd be approved, no problem. She'd seemed particularly enthused that they were interested in a school-age child and were open to two siblings.

Laura knew having foster kids would test them and might even be stressful at times, but it felt like they were on the right path, and she couldn't wait until they were matched.

Even though Laura wasn't that familiar with Milwaukee, she found the hospital without any trouble. She'd been worried about getting lost or not knowing where to park, but everything was clearly marked, and they had valet parking, another miracle of modern times, second only to GPS. So many times over the years, it seemed like no matter what Laura did, nothing worked out. Other times, life seemed to be made up of clear skies and nothing but sunshine. Today, she decided, was the latter.

After going into the hospital, she checked in at the front desk and was directed to the indoor courtyard, where a crew of three men had already carefully unpacked all her pieces and was beginning to assemble it. A mechanical platform that resembled a cherry picker elevated one of the workers, while the supervisor, Matt, yelled out directions from below. A third man scanned the diagram she'd sent with the shipment. "You started without me?" she asked in mock indignation after introducing herself.

The guys were apologetic then. The one up in the air froze, his arm partially extended, as if he'd been caught doing something wrong. "Sorry!" he yelled down.

"We just got started," Matt told her.

"It's fine," she said, in a way she hoped was reassuring. From then on, they checked with her before attaching each piece. Honestly, though, it turned out they didn't need her at all, but she was still glad to be there as it came to life. Once it was assembled and perfectly balanced, they turned on the floodlights. Lit up, the mobile was breathtaking. And when the guys attached the plaque on the base and she read the words, "*This Thing Called Life* by Laura Sutton," it put her over the edge. Seeing her name on that plaque made it real. She was an artist who had created something of worth. She stood there with tears streaming down her face, alarming the guys in the maintenance crew.

"Is it okay?" Matt asked, gesturing to the mobile. "We can make adjustments."

"No, no, it's perfect," she said, rummaging through her bag for a tissue. "I'm just overwhelmed." She wasn't sure he completely understood, but he nodded as if he did. Long after the guys had packed up their equipment and left the courtyard, she was still parked on a bench, admiring her work. She'd taken photos and filmed a video clip and sent them to Paul, who texted back: *Love it! So incredible!* Followed by: *When do you think you'll be home?*

She'd texted back: *Leaving in half an hour.*

Mesmerized was the word that came to mind as she watched the mobile rotate and shimmy in the light. She'd envisioned this, dreamed it, and put it on paper, and now it was real and casting rays of light in every direction. A dream come to life.

Lost in thought, Laura didn't initially notice the woman who wandered into the courtyard until she took a seat on the next bench over. She was strikingly pretty, even without makeup, and her hair was pulled up into a messy bun. She wasn't wearing scrubs or an ID, so she wasn't a hospital employee. Laura guessed she was the mother of one of the babies in the NICU.

The woman gazed up at the mobile. "This is new." She leaned back on the bench to get a better view.

Laura nodded. "Just installed today. Do you like it?" It was on the tip of her tongue to say she was the artist and explain what it symbolized, but she held back, wanting the work to speak for itself.

"I absolutely love it," the young woman said, a delighted smile slowly coming over her wan and tired face. "There's something about it that's very calming. Comforting." She kept her attention on the mobile, even as she kept talking. "My daughter, Fiona, is in the NICU."

"Fiona is such a pretty name. I bet she's adorable."

"She is. Everyone says so." Her voice was tinged with motherly pride. "All the nurses were shocked at how much hair she has for such a teeny thing. Here, look." She got up and came to sit next to Laura, her phone held out.

"She's gorgeous," Laura said, admiring the image of a sweet little baby with a wrinkled face and glossy black hair.

"Fiona's a miracle baby. They weren't sure she was going to make it, but she's a fighter. She should be able to go home in a few more days."

"I'm glad. You must be overjoyed."

As if just realizing the conversation was going one way, Fiona's mother turned to look at Laura. "Do you have kids?"

She hesitated for only a second. "Not yet, but my husband and I applied to be foster parents, and we're hoping to get matched by the end of the year. I'm looking forward to being a foster mom." She felt her face color at having put out so much personal information to a total stranger. Would this woman, who'd just given birth, feel like foster children didn't count by comparison?

"That's wonderful! You're doing a really good thing," she said enthusiastically. "I was in the system myself. I had two foster families that didn't work out, but my last one was the family who adopted me. I couldn't have a better mom and dad. They've been coming to the hospital every day to see Fiona. They're so excited to be grandparents."

"Really," Laura said, because she didn't know what else to say. The woman's reaction was just what she needed to hear. Inside, she felt a wellspring of warmth radiate through her, just the way the mobile's reflected lights filled the courtyard. She'd wanted to be a mother so badly for so long, and soon there would be a child in their home. The longing and the dream never went away. For a long time, it had seemed like it wasn't going to happen, but now she knew that all her hopes had led her here. It wasn't the way she'd envisioned her life. She knew that having foster kids in their home might not be an easy path, but this woman's story proved it could have a happy ending for parents and child alike.

Laura took it as a good omen. As it turned out, Paul wasn't the only one who could receive a sign.

CHAPTER FORTY-THREE

Logan had asked to go back to visit her many times, but Grandma Nan wasn't convinced it was a good idea until his therapist agreed. "He's made such progress," Dr. Meyer said. "He has more confidence and a higher sense of self-worth. Considering what he's been through, he's doing remarkably well. If he feels the need to touch base with her, I say do it. It will be a bridge from his old life to his new life and give him a sense of closure. I think it would do him good."

Logan had been there when Dr. Meyer had told this to his grandmother and had looked at her, pleading with his eyes. He had been overjoyed when she'd finally agreed, deciding they'd make the drive back on his first free day from school, a Friday in October slated for a teacher's in-service day. They'd leave the night before and stop at a hotel along the way. "We'll find a hotel with a pool. What do you think of that?" she'd asked.

"Yes!" He'd punctuated the word with a fist pump in the air.

"It's not Disney World," she'd said, teasing him.

But it might as well have been Disney World as far as Logan was concerned.

So much had changed in the last eight weeks. He'd started back at school, the same school where he'd attended kindergarten and first grade. The therapist had worked with him on what to say when other kids or adults asked why he had returned and was now living with his grandmother. Grandma Nan was so proud of his progress, and Logan saw it too. Looking in the mirror, he saw a different boy. For one thing, he'd gained weight. A lot of weight. His ribs didn't even stand out anymore. That, along with the new clothes and regular haircuts, made a world of difference in his appearance.

Dr. Meyer had been the one to tell him that his father had confessed to pushing his mother down the stairs, telling everyone it had happened just the way Logan had said. "This means you won't have to testify," he said. "Your dad said to tell you he is sorry."

Sorry was not a word Logan had ever heard his father say, and he wasn't convinced he meant it. "Will he stay in jail?" Logan asked.

Dr. Meyer nodded. "He'll be in prison for a long time. You can write him a letter if you want to, but you don't have to."

"I don't want to."

"It's up to you. You might change your mind, but if you don't, that's fine too."

When he'd first arrived at Grandma Nan's, he'd been amazed to find she'd kept all his old toys, the ones he'd played with when he used to go to her house years ago while his parents were at work. His Tigger was there, along with his teddy bear, his Wiffle ball and bat, the board games, and the ancient Nintendo with all its games.

"You still have them?" He'd looked at her, astounded.

"Naturally. I wouldn't get rid of anything of yours. I was counting on you coming back to me."

He'd walked around the house, stopping to stare at the framed pictures on Grandma's wall. The ones he was most interested in were those of his mother. Grandma had photos from when his mom was a baby all the way up to one of her holding Logan in her lap when he was about four. He'd forgotten about that picture. Looking at it gave him mixed feelings. He loved her so much, and it was good to see her face, but it also reminded him that she was gone. "I miss her," he said.

"I do too," Grandma Nan had replied.

"It hurts," he said, tapping on his heart.

"I know, and that never changes. I can think about her now and remember the good times, but sometimes I still get moments when the sadness comes back, and it's awful."

"When will it get better?"

She had tilted her head and thought. "No one can say for sure. It takes time. A long time. And that's to be expected because she was my daughter and your mom, and we really loved her then and still do. Grief is one of those emotions that hangs on, popping up when you don't expect it. All we can do is keep going and cherish the ones we love, like I cherish you." She had pulled him into a hug, so tight he felt trapped, but he didn't want to hurt her feelings, so he allowed it. When they pulled apart, she had tears in her eyes but was smiling.

So now they were in a car, heading back to where he'd been before, going to visit and cherish someone he'd once loved and still did. They'd left the hotel midmorning. With a stop for lunch, Grandma Nan had estimated they'd arrive at the elementary school right at the end of the day. Logan buzzed with anticipation, wondering how it would go. The place would be the same. He was the one who was different: older, stronger, less afraid now that he'd found his voice.

When they crossed state lines and saw the sign announcing they were in Illinois, he leaned forward in his spot in the back seat and voiced the concern lodged in the back of his mind. "Do you think she'll remember me?"

"Of course! I talked to her, and she knows we're coming. She can't wait to see you."

"You didn't tell her about the present, did you?"

"No. I know you wanted it to be a surprise."

He sat back, satisfied. There were so many things in his life he'd like to forget, but he wanted to remember everything about Ms. Tracey. Sometimes during his hour in her room, he'd get lost in thought because he was so busy admiring her wavy red hair and the freckles sprinkled across her nose, like glitter on an art project. Her voice was so nice too. She never got impatient or annoyed with him. Every word was kind. All she ever wanted to do was to help the kids who came to see her. Older kids, little kids, all of them with some kind of speech problem. But he'd been her favorite. She'd said so, and he'd believed it.

Someday, when he was a grown-up, he hoped to find a lady just like Ms. Tracey, and then they'd fall in love and get married and have children. Their house would have lots of laughing and no yelling, unless it was the kind of yelling that people did when they were joking around. There would always be plenty to eat, and the kids would have good-fitting clothes, and they'd each own more than one pair of nice shoes. In the wintertime, all of them would have warm jackets and gloves and waterproof boots. They'd be happy, so happy, and they'd love each other.

Having a life like that would be the best thing ever.

When Grandma Nan pulled into the parking lot of his old elementary school, Logan could see that the school day was over. They'd passed the crossing guard on the way in. She was chatting with a mother holding the hand of a little boy who looked like a kindergartner. The buses that usually lined up along the sidewalk in front had already gone. A few stragglers, kids with their moms, were heading to their cars. One of the moms held an art project, pictures taped to a poster board, which she struggled to keep hold of as it kept rising up in the breeze.

"They didn't have off today?" he asked, craning his neck to see.

"No, they're on a different schedule than your school." Grandma Nan pulled into a space and turned off the engine. "Are you ready, Logan?"

"I'm ready." He grabbed the wrapped package from the seat next to him, and together they walked to the front of the building, up the steps, and into the front door. He felt like he'd grown six inches since the last time he'd gone through that door.

Miss Barnes was at the desk, just the way he'd remembered. She called out, "Hi, Logan," and waved, right before buzzing them in. He waved back. She'd always been so nice to him.

"I'll show you the way," Logan said, picking up the pace.

"Just remember I'm an old lady and can't go as fast as you can."

He slowed then, even though it seemed to take forever, and he wanted to be there already. When he got to the end of the hallway, Ms. Tracey's door was ajar, just the way he remembered. He pushed it open, and there she was, sitting at the little table, waiting for him. "Logan!" she said, standing up. She came right over and gave him a hug. When he looked up, he saw her hair was pulled back, and she wore the white round earrings with the smiley faces on them. "I'm so glad to see you."

"I'm glad to see you too." He wasn't talking loudly, but his voice seemed to echo in the tiny room. He grinned at seeing her shock and delight that now he could talk. He'd tried so many times in this room and could never do much more than make the tiniest of noises when exhaling, and now he was fine and could talk like everyone else.

"I knew you'd have a beautiful voice." She tousled his hair in an affectionate way. "I knew it all along."

"He does have a beautiful voice," Grandma Nan said. "I'm so lucky that I get to hear it every day now."

"Did Logan tell you he was my favorite?"

"No, but I'm not surprised."

Ms. Tracey invited them to sit at the table, and then she got a small cooler out from underneath, setting the table with three wineglasses and pouring sparkling grape juice, then setting out paper plates, napkins, and cupcakes for each of them. "This is a regular celebration," she said. "I was so excited to hear you were coming all the way from Nebraska to visit me. I'm so honored."

They talked for a bit, Ms. Tracey asking questions about his new school, and Logan answering in between bites. She acted as if each word he said was a miracle, and in a way, it was. Funny how much better things were once you had a voice.

Grandma Nan added to the conversation, telling Ms. Tracey that Logan would be getting a dog soon. "When he was little, he was afraid of them, but lately he's become quite the dog lover."

"I have a dog named Mimi," Ms. Tracey said, pointing to the picture on the bookcase. Logan had seen it many times before. Mimi was a little fluff of a dog. In the picture, she looked like she was smiling. "I adore her. She's better than most people."

"Mimi is cute," Logan said, not wanting to hurt her feelings, "but I want a big dog."

"Big dogs are great too," Ms. Tracey said.

At the end of the visit, Grandma Nan reminded Logan about the wrapped gift sitting at his feet. He hadn't forgotten. He just wasn't sure how to give it to her.

"For me?" Ms. Tracey asked, her eyes widening in delight. After he set the present in front of her, she tore at the paper and then lifted the lid of the box. Nestled in the tissue paper was a framed photo of Logan, taken just last week. Her hand flew to her mouth, and she looked as if she were about to cry. "Oh, Logan, I absolutely love it. I will cherish it always."

He rose out of his chair to point excitedly. "Push the button."

When she pressed the button at the bottom of the frame, a prerecorded audio message was activated. It was Logan's voice saying, "Hi, Ms. Tracey. Thank you and I love you. This is Logan, by the way."

Now Ms. Tracey was the one who couldn't speak. She opened her mouth, but nothing came out, and a tear escaped from one eye.

"I didn't want you to forget me," Logan said, while Grandma Nan handed Ms. Tracey a tissue.

"Oh, honey, I could never forget you."

When they left, Ms. Tracey gave Logan another hug and then hugged Grandma Nan too. "I can't thank you enough for coming back to see me. You keep in touch, okay?"

They exchanged e-mail addresses, and Grandma Nan promised to keep Ms. Tracey updated and send her photos of Logan's dog once he got one. And Logan knew she would, because Grandma always kept her word.

ACKNOWLEDGMENTS

I owe a debt of gratitude to my editor, Danielle Marshall, for seeing the potential in *Half a Heart*, acquiring it for Lake Union Publishing, and guiding it through the publication process. I knew after our first conversation that my novel couldn't be in better hands.

Thank you to the entire Lake Union and Amazon Publishing teams for all your hard work. The way you turn a manuscript into a book and then match it with the appropriate readership is magic. You guys are simply the best!

To those who gave me early feedback on the manuscript—Kay Ehlers, Geri Erickson, German Fiscal, Alice L. Kent, and Michelle San Juan—I am grateful for your time and insights. Any remaining errors are mine and mine alone.

My husband, Greg, and my kids—Charlie, Maria, and Jack—had nothing to do with the actual writing of this book, but they make me happy, and I love them very much.

I also want to acknowledge the readers of all my books. Because of you, I get to write novels for a living, which is no small thing, believe me. If you enjoyed this book, a short review on Amazon or Goodreads would be very much appreciated. I read all my reviews and enjoy hearing readers' thoughts on my stories. As long as you keep reading, I'll keep writing. Thank you!

ABOUT THE AUTHOR

The bestselling author of *Hello Love*, Karen McQuestion writes the books she would love to read—not only for adults but also kids and teens. Her publishing story has been covered by the *Wall Street Journal*, *Entertainment Weekly*, and NPR. Karen has also appeared on ABC's *World News Now* and *America This Morning*. She lives with her family in Hartland, Wisconsin. To find out more about Karen and her books, follow her on Twitter (@karenmcquestion) or visit www.KarenMcQuestion.com.